THE
NARRATOR
K.L. SLATER

bookouture

First published as an Audible Original in August 2022 by Audible Ltd. This edition published January 2023 by Bookouture.

An imprint of Storyfire Ltd.
Carmelite House
50 Victoria Embankment
London EC4Y 0DZ

www.bookouture.com

ISBN: 978-1-80314-931-8
eBook ISBN: 978-1-80314-930-1

To my daughter, Francesca Kim, who was still a 'Miss' when I wrote this book!

ONE

TEN MONTHS EARLIER

She waits at the agreed pickup point, her stomach roiling in anticipation of the evening that lies ahead. The latest instalment in the bestselling Tower series is widely tipped to take the coveted Smoking Gun Award for the Crime Fiction Book of the Year.

Tonight will be the culmination of years of hard work. The ultimate pay-off when she will finally receive the accolade she deserves. The books have won so many awards over the years and yet none of them have really meant anything to her until now. This is the biggie, the one that every author wants to win and the prize she has been waiting for.

When she hears those long-anticipated words from the celebrity presenter: '... and the Smoking Gun Award's Crime Fiction Book of the Year is... *Deathly Betrayal* by Phillipa Roberts!', she will gather her courage to rush up to the stage and speak to the publishing world and more importantly – via livestream – to the millions of readers who have universally adored and loyally supported the books.

For now, though, she scans the quiet street waiting for her lift to the venue, self-consciously patting her fresh blow-dry and batting the false eyelashes the make-up artist carefully applied just a couple of hours before. She's splashed out on a glitzy cocktail dress and expensive designer heels so she will look as perfect as possible when her big moment arrives on stage and the press cameras start flashing.

She can do it. She has promised herself that tonight, she will finally own her success. A culmination of everything she has worked for.

At last, movement catches her eye and a sleek, black limousine cruises smoothly down the empty street. It slows and stops in front of her, the pristine bodywork and polished alloy wheels glinting in the early evening light.

She opens the passenger door and peers inside. Her face drops. 'Oh, it's you!'

'Surprise! I offered to do the honours... I'm glad you're pleased,' the familiar voice says drily, as she climbs in and gets comfy on the soft, cream leather upholstery. 'I thought we could chat on the way to the event.'

She doesn't reply. The last thing she wants before this evening is to justify her decision all over again.

Once she's secured her seatbelt, the car starts to move again. 'Open the glove compartment,' the driver says. 'There's a surprise in there for you.' She leans forward and pops it open to find a mini bottle of pink champagne and a glass. 'It's a special night. Go ahead and pour yourself a drink.'

She doesn't really feel like drinking while travelling, but she does feel more nervous than expected at the thought of speaking on stage later. She could do with a booster. The foil has already been removed on the perfectly chilled bottle and, as it is a very special evening, she throws caution to the wind.

She unscrews the plastic cork and pours out the fizz. It is a nice thought, but it doesn't change anything. 'If you think you're going to convince me to carry on writing, then you can just think again.' She takes a sip, and the bubbles dance across her tongue. 'I've written the last title in the Tower series and nothing you can say will change my mind. I'm sorry, but the party's over.'

There's a tense silence filled with desperation and denial.

'But what are the readers going to say? This is no way to repay their loyalty over the years.' The limousine swerves slightly, and a tiny amount of liquid spills into her lap. She grabs a tissue from her handbag.

'I'm sorry, but it's been ten long years, and now it's time for me to move on.' She gives her firm reply as she dabs her dress. She has every right not to write another word and that is what she's decided to do. Tonight she will share it with the world. 'The readers will understand, they'll soon find a new favourite crime series.'

After a bigger gulp of champagne, she looks out of the window, trying to ignore the wave of tension rolling in from the driving seat.

'Which way are we going?' Her voice is tight with tension. 'We don't want to be late.'

'Relax. I've planned a bit longer route that takes us around the edge of town. Less traffic, more time to talk.'

She can feel a headache coming on. Why didn't she just get a cab? It would have been quicker and a lot less hassle. Suddenly, out of the corner of her eye she catches a glimpse of the hotel hosting the awards a few streets away. Its foyer is an explosion of violet neon light invading the fringe of planted trees around the foyer. She cranes her neck as the limo sails by.

'Turn back!' She lurches forward, spilling a little of her drink as her head pounds with the impending headache. 'We're almost...' She gathers her thoughts and tries again. 'There... there's no sense in driving... out of our way...' Her words sound strange, all soft and unformed at the edges. 'There's no... sense... in...'

'Rest your head back and close your eyes,' the driver says, more relaxed now and turning the car onto a road that will eventually lead them far, far away from the hotel. 'Leave everything to me now. You don't need to worry.'

'But... late... we...' Her voice sounds so faint to her now, as if she herself is fading away. 'We can't... be... late...'

She is floating. Out of the car and off towards the peaceful darkness in her head.

'That's it. Close your eyes.' She hears the voice beside her soften. 'Nice and easy does it. You've been so confused, but when you wake up, you'll feel altogether different about everything.'

* * *

When she opens her eyes, it is pitch dark and utterly silent. Where is she? How long has she been here? The thoughts are painful. It hurts her head to even think.

She pats her hands over her limbs. Every inch of her feels bruised, and yet she can't find any cuts or lumps where she has hurt herself. Her head is a mess, a tangle of flashes, unanchored flashbacks. The last thing she can remember is getting ready... make-up, high heels, new dress. Where was she going? How on earth did she end up *here*?

She coughs, the invasive stench of damp extending its foul tendrils into her nose and chest. Her throat is painfully raw and parched; the thirst is off the scale. She has a banging headache that ricochets around her skull every time she moves her head even slightly.

With great effort and difficulty, she pulls herself to her feet, unanchored and completely blind.

She spreads her fingers wide and places her hands on a

slimy, damp stone wall, patting, her fingers searching out any detail with each tentative step. She thinks she must be in a disused basement. This place has not been finished even to the most basic standards.

Her joints ache like last year when she came down with a bad case of flu. She thinks it was last year, but her grip on the past is wrecked. She looks down and sniffs, aware of a stench that clings to her. Tentatively, she presses her fingers between her legs and feels the clammy damp of her underwear... Oh no...

Her glittering dress is gone and, in its place, a billowing, thin garment that feels rough like a shroud. Her underwear is still intact, although now it's uncomfortably wet and smelly, but the elegant Jimmy Choos are missing, and her feet are cold and bare and immersed in the ripped-up papers that litter the cold, concrete floor.

With great difficulty, she manages to inch her way all the way around the room. She counts the corners until she has touched four walls and one cold, steel door with no handle and no glass panel.

She bangs on the door with flat palms. 'Hello? Is anyone there?'

She stands very still to listen to a silence so thick and impenetrable it almost has a sound of its own.

She slides down the wall and sits with her knees drawn up. Wrapping her arms around her legs, she lays her cheek on top of her knees, squeezing her eyes shut.

How did she end up here? What on earth happened after she'd got all dressed up and left the house?

Her brain feels like pea soup. Full of mixed-up thoughts she can't quite access.

She remembers the sequinned flash of her cocktail dress, the blur of a bolder lipstick than she'd usually wear in a mirror, and now... now here she is. In hell.

She stretches out her legs and the littered papers rustle all around her. She grabs a handful and realises, for the first time, the pieces of paper are all the same size. Identical oblong squares, each with one long edge that has been torn.

Book pages, the size of a paperback. A thick layer, all over the floor.

She picks up a single piece and holds it in front of her face. Although she can't see a thing, a disturbing idea presents itself. A fresh curl of discomfort begins in her already churning stomach.

Could they be pages torn from the books of the Tower series?

What if she has been taken prisoner not because of who she is, but because of the words she has written?

TWO

EVE

I stare out at the weed-strewn back garden of my mum's terraced house, tapping my fingers on the windowsill to the radio.

This place feels harder to escape with each day that passes. I climb down the short ladder and lay the paintbrush on the lid of the olive-green paint, wiping my hands on the legs of an over-sized pair of paint-spattered overalls of Dad's I found in the garage.

Two years ago, I was living what for me was my perfect life. Home was a modest but cosy house with my handsome businessman husband, Hugo, and our five-year-old daughter, Scarlet.

From being a kid, I'd always dreamed of being an actor... a movie star, even. That hadn't quite materialised, but I'd found myself something nearly as good. I'd clawed my way into a career as a successful audiobook narrator, reading mainly crime fiction – my favourite genre – for a handful of publishers.

But one day eighteen months ago, everything changed virtually overnight.

My dad walked out of the house to get bread and milk from

the local shop and never returned. Nottinghamshire Police launched a county-wide search both on the ground and on social media. A few sightings came in, but a week later, they pulled his body out of the river Trent. In trying to support Mum and come to terms with Dad's death myself, I swiftly spiralled downwards. But there was more to come.

Six months after Dad's death, I found out my husband was having an affair with Saskia Peterson, a colleague I'd been foolish enough to introduce him to at a publishing event.

Two months after this bombshell, Phillipa Roberts, the best-selling crime author who was a personal friend and whose books had launched my narrating career, went missing. I had built a solid catalogue of work, but Phillipa's audiobooks were the jewel in my narrating crown. When all this stuff converged, my head had exploded. My doctor diagnosed severe depression and anxiety and put me on medication.

Within the space of a few days, my life – including my career – collapsed like a Jenga tower.

Hugo had left home soon after I discovered his affair, and Phillipa never returned. After an initial blaze of interest, the story died down. Although the police insisted they were still actively looking for Phillipa, it was fairly obvious they had downscaled their operation. New missing people's faces appeared in their Facebook posts; the fly posters publicising Phillipa's disappearance curled at the edges and faded. Now the discussion of what happened to the much-loved crime novelist was limited to online forums where the fans still mourned her absence.

I left London with Scarlet and gratefully accepted Mum's offer for us to come and stay for a couple of months. Now, ten months since Phillipa disappeared, I am back living in the small, stifling town I grew up in, but I feel much better now. I feel well again.

The day I'd turned up at the door with Scarlet and a couple

of large suitcases, my mum, Viv, had looked at me pityingly. 'Don't be too hard on yourself, Eve, love,' she'd said gently. 'Plenty of people go to London searching for their fortune, and for most, it doesn't work out. But at least you tried and that's what counts.'

But it *had* been working out. It was working out brilliantly before Dad died and Hugo decided he wasn't happy being Scarlet's dad and my husband.

Five years ago, when we'd all gone up to Edinburgh, when Dad's sister, Aunt Mabel, turned eighty, that was when I first met Phillipa. Everyone was in awe of this successful writer who Aunt Mabel had taught in primary school. She'd been so down to earth. We'd broken away from the tea and cake brigade and found a quiet corner with two glasses, a couple of tins of aromatic tonic and a bottle of rhubarb gin. I'd asked Phillipa about her career, hanging on every word about how she broke into publishing at a mature age after a career in travel. It had all seemed so glamorous. She'd suddenly stopped speaking mid-sentence and said, 'Your aunt Mabel instilled the belief in myself that I could write. She's the reason I achieved my dreams. What are your dreams, Eve?'

'I'd like to be an actor,' I'd told her without hesitation, bolstered by my third glass of Prosecco. 'I suppose I just want to perform really.'

It was Phillipa who'd encouraged me in my career. Suggested it, in fact. Later, in that quiet corner, she said, 'You've got a fabulous voice, Eve. Here, read a bit of the latest book in the series I'm writing.' I'd read a few paragraphs of her book *You Die First* into a Dictaphone, and when she played it back, I was surprised how relaxed and clear my voice sounded. 'You've got a lovely bit of local accent in there, not too much. It's the kind of voice that can transport the reader and showcase the story.'

A month later, she took me down to London to the recording studio and the rest is history. I've narrated all nine of her incredibly popular police procedural novels. The first few had used various narrators and they asked me to re-record those for continuity. Thanks to Phillipa giving me a chance, I quickly built a thriving career as a narrator with Harris-Lasson, her publisher, being my biggest client.

Phillipa and I stayed in touch. We met up a couple of times in London and periodically emailed. She invited me to her fiftieth birthday and that's when I got to meet her family. Fleur, her lovely wife, and Phillipa's stepson, Milo.

Then, on the night of the biggest award ceremony of her life, the Smoking Gun Crime and Thriller Awards, at which she was expected to win a major prize, Phillipa went missing. The last person to see her was Fleur who'd left home earlier for the venue when Phillipa said she had a last-minute call to make.

Harris-Lasson, her publisher, had reeled in shock. Her readers were distraught. All sorts of theories were thrown around online and in the press. Had Phillipa been kidnapped for a ransom, perhaps? Had she had a terrible accident the police hadn't discovered yet, or had she simply decided to leave her life behind and start afresh under an alias?

My sense of security had exploded like single-paned glass. On top of everything else I was dealing with at the time, I had simply felt unable to carry on in London. I felt I had no choice but to come home.

I turn away from the narrow bedroom window now. It's no good looking back filled with regrets, is it? Although there is undeniably something utterly depressing about turning thirty-six years old, as I had done last month, and still be living with your child in your mother's house.

Still, I was so much luckier than most because I had Scarlet: the light of my life and the reason I kept going. For Scarlet, I kept hoping for a better future without really feeling anything would change.

When I turned thirty-six, Mum had made me a birthday

cake with candles, and Scarlet had loved helping me blow them out. Mum had regarded me with sad eyes and said, 'I know this isn't the life you'd hoped for, Eve, but I see it as a bonus you're back home where you belong.'

But I didn't belong here, not anymore. I knew Mum came from a place of trying to make me feel better, but it felt like I'd finally hit rock bottom. Since Dad died, Mum understandably wants to keep me and Scarlet close. She wants me to settle down in my hometown, be satisfied with the life we have here.

Mum means well in her own way but there are times she makes me feel like I'm still back at school. Yes, we have a roof over our heads. Yes, I have someone I can trust to watch Scarlet when I work shifts for extra money at a local brasserie and bar.

But every day we stay here, I feel a little more of my spirit drain away.

It's the small things that stack up and bring me down. Like when I tell Scarlet no more television and my mother over-rules with, 'Let her have just five more minutes.' Or when I return to my bedroom after taking Scarlet to school and see that yet again, my books and magazines have been tidied away from the side of my bed, losing marked pages or articles of interest. These are the times I feel something inside me splinter.

I pick up the paintbrush again. I'm just doing this one wall in the olive green and leaving the rest. The endless magnolia walls that feature in every single room in the house – apart from Scarlet's bedroom which has wall-to-wall unicorn wallpaper – have finally broke through my resolve to put up and shut up.

With each brush of thick, luxurious colour I apply, there is a feeling of burying my past mistakes and creating a new canvas that is ripe for possibilities. If only life were that simple.

The one o'clock news comes on the radio, and my mind begins to wonder about what there might be for lunch. Then, a few news stories in, my hand freezes, the paintbrush suspended in mid-air. Large drops of dark green paint drip down onto the old dustsheet I've used to cover the carpet.

The newsreader's voice is deep and confident. The words he is saying are about to rock my world.

I climb back down the ladder in a daze, lay the paintbrush down on the lid of the tin and stand listening to the news report in disbelief.

THREE

BBC RADIO NEWS REPORT

Bestselling historical fiction author, Phillipa Roberts, who became one of the UK's most high-profile missing persons some ten months ago, is again hitting the headlines. Ten months after her disappearance, Roberts's wife, Fleur de Bois, has discovered a hidden manuscript in the riverfront house they shared together in Chiswick.

Ms de Bois told the Metro, *'Planned renovations were being carried out at the house, and during a clear-out of the attic, a hidden, complete manuscript written by Phillipa was discovered.'*

Roberts's publisher, Harris-Lasson, confirmed the book is currently being edited and will be published in spring 2023 as the tenth book in Roberts's global bestselling Tower crime series.

Roberts's editor, Jules Handley, said, 'We all think about Phillipa every single day and we live in hope that, one day, she will be found safe and well. This book will honour her continued legacy as a global bestselling author. We are privileged to be publishing the story across all formats including a full audio production next year.'

Despite a prolonged police investigation, Roberts has never been located. Due to a lack of leads, and although the Metropolitan police insist the investigation remains open, it is widely thought that Roberts might have orchestrated her own disappearance for unknown reasons. Her wife has always strenuously denied this.

Fleur de Bois told the BBC, 'Phillipa loved her career and our family life. As much as I'm exhilarated that this secret book will keep her foremost in the nation's memory, I'm appealing to her millions of readers and fans to get my message out there. I'm begging anyone who has the slightest shred of information that might help find my wife, to please, come forward.'

FOUR

EVE

I turn off the radio and rush across the room to snatch up my silenced phone. I have two missed calls, a new voicemail notification and several text messages.

I check the missed calls first and my heart soars. Both are from Jules Handley at Harris-Lasson, Phillipa's editor of ten years. I press on the voicemail link and Jules's familiar North-East accent fills my ears.

'Eve, Jules here. Hope you're well. I'm sure you've heard the news about the secret Phillipa Roberts manuscript – it's trending on Twitter. Give me a call back soon as you can.'

With my heart hammering, I check the texts. The first one again from Jules.

Hi Eve, I've left you a voicemail. Call me! Jules

The bedroom door opens, and my mother cranes her head around.

'I've made you a cuppa and a slice of cake.' She frowns at the half-painted wall. 'I wouldn't leave it like that, Eve. If you don't complete each coat, you'll overlap and get a dark join.'

I jump up, waving my phone. 'Mum, something amazing has happened. They've found a Phillipa Roberts manuscript... a secret book she wrote that nobody knew anything about!' I babble, not making much sense.

Mum presses her lips together, unimpressed. 'Have they found Phillipa as well?'

'No, I don't think so. But it's incredible there's another book.'

'It all sounds like a publicity stunt to me – her going missing and then, lo and behold, there's a secret book found. Perhaps her publisher is in on it.'

'She was kind to me, Mum. She helped me to break me into the industry and you shouldn't say things like that.'

'Like what?'

'Stuff about her publisher. We still don't know what's happened to Phillipa and the police seem to have all but given up. It's awful for her family.' I reach for my phone. 'I need to call Harris-Lasson back. They've left messages asking for me to contact them.'

'Surely you can do that after you've had your tea and cake.' Mum sniffs.

A wave of irritation floods into my chest. 'I'll come downstairs when I've made the call.'

Mum's face flushes as she steps back on to the landing. 'I wouldn't get your hopes up, Eve. It might all be a storm in a teacup.'

I close the door behind her, wishing I had a lock on it. I check the time. I still have a couple of hours before I have to pick up Scarlet from school. Jules picks up on the second ring.

'Eve, there you are! I was just about to call you again. Have you heard about Phillipa's hidden manuscript?'

'Just now, it's incredible! I heard it on the radio and then I saw your messages.'

'Incredible is precisely the right word. We've known about

the book for a few weeks, actually. The first time I read it, I literally couldn't put it down.'

'It sounds amazing,' I say. Then, 'I wonder why Phillipa would write a whole book and then hide it away?'

'This can only be a positive development. If nothing else, it will raise public awareness of her disappearance again.'

'I assume the police know all about it?'

'Yes, Fleur got in touch with the police immediately. They seem to think it further proves Phillipa was in a very confused frame of mind when she took off – if that's what happened.' After a couple of months with no contact from anyone and no demand for money, the police had concluded there was little chance Phillipa had been abducted.

'It's so frustrating,' I murmur.

'Anyway,' Jules continues. 'The reason I wanted to speak to you today is that we'd very much like you to narrate the new book!'

'Wow!' I feel slightly dizzy with the magnitude of the news. I sit down on the bed. 'That is amazing, and the answer is yes... thank you so much! I'd love to be involved.'

'Amazing! It'll be a fixed fee on a par with your previous contracts with us. I'll email over details later today.' Jules hesitates. 'I should warn you we're back to all systems go at this end, Eve. It might be tough for you to see people getting on with the job again despite Phillipa's absence.'

'I'm pragmatic about it,' I say. 'Phillipa once told me that authors want their stories to be read. She'd want this book in the hands of her readers, I'm sure.'

'Excellent! Everyone will be so pleased you're on board, and let's face it, who else could do it? You've done such an amazing job with the series, and we all said, if Phillipa were around to choose, there'd be no doubt in her mind you're the best fit. She believed in you and so does everyone at Harris-Lasson.'

I feel quite choked. 'I'm honoured. Thank you so much.'

Jules pauses for a moment before speaking. 'With this book being so high profile, I should mention that Alicia Kent herself is personally overseeing it when usually she'd have little input. In practical terms, it means I'll need to report to her at every stage of the audio-recording process.'

'Fine by me!' I say brightly. I haven't had a lot to do with Alicia, I met her briefly when she joined Harris-Lasson as the new CEO just a few months before I left. All I know is that I've been thrown a lifeline in getting my life back on track. I feel light and free... and I haven't felt like that in a very long time.

Jules's voice drops lower. 'Between you and me, Alicia can be a bit of a micromanager. But let's not worry about all that for now. It's going to be great. *You're* going to be great!'

'It's a dream come true to be asked,' I say, smiling to myself. 'What's the next step?'

'Well, I know it'll be a bit of a push, but can you possibly come to London? Monday morning would be amazing if you could do it.'

Monday would be a *very* big push. I still have to tell Mum I'll be going to London again and I also need time to explain properly to Scarlet. It's already Friday afternoon and Scarlet is breaking up from school for the summer today. I'd love to spend the weekend doing something nice together instead of scurrying around trying to get everything ready to go to London early Monday morning.

'I don't suppose we could make it Tuesday? It's just that—'

'I'm so sorry, Eve. Alicia wants everyone involved in the project present at a team meeting at ten on Monday morning.' She hesitates before saying, 'She'll notice who's not present. It really is vital you come.'

There will be a thousand other narrators snapping at my heels if I put so much as a foot wrong on this job.

'I'll get a train and hotel booked.' I'll have to grovel to Mum who'll be left looking after Scarlet alone during the summer holidays.

'That's fantastic, Eve, and if you're looking for a temporary flatshare, I might have a contact here.'

'That would be so helpful.' Affordable accommodation will be a major problem for me in London, so this is incredible news.

'Perfect!' Jules's voice is bright before she adds, 'Are you one hundred per cent in?'

The brief silence is loaded with her expectation.

This is my chance to claw some self-respect back and take a massive step in rebuilding my career and making a new life for us. But the worry of having to leave Scarlet here with Mum in the meantime manifests itself as a dull ache in my stomach.

I take a breath and close my eyes.

'I'm one hundred per cent all in,' I say. 'See you Monday.'

FIVE

CHAD

He printed off the final report from Google and slid it into the plastic wallet. He'd bought a lever arch file specifically to gather every single detail of Phil's disappearance and he filed it away in here.

Phil is what some of her friends called her. Phil was her nickname, although he didn't care for it himself. Phillipa sounded pleasingly formal, but sometimes he liked to refer to her by the shortened version because it showed he wasn't just a run-of-the-mill clueless fan like all the others he encountered online.

He glanced at the bulging file. There had been so much activity ten months earlier when she first went missing. The press, the online fan forums, her publisher making regular statements, the police appealing for help. He had felt powerful, as though he stood in the eye of the storm, the man with all the answers.

And then, almost as quickly as it had blown up, all the fuss blew away. He didn't mind admitting he had been furious. Furious at them all. The police, the publisher and particularly Phillipa's feckless wife. It seemed obvious to him she courted the publicity for herself. Insisting all that mattered to Phillipa was family life when she was so much more than that.

He refreshed the Google search, but there was nothing new there. He shouldn't get himself all het up about the situation, particularly now there had been such a momentous announcement.

There was to be another book. Another book! After everything, after worrying there would never be another title in the unrivalled Tower series, there was to be one after all. He knew every one of the characters like they were family members. DI Jane Tower's team, the hidden problems of her colleagues, her family history. He had even visited many of the actual locations mentioned in the books, taken selfies of himself at each one.

Chad had an almost photographic memory, aided by the hours he'd spent studying the plots and character arcs of the books.

But he confessed he felt irritated with Phillipa. She had played a silly game writing an entire novel and hiding it away.

He'd think it through, sleep on it and his brain would inevitably come up with suggestions. That's what he always did. He knew he was different to other people in the way his mind worked, but he was good at putting on an act. He was skilled at appearing 'normal.'

He knew far more about Phillipa Roberts than anyone would imagine.

That fact alone gave him a warm glow. A secret little *thrill* deep down inside.

SIX

It's impossible, in the pitch dark, to keep track of time. How long has she been trapped in here? Her throat is raw, and she can't keep track of a line of thought for more than a few seconds before it evaporates like smoke. She tries counting the seconds to accrue minutes, but it's too easy to lose track and forget where she was.

She shivers, but she doesn't feel cold. Her skin feels hot and clammy, her face flushing with heat. She takes in some deep breaths and exhales slowly.

Think, think, think.

She can remember preparing to go out. Days before... or hours before now, she can't tell. There had been so much to do. Hair? She thought so. That was one thing.

She could vaguely remember writing the last book. It had been a difficult one to write because she had had to force herself. She can't remember the story. The details of the plot and the characters are just out of her reach. But she can recall the feeling of frustration and panic when it just wasn't coming together.

Life had been normal, she thinks. Whatever normal was.

But then... then something had happened. Something that caused a big gap in her memory.

She coughs. Her throat feels like she has swallowed razor wire. She desperately needs water. She feels around the wall again until she reaches the cold steel door. Then she balls her fists and bangs on it as hard as she can.

'Water!' she shouts out. 'I need water. Let me out!'

Silence. Not just quiet... but an echoing vacuum that tells her she is alone, not just in this awful space but in the whole building. Whatever and wherever this prison is.

She assumes someone will come, but what if they never do? What if she is simply left here to die of dehydration and starvation?

Her breaths come fast and shallow now. Sweat pools in her armpits and then an icy wave of shivering begins, shaking her entire body.

Breathe, she tells herself. *Slow down and breathe.*

Her throat tightens. She feels sure this is it... She is going to die here.

Her heart bounces off her chest wall and she slides down, lies on the floor with its carpet of papers and waits for death to take her.

SEVEN

EVE

After the call with Jules at Harris-Lasson, I allow myself the luxury of lying back on my bed and just enjoying thinking through everything she'd said. I'm back in the game with what will be the most talked-about book of the year. There'll be so much attention from the press, the work should come rolling in. I pray that's the case, anyway.

After a short time I sit up and spend a little time looking at the cost of a train ticket, making notes about what I might need to take with me. I pray Jules's flatshare contact comes through. But I ought to budget for a couple of nights in a B & B or something just in case it doesn't work out.

When I can't put it off any longer, I go back downstairs.

'You're *what*? You're seriously thinking of going back to London?' Mum's mouth sags as she puts down her mug.

'I'm deadly serious,' I say confidently, even though guilt about leaving Scarlet continues to grumble inside me. 'It's an amazing opportunity I can't afford to turn down.'

She takes a crumpled tea towel off the counter and begins to fold it carefully. 'Well then, I'm very concerned.'

'Concerned about what?' I lean back against the worktop

and brace myself. The feeling of relief is fading fast. Mum has always had the ability to zero in on my insecurities within seconds.

'I'm concerned about my granddaughter. I'm concerned her thirty-six-year-old mother hasn't learned from her mistakes and is willing to drop everything and uproot her yet again.'

'My career isn't a mistake,' I say, wounded. 'It was going well before Hugo left and Phillipa went missing.'

'The operative word being *was*.' Mum looks up from her folding. 'I'm sorry the bottom dropped out of your career, Eve, but you need to wake up to reality.'

The old inferiority rises like a wave inside me. 'It wasn't my career that failed. It was ruined by everything else that happened around me.'

Mum shakes out the tea towel and starts folding again. 'If you'd been able to come to an agreement with Hugo, he'd have helped look after Scarlet, I'm sure. You'd have had more freedom and more time to get yourself another job sorted out. A *decent* job.'

Mum doesn't approve of me working at the brasserie bar in the middle of town three nights a week. 'Hugo hasn't wanted anything to do with her until recently. You know that!' Scarlet's father has a brand-new business and a newly pregnant girl-friend, Saskia, to keep him busy now. There has been no room for a five-year-old girl in his plans, and he has only just started paying me regular maintenance. 'I just want to get back to doing what I love. As well as being a mum to Scarlet. It's not too much to ask to want both.'

I always find myself on the back foot in my conversations with Mum.

'I deserve another chance,' I say.

At last, Mum puts down the tea towel and sighs. A long, weary sound. 'I know only too well about career disappointments. I decided to put you first all those years ago, Eve. Now it's time for you to take stock and think about Scarlet.'

I say nothing. I can't stomach the story, yet again, of how, by simply being born, I managed to ruin Mum's planned career as a midwife. But she's on a roll now and there's no stopping her.

'I know not everyone is as unselfish as I was, but'—she looks at me—'you had your chance in London, and it didn't work out, love. Can't you just accept that and focus on the best job in the world: being a good mother?'

'Life's not about just the one chance, Mum.' I allow my arms to relax down by my sides. 'You get knocked down and you pick yourself back up again. You keep reaching for your dreams and never take no for an answer. That's the lesson I'm teaching Scarlet.'

'What are you trying to say? That I gave in too easily?'

'Of course I'm not, I just mean—'

'I was eighteen years old when I fell pregnant with you, Eve. Eighteen! I made the decision to shelve my dream to be a midwife. I married your father and became a housewife and mother.'

'I understand you feel as if you missed out, Mum. But nowadays, women don't have to choose just the one role.'

'Sometimes you have to step back and put others first,' Mum says, her voice softening a little. 'The way I did for you and your father who, thanks to me, succeeded in his management aspirations.'

An ache starts in my chest when I think about Dad. The gap he left in our lives will never be filled, but since the day he left, Mum steadfastly refuses to talk about it.

I was always closer to Dad growing up. We liked the same things: spending time in the garden, walking along the towpath, playing board games and doing puzzles. Dad acted like a safe middle ground for me and Mum to get along. He'd diffuse arguments, suggest things for us to do together to bring us a bit closer.

When he died, the dynamic changed between me and Mum. Dad had been the glue that held us together, and now... well, we felt miles apart most of the time. But Mum and Scarlet adore each other, and Mum has been good enough to put a roof over our heads for the last eight months.

She sighs and touches my arm. 'You'll never find happiness while you're chasing your tail, Eve.'

I blink the hurt away. I need to keep focused. 'Mum, I'm asking you to keep Scarlet here for a month at the most.'

'And what's Hugo going to say about it all? What's he going to think about Scarlet being put through more upheaval?' She sighs. 'I know he did you wrong, Eve, but you two have a daughter together. You must get over your resentment for Scarlet's sake.'

I bite down on my tongue and the retorts that lie there. If Hugo had seen Scarlet regularly after we split up, I'd have no problem in asking him to help out now. But I don't feel comfortable leaving her in what, essentially, will be a strange situation for her with her daddy and his new girlfriend who weirdly used to be my colleague.

'What Hugo thinks isn't my problem, but I'll call him later and explain.' I sigh. 'Look, Mum, I'm grateful to you for taking us in, and when I get paid for this job, we'll be out of your hair. Can you do this for me? For your granddaughter?'

'Of course I can.' Mum smiles tightly. 'After all, I've been putting myself last for my family's sake all my life.'

She can't dampen my spirits. Not now.

'Thank you,' I say, and I feel a rush of opportunity.

At last, the future is starting to feel like a bright glow on the horizon rather than the dull, shapeless blot I had started to believe might be here to stay.

EIGHT

I've got about an hour before the school run so I get changed out of Dad's painting overalls, pull on a pair of jeans and a tunic top and head into town. I desperately need some new clothes for London. I just wear jeans and a T-shirt at the bar, and apart from that, I don't go anywhere but the school.

Money has been tight for a while now, so I head to trusty Primark. I walk around quickly, selecting a couple of pairs of tailored trousers and blouses. But I can't find sleepwear. I stop and ask an assistant who's striding purposefully across the shopfloor.

'I'm heading over there now, if you'd like to follow me,' she says.

I've just set off in the assistant's wake when a man with swept-back hair and angular features appears suddenly in front of me, forcing me to stop walking. He's average height – I'd guess about five foot ten – quite stocky, with a spotty complexion. For some reason he looks familiar, but I can't place him.

'Can I be of any help?' he says politely. He's wearing black-rimmed spectacles and a paisley-print shirt which looks too long in the arms for him. He's not wearing a Primark uniform and I can't see a name badge. I'm not sure if he is a member of staff or a fellow customer just trying to be helpful. I glance at the female garments draped over his forearm. 'Just picking up a few things for my mother,' he says, raising his arm slightly.

I stand on my tiptoes and crane my head over his shoulder, searching for the uniformed assistant I'm supposed to follow. 'Thanks, but someone is helping me, and I'll lose her if I don't rush.'

I start to move forward but he doesn't step aside.

'I know who you are,' he says. His voice is pleasant, but his pale-grey eyes are intense. 'You used to narrate Phillipa Roberts's books but now you work in Jinksy's Bar.'

I freeze for a moment or two. Then I realise that's why he looks so familiar. He's a regular customer at the brasserie. He often sits at a corner table in the early evening, sipping a latte and reading, sometimes for a couple of hours.

Maybe I should be flattered to be recognised in a professional capacity for the first time in my life, but instead I'm a bit taken aback. 'I... yes. I've seen you in there.'

'I'm a massive Phillipa Roberts fan,' he says, his eyes burning into mine. 'I've heard you speaking to customers at the bar but it's always noisy in there with the coffee machine and the background music. Hearing you speak just now I realised where I recognise your voice from... it's the Tower series.' He holds out a hand. 'Pleased to meet you, Eve. I'm Chadwick Belton. My friends call me Chad.'

He knows my name.

A little shiver tickles the back of my neck. I don't know how he's picked up on my voice. I don't really use my 'own' voice when I work on books. I mean, obviously I do, but it's all acting, really. Getting into the heads of all the characters.

'That's incredible...' I say lightly. 'That you were able to discern who I was just from hearing a few words.'

He smiles and watches my face closely, his head tipped to

the side, not moving. I've seen him do that in the café, too, when I look up from the coffee machine or when I'm serving another customer. Frankly it's a bit creepy. I begin to feel slightly uncomfortable even though there are other customers milling around us.

He straightens his head and says, 'I've always been good with voices. I'm so glad I bumped into you because I've just heard the news about Phillipa's newly discovered book.' He trains his incisive gaze on me again. 'Will you be narrating it?'

I'm rattled by his direct manner. In other circumstances I might even be flattered... if I was on the lookout for attention, that is. But I'm not a big believer in coincidences. The fact he's 'happened' to bump into me at the shop just as Phillipa's hidden book is discovered, as well as frequenting the bar I work at makes me want to run a mile.

'Sorry, I really must go. It was nice to meet you.' I stepped forward, and because he still doesn't move, I find myself awkwardly close to him. Close enough to smell his cheap, cloying aftershave. I step back again and look back at him questioningly.

'I hope you don't mind me saying, Eve, but I think you have the voice of DI Jane Tower all wrong,' he says. I glance around to see if anyone has noticed we've been stood here a while, but the people around us all have their backs to us or are busy rifling through the stand of cheap T-shirts in every colour you could imagine. 'Phillipa wrote Jane Tower as a strong woman with a vulnerable core, and I think you've missed that subtlety. At times, you portray her as rather bolshy and unfeeling.'

I feel a rush of indignation. 'I'm sorry if you feel that way. Phillipa herself selected me as her narrator and I happen to know that she fully approves of my portrayal of the detective.' I give him what I hope is a disingenuous smile. 'Have you actually met Phillipa, Chad?' His eyes narrow and a muscle in his jaw twitches. 'No, I thought as much. Now, if you'll excuse me.'

My heart is hammering but I keep my expression impassive as I step forward again. When he fails to move a third time, I just kept going. My shoulder grazes his and he stumbles slightly as I plough on ahead. My heart bangs on my chest wall, and I have to force myself not to run as I catch sight of the shop assistant I'd asked for help about twenty yards in front of me.

'I heard she was a family friend,' he calls spitefully after me. 'Of course she gave you the job!'

Imposter syndrome pecks at my heels and I feel alarmed that this stranger – Chad Belton – knows so much about me.

But I don't stop walking and I don't look back.

NINE

I arrive at Scarlet's school a few minutes early. I park Mum's ten-year-old Ford Fiesta down the street and scroll through my phone, reading the many news reports about the discovery of the new Tower book. Dramatic headlines scream for my attention on the news websites.

Missing author leaves hidden legacy for loyal fans.

More mystery surrounds missing writer.

None of the articles tell me anything new. They all mention publication of the new book will start with the audio and hardback formats, but my name isn't mentioned specifically. Social media is alive with the news. It is trending under #SecretTowerBook and everyone has an opinion they feel the need to express.

@Crimeficfan76 Great news about book but will they ever find @PhillipasTower1952?

@Tina_Turtle1 Can't wait for new book but something feels odd about this. Why hide a book then disappear??

@MAgazinebabe11 Seems disrespectful for @HarrisLassonUK to publish when @PhillipasTower1952 is still missing. Must be awful for her family.

The guy in the shop – Chad – had heard about the new book because everyone in the reading world is talking about it. Yes, he knew my name, but then most of Phillipa's ardent fans probably would.

I exhale and glance at the digital clock on the dashboard: 15.29. The school bell will sound in under a minute's time. I power my phone down and get out of the car.

At the gate, I hover around, standing a little way apart from the gossipy clusters of parents. Mum picks up Scarlet quite a bit because of my shifts at the bar, so I haven't got to know that many people. There are one or two faces I recognise from my own schooldays. People who have stayed in the area had kids themselves and are now living the same life on repeat. Fair enough, some people crave familiarity, but it's not for me. I don't feel as if I belong around here anymore.

Scarlet runs around the corner of the school building and spots me right away. She waves and her face brightens. I wave back and she rushes over and wraps her arms around me.

'That's a lovely welcome,' I tell her, taking her little pink rucksack and leading her towards the car. 'Fancy calling at the park on the way home?'

'Yesss!' She punches the air.

The park is just a five-minute drive from school. 'I wanted to talk to you about something,' I say carefully, as we buckle up. 'Remember when we lived in London and Mummy worked for the publishing company?'

She nods. 'You read the books out loud, so people could listen,' she says.

'That's right! Well, I've had some exciting news today.' The car feels like an oven, and I roll down the windows a little more. 'Harris-Lasson want me to work for them again.'

'Cool,' she says blandly. 'Can we get an ice-cream at the park, Mummy?'

'We'll see,' I say, slowing as the lights turn to red. I turn in my seat to face her. 'Thing is, Scarlet, to do the job for Harris-Lasson, I'll need to go back to London. Just for a while.'

'Do I have to go to London, too?' She frowns and looks at me. Her cheeks are pink and her fringe is stuck to her forehead. 'I like it at Gran's house.'

I feel my shoulders relax a little. 'No, you can stay here. It won't be for very long, and Gran will look after you. I'll call you to chat every day and come home every weekend. Are you OK with that?'

She nods. 'Jemima is going to ask her mummy if I can have a playdate at her house this weekend.'

'That sounds exciting,' I say with relief. She doesn't seem in the least bit concerned about me working away for a while. Everything is falling into place.

* * *

After tea and while Mum sits and reads a book with Scarlet, I go upstairs into the tiny box room where I'm keeping all my personal items. The bigger things and the few sticks of furniture I kept are currently stashed at the cheapest storage place I could find until we get our own place.

The box room is stacked full of my stuff. Mum must be sick of the mess now, especially as I told her we'd only be staying a couple of months, but she never complains. I'm so grateful she's never made me feel like we're overstaying our welcome. In fact, it's been the opposite. Whenever she gets the opportunity, she encourages me to stick around. I think she must have been lonelier than I thought after Dad died.

I scan the stacked brown boxes until I find the right label. I peel off the masking tape, open the box and lift out, one by one, the nine Tower paperbacks I packed so carefully in bubble wrap before we left the old house. These books are all first editions gifted to me by Phillipa, and they're very special since each one is signed to me personally. I pick up the very first in the series and open the cover, running my finger across Phillipa's signature. I read the dedication out loud:

To Eve, the voice of my stories. Love and best wishes, Phillipa Roberts

Her official signature features a flowery dramatic script, the P and the R of her name oversized and ornate.

I've never read a book on handwriting analysis, but I've always felt Phillipa's handwriting is special. The ornate capital letters seem to represent her public persona, but the more tempered, plainly printed letters feel like there's a real person hiding underneath.

Phillipa can be showy when she's performing to her adoring fans, but she is also introspective and deep. That's what makes her so special. It's how she can accurately tap into her readers' feelings and fast-track straight to their hearts.

I replace the book and take out the ninth instalment Harris-Lasson published last year: *The Final Betrayal*. Sadly, I haven't got time to read all the titles again before I record the new book, but I'm going to refresh my memory with this, her last one.

TEN

TWELVE MONTHS EARLIER

Phillipa Roberts opened her eyes and looked around her pure-white bedroom – diaphanous white drapes that moved slightly in the breeze entering through the window, white walls and paintwork and white bedding.

Her wife had a thing about pale perfection for the house interior and what Fleur wanted, Fleur usually got. With wealthy parents, it had been the pattern of her upper middle-class upbringing.

Phillipa had been born working class and her life had not been without tragedy. Her father, who'd died in an accident at work when she was still a baby, had been a shipbuilder at South Shields. Her mother had worked two cleaning jobs while raising Phillipa and consequently, she knew what being poor felt like. She'd seen empty food cupboards, shivered in the depths of winter when the inside of the windows had iced over in their tiny back-to-back house with its shared outside loo.

Fleur's all-white aesthetic at home was tough on young Milo, Fleur's twelve-year-old son by her ex-husband, Simon.

Phillipa was close to the boy, and they had a bond, not least because she spoke up when she felt Fleur was harsh. Thanks to the perfection of downstairs, Fleur dictated that virtually any activities Milo wanted to do had to be done upstairs. Even stuff like gaming or watching TV.

'You can do that in your bedroom,' she'd tell him disapprovingly. 'You're making the place look untidy.'

'It's not fair on him,' Phillipa had said, trying to reason with her wife. 'We don't want him to feel like he's a nuisance. We want to spend more time together as a family, not less.'

'Nonsense! He's got a fifty-inch TV to play his games on. There isn't a kid alive who wouldn't trade places with him.'

Phillipa had been forty-one years old when her first book in the Tower series was published nine years ago. After years of sending out submissions, trying to get an agent and a publisher, her sample chapters were picked up from a stack sitting on a desk in the Sage Heathfield Literary Agency by a talented young assistant, Jasmine Sanderson. The following day the young woman brought the manuscript to the attention of Sage herself. Over the course of the next six months, Phillipa, Jasmine and Sage had worked tirelessly together to polish up the story ready for submission.

Harris-Lasson Publishing had acquired the first three books in the Tower series and the rest was history. Nine books now published with almost ten million of the series books sold globally. She had more awards than she could shake a stick at and, best of all, her career was still going from strength to strength with her literary agent in talks with several big streaming services about adapting the entire DI Jane Tower series for screen.

If she won the Crime Fiction Book of the Year she'd be inaugurated into the coveted hall of crime fiction fame. An accolade bestowed on some of the most legendary authors of the genre.

Phillipa had waited so long to achieve this dream and yet now, she sometimes felt the fight was behind her. She was living a fairy-tale life, but she often had the sense it had somehow fallen flat.

Writing was hard work, and most people didn't realise it. There was no escape from the world of the Tower series and its characters because they resided in her head. They were a part of her, just like her own life and the real people in it. If she was going through a difficult time, then she also wanted that for her characters.

Fleur was the only one who understood. At least she used to understand. After six years together, Fleur seemed fed up and Phillipa felt guilty her wife was the one who kept the house running and looked after Milo.

They had met at one of her many promotional events. Fleur had been the assistant manager at a newly refurbished two-storey independent bookstore on Kensington High Street. The shop had been woefully unprepared for the queues of readers wanting to take part in their 'Meet the Author' event.

Once the shop had quickly filled to capacity, the staff had tried to close the doors and minor scuffles broke out. Actual pushing and shoving and screeching amongst Phillipa's core army of fans that largely, it had to be said, consisted of middle-aged ladies.

Fleur had whisked Phillipa into a tiny, cluttered storeroom for her own safety. They'd peeked through the door, both almost crying with laughter at the sight of so many cultured Tower fans shouting at the top of their voices and, in the case of one particularly affronted lady with a blue rinse, walloping a member of the security staff with her overfilled Radley handbag.

'I just don't know what we're going to do,' Fleur had wailed at that point, clearly anxious, despite the hilarity of the situation. 'You're only booked with us for an hour. It would take at least double that to get through everyone who's turned up.'

'It doesn't matter,' Phillipa had said, enjoying the other woman's company. 'I'll stay as long as it takes.'

Fleur had breathed a sigh of relief. 'In that case, I'll take you out for dinner afterwards. That's if you're free, of course?'

'Best offer I've had all week.' Phillipa had inhaled Fleur's warm vanilla scent. She knew her eyes were twinkling, and felt relieved only she could feel the butterflies in her stomach.

She'd known *that* early there was magic between them.

The evening had been an enormous success. The staff were delighted to shift nearly a thousand hardbacks of Phillipa's new novel. The initially rambunctious fans were calmed and thrilled to meet Phillipa to get their selfies taken and their books signed. Fleur basked in the flurry of compliments from the shop manager, who was both relieved and impressed Fleur had managed to rescue the situation before the shop windows got broken.

Over dinner, Fleur had explained how she and her husband, Simon, had separated a year earlier. 'The decree nisi came through last month. It's been over for me for a long time, but Simon can't accept it. He lurches from begging me to come back to drunk-dialling and calling me a drug addict who needs help.' She saw Phillipa's alarm and laughed. 'Honestly, I'm not an addict. That's just his take on the antidepressants I was prescribed after my parents both died in a car crash five years ago.'

'That's awful,' Phillipa had said softly, placing a hand over Fleur's slender, manicured fingers. 'I'm so sorry you had to go through that.'

Fleur didn't move her hand away. 'It was tough. But thanks to the medication and regular therapy, I got through it. The funny thing was, I thought Simon was being supportive at the time. Little did I know what he was really thinking. Or what he was capable of.'

Fleur had already been through so much in her previous marriage, Phillipa had tried everything to stop her finding out the truth.

But now something was happening. Something out of her control. It broke Phillipa's heart that she didn't know if there was anything she could do to stop everything falling down around their ears.

All she knew was that, if she found a way out, she'd take it. No matter how risky or how hard it was going to be. The alternative was unthinkable.

ELEVEN

She sits bolt upright, her eyes wide open but unseeing in the pitch dark. Death did not take her after all. The smell of damp and the stale urine stench on her is so strong now, it's difficult to breathe.

There is noise. Lots of noise... above her, or outside the door, she cannot tell.

She cries out into the thick blackness, a plaintive wail that rips through her throat and emerges as a whine. 'Someone... please, help me...'

Her heart lurches at the sound of a bolt being drawn across on the other side of the door. She shuffles back against the wall, brings her knees towards her and wraps her arms around them.

Her bowels cramp at the sound of bolts sweeping back. Banging, scraping and then the steel door swings open and very weak strains of light flood in. Just enough for her searching eyes to look around and see the filth, the tendrils of black mould climbing up the walls.

The room is like how she'd imagined it, but worse. Bare walls, constructed of dark stone blocks and glistening with damp, a dull steel door with no handle, only a sealed steel hatch set close to the floor. A sea of torn pages from paperback books litter the room so she can't see the floor at all. The print is too small to decipher without her reading glasses.

Her head swivels to a figure in the doorway as a sudden blinding light dazzles her.

'Please,' she calls out. 'I need water. I need... to get out of here.'

As the figure moves quickly towards her, she glimpses a flash of someone dressed completely in black wearing a bala-clava, gloves, heavy boots. She can't get a handle on size or gender. She whimpers and runs to the corner of the room as the figure moves towards her.

She yelps at the bright glare drumming into her eyes and squeezes them shut again, opening them slowly in tiny increments.

'You have to let me go! I feel so ill... like I'm going to die.' Ringing starts in her ears, filling her head with more pain. She drags in air, erratic and shallow as if invisible hands are squeezing her neck. 'I can't stand it... I can't breathe...'

A small bottle of water rolls across the floor to her.

'Make it last. No more until tomorrow.' The robotic voice is deliberately distorted with some kind of device. It sounds like the Daleks she used to watch on *Doctor Who* as a child.

She staggers to her feet, reaches for the water in panic. Water means she is staying here. She squints at the figure again, but the light is just too bright to see anything other than a dark human shape.

'Who are you?' she whispers. 'What do you want from me?'

'All will be revealed in time,' the disembodied voice replies. 'If you make it through the night, that is.'

The figure moves quickly forward and crouches down beside her, raising a hand. The shield of light moves with it, and she cowers back against the wall, retching when damp slime covers her skin and invades her nostrils. A gloved hand comes down and she flinches. It rests gently on her head. Then it grabs at her hair, and she lets out a yelp, coughing as her throat burns.

'You'll do as you're told. There are no choices.'

'What is it you want me to do? Why am I here?'

She looks up, hoping to get a glimpse of the person behind the mask. But the angle of the light throws them into shadow.

'I don't know why I'm here,' she whimpers. 'I'm begging you to please, please let me go. Is it money you want? I can get you money.'

The figure points, and she picks up the water, unscrews the plastic top. She holds the bottle up to her lips and drinks. Long and deep, it soothes her burning throat, but she takes too much in and chokes and splutters. The figure watches her dispassionately. She tries again. This time she is more careful and takes only small sips.

'Don't insult me with your bribes,' the figure snaps. 'I want something far more valuable than money.'

'What do you mean? What is it? Tell me and—'

'Enough!'

She feels her entire body lurch forward, past the figure. Her legs give way, she falls and scrabbles across the filthy floor like a crab, desperate to reach the square of light beyond the door.

They yell out in fury and grasp her leg. She kicks hard and feels satisfaction when her foot makes hard contact. She hurls herself forward another couple of yards and then the room explodes.

Excruciating pain shoots through her entire body, and for a moment she thinks she is exploding from the inside out. Her body is rigid, every single muscle tense with cramps as if she's just been hit by lightning.

She rolls onto her back, unable to move, crying out with the unbearable pain. Above her, the figure wields a taser gun above her.

'Want some more?' She is kicked hard in the side, and she cries out. 'Please... just let me go. I promise I won't say a—'

'Enough! Try that again and I'll zap you once an hour for a whole day.' The voice is monotone, artificial. It's the most chilling thing she's ever heard.

The figure steps over her and heads for the door.

'Please, don't leave me here. I can't stand it, I can't!'

The figure does not look back. The door slams shut, and she is plunged again into a sightless world.

A whole day. The cruel words echo in her ears, taunting her. She can't stay here for another hour, never mind a full day.

She can't survive here. It's just not possible.

TWELVE

EVE

Earlier I had arranged to speak to Hugo on Facetime at eight o'clock when I knew Scarlet would be in bed. He finally calls me at 8.25 p.m.

'Hello, Eve,' he says in the deep laconic voice that sent shivers down my spine when we first met. 'How are you?'

'Fine, thanks. You?'

He looks up over his iPad screen and a smile plays at the corners of his mouth. He's probably making eye contact with Saskia, who I gather must be in the same room. 'We're perfect.' He smiles, displaying a new set of sparkling white veneers to add emphasis to just how wonderful life is.

'Is Saskia feeling OK? I hope everything's going well with the baby.' Hugo told me their baby news about a month ago when Saskia was three months pregnant. He'd called on Face-Time to tell Scarlet the news, but I'm not really sure it sank in because she has barely mentioned it.

Right on cue, Saskia's face appears, filling half the screen with smooth brown skin and perfectly arched brows. Her shining, caramel-coloured hair falls naturally to one side in soft waves. She looks radiant. I remember when I was pregnant with

Scarlet, I'd suffered from extreme exhaustion for the first trimester. My hair came out in handfuls and hung lifelessly around my constantly pasty face that no amount of make-up could conceal.

'Eve! So lovely to see you!' Saskia purrs. 'Hope you and darling Scarlet are well. Sorry to rush, but I'm doing a feature in ten minutes for a pregnancy fashion website. Speak soon, we're well overdue for a catch-up!'

She's gone before I can respond. She was always the same when she worked at Harris-Lasson. As Phillipa's PR manager, she was known for dashing around, constantly busy and buzzing with energy. Phillipa used to call her 'Miss Dynamite', even to her face.

I tried to blame Saskia as much as I blamed Hugo when I found out about the affair. She apologised, begged my forgiveness and said she felt so ashamed. Clearly not ashamed enough to ditch my husband, it has to be said. But I know Hugo and I know what he's capable of. How he can manipulate so skilfully, you don't realise you've been had until it's too late.

Back then, I'd sensed a restlessness in him for a while. He'd told me he felt panicky now he was getting close to forty. 'I feel like I might never achieve what I want to achieve,' he said after too much after-dinner brandy one night.

Hugo liked to call himself a businessman, an entrepreneur. But he wasn't a very good one. He'd taken out loan after loan, securing the biggest one on the house and taking the last of the equity in our property. He was a skilled salesman, seeming to have no trouble convincing people to invest in his innovative business ideas, only for them to lose every penny in record time. But Hugo never cared about that. When it came to business, he saw investors as fair game. Collateral damage in his quest to silence the voice of his late, critical father who'd said, at every opportunity, that Hugo hadn't got the fire in his belly needed to succeed in business.

Hugo met Saskia Peterson at a publicity event for Phillipa's last book. 'These things are always so dull,' he'd complained when I'd shown him the invite. But he'd dragged himself along without too much fuss when I'd assured him there'd be free champagne.

When we arrived, I'd introduced Hugo and Saskia, so he'd have someone to chat to when I got called away to record a podcast interview. It simply hadn't occurred to me that Saskia was young and beautiful, a part-time model in addition to her blossoming publishing career. Naively, I never thought to question Hugo's fidelity in any way, or indeed his commitment to our marriage.

Saskia and I had always got on well. She'd been one of my favourite people at Harris-Lasson. Imagine the irony when three months later I found a deleted selfie of the two of them kissing in the trash folder on Hugo's phone.

Now I believe Saskia is essentially a good person who got herself caught up in a lie when she swallowed Hugo's story that he and I were secretly estranged. Sadly, before the truth could show itself, she fell in love with the liar. For that reason, I decided to be civil with her. Polite. And for the sake of Scarlet really, although thanks to Hugo, Saskia hasn't really seen much of her.

'Looks well, doesn't she... Saskia,' Hugo says, pulling me back into the conversation.

'What? Oh yes. Yes, she does. So... what was it you wanted to talk about?' I prompt him.

Hugo laughs insincerely. 'Same old Eve. Cut out the small talk and straight down to business, eh?'

'It's just that I've... well, I have stuff to do. That's all. I've had a work opportunity just come in.'

'Really? That's good news; you've been out of the game for a while now.'

I open my mouth to reply but he speaks over me.

'That's quite a coincidence actually because here's the thing.' That has always been his favourite pre-empt to saying something I'm not going to like. 'I haven't told you this until now largely because we didn't know if it was all going come off. But we've bought a new place. A four-bed thatched cottage in Oakham, Rutland. Huge garden, next door to a private horse-riding school.'

'Wow... congratulations.'

A horse-riding school. Scarlet's ultimate dream. My mouth tingles as if I've chewed on something sour.

'Thanks. We're over the moon about it. Saskia's already playing interior designer – she has a flair for it. Anyways, what we thought would be lovely, is if Scarlet comes down and spends the summer with us at Bee Cottage, so she can see her bedroom and get to know the place... and Saskia, of course.'

Bee Cottage. Sounds idyllic.

'Well, the whole summer is out of the question. That's far too long, but perhaps we can sort something—'

'Then Viv rang and told me you're going to be working in London again, and now it couldn't be a more perfect time!'

He's already spoken to Mum? I know they keep in touch. Mum has never said as much, but she's always thought the world of Hugo, despite his shortcomings.

'Didn't she tell you? She called me earlier and told me you're going to be working in London for about a month. It was Saskia's idea. She said, "Wouldn't it be lovely to have Scarlet here for the summer while Eve is working away?"'

'Well, I—'

'It would give Scarlet time to feel part of the family before the new baby arrives. Saskia's an accomplished rider, too, so she's desperate to get her going with some horse-riding lessons. What do you think?'

For a few moments, I'm struck dumb. I feel a bit betrayed by Mum, but she's done this before – called Hugo and told him things about Scarlet before I've had the chance. I've asked her not to do it, but she doesn't seem to think she's doing anything wrong.

Thoughts swirl around my head. Scarlet staying with Hugo and Saskia for a whole month? Sure, Scarlet will love the horse-riding and seeing her new bedroom... what five-year-old wouldn't? But there's more to keeping a child stable and healthy than that.

Scarlet has already been showing signs of mood changes and the timing is dreadful because I've just enrolled her in several holiday activity clubs at her school, paying the first two sessions up front. All her little friends will be going, and she's been looking forward to it. My hands and throat start to itch.

'That all sounds wonderful, Hugo, but a month away from home is too long for Scarlet. What would be lovely is for her to come to you for a weekend, initially. That, we can talk about. Staying away any longer is out of the question because of the activity clubs which keep her in touch with her school friends.'

My chest burns when I think of Scarlet being seduced by a life riding horses at the new cottage. Hugo knows perfectly well how to bewitch a five-year-old over the summer. Sustaining that interest is likely to be the more difficult thing for him, judging by his track record as a father.

Something just doesn't feel right about Hugo's proposal. Something I can't quite put my finger on.

On the monitor, Hugo shakes his head in disbelief. 'She's *five*, Eve,' he says in that 'I can't believe you're being so stupid' tone I got to know so well during the last year of our marriage. I wonder if Saskia has heard it yet. Probably not. 'Missing out on a silly school holiday club won't make any difference at all to her when she's this young. I mean, what do they do there? Probably sit them in front of *Peppa Pig* all day.'

'It will make a big difference to Scarlet. They have their little friendship groups, even at this age. It's important she has the same chance of integration as the other children in her new class this September.'

I watch as the amiable expression slides from Hugo's face. 'I'm disappointed you're being so awkward about this, Eve. You're off to London on a jolly for a whole month and unable to look after Scarlet, but you don't want me, her father, to step in to help out. Am I reading this right?'

'It's not "a jolly", Hugo – it's work. A very important step in my career, otherwise I wouldn't be leaving her.' He presses his lips together in an amused expression and says nothing, but I know what he's thinking. I know what they all think about my career, including Mum. 'I simply want to avoid more upheaval in her life.'

'Upheaval caused in the first place by you sodding off back to middle England, you mean?' he snaps.

'No, Hugo. I mean the upheaval caused by your affair with my colleague, and me being forced to sell the house when you left me and Scarlet to be with her.'

He shakes his head slowly, as if he's forgotten just how petty I've become. As if, by mentioning his affair with Saskia, I've done something unforgivably distasteful. 'I'm sad you're reducing what we want to do for Scarlet down to a few smutty words, Eve. I honestly thought you were better than that.'

As the indignation rises in my chest, I observe the need to explain, to defend myself and I take a breath. He's always done this. This exact thing. Deflecting any blame or responsibility of his by highlighting *my* shortcomings. It doesn't sound much, but it's very real, and it's one of his favourite games. He's good at it. Hard to explain just how bad it used to make me feel, and now he's trying to do it again. Well, my days of playing his games are over.

'Thank you for the offer, but the answer is no. Scarlet can't come to stay with you for a whole month, but if you like, we can sort out a few days.'

He glances over his shoulder. A quick, sly movement to check Saskia has left the house before his features knit into a snarl.

'Don't make the mistake of thinking you have the upper hand here, Eve.' He lowers his voice to barely more than a whisper. 'If I wanted, I could get custody of Scarlet in a flash. You'd do well to remember that. If you don't want Scarlet staying here then maybe you ought to be turning down jobs you aren't in a position to fulfil properly. You can't just abandon our daughter every time London calls.'

My heartbeat starts racing but I keep cool.

'The custody of Scarlet has been decided, Hugo, and you have to abide by that.' He'd kicked up a fuss when we first split up, forced me to go to court to get custody of our daughter. I'd have been happy with shared, but in the end, I went for full custody, and he didn't contest it.

Hugo had lost interest in the fight for Scarlet when he became embroiled in his exciting new life with Saskia, when he realised the gravity of what being a hands-on dad would mean to his fancy lifestyle. He had disappointed Scarlet countless times.

He had lacked the emotional strength to maintain both sides of his life: the old and the new. He'd sacrificed our daughter and run away from his responsibilities, and now he wanted in again because it suited him. Well, it wasn't that simple.

We stare at each other through our respective screens. Two people who used to love each other deeply, who created another small and wonderful human being called Scarlet who needs us both in her life. These days, it seems, we are quietly at loggerheads but succeed most of the time to conceal it from ourselves and others. That's not the case right now.

His eyes narrow dangerously. 'What do you think a family court might say if it had to choose between a child's parents?

The father, a financially secure businessman settled in a beautiful home who can offer wonderful opportunities to his daughter. Or the mother who is basically transient and back living with her mother with no substantial income to speak of?'

I realise then why something had felt so wrong about his "caring father" attitude... It wasn't the Hugo I know. A rush of painful memories surges forward. The times he'd let Scarlet down on their planned outings in the weeks and months after he left us. The way I'd had to console her when she finally walked away from watching out of the window. Realising, at such a tender young age, that she couldn't count on her daddy coming to see her as he'd promised.

Scarlet is a child who can easily become anxious. When we moved back to Nottingham, there were one or two incidents of concern at her new school involving a child getting an injured finger and another being left with a ruined piece of artwork. Both had cited Scarlet as the aggressor. The school were very supportive and together, we ironed out her behavioural problems. Now Scarlet is far happier and stable at school and has made new friends. That's why it's so important her integration is continued over the summer break.

For me to agree to her spending a whole month in his care, I'd have to feel completely reassured that Hugo would stick to his word and put Scarlet first. Sadly, I haven't got that sort of confidence in him.

'A month is out of the question,' I say firmly. 'It's not up for negotiation.'

I press a button and Hugo's face disappears. I shouldn't have done that, but at least I can breathe again. Ever since I've known him Hugo has been full of big ideas that he pursues with gusto and then quickly tires of them and abandons his plans. But this is not just one of his hare-brained business ideas. This is about our daughter.

Hugo's spiteful threats have struck a chord. He's planning

something big. A change. This is not me unduly worrying; he's just said as much. I'm not in a great position right now. My personal circumstances leave room for improvement, whereas Hugo is flying high. It's a real threat and I'd be foolish to under-estimate him.

I need to get my life back in order, for my daughter's sake. It's my only weapon against Hugo if his intention is to apply for custody of Scarlet.

THIRTEEN

CHAD

It had annoyed Chad the way Eve Hewitt had dismissed him so easily in the shop on Friday. She'd treated him like some crackpot fan, and he was far from that.

Eve had made the mistake of lumping him in with the other so-called superfans. It was a label he hated, but one that, over the last couple of years, had brought too many benefits for him to shun membership of the sad little groups Phillipa Roberts's PR people had dreamed up. Most of them made up of readers who didn't know the first thing about the intricacies of the Tower series nor the hidden subtleties of the characters.

If Eve knew what he knew, if she realised the power he could wield if he so wished, well... perhaps she wouldn't be so flippant then.

When Chad had tried to engage her to discuss her representation of DI Jane Tower, she had instantly become defensive and had ended up barging past him like he was nothing. A nobody.

They all thought they knew Phillipa. But nobody really knew her, not like he did.

He looked around now at this, his special room, the basement he'd finished all by himself. He'd plastered the walls, screeded and painted a new floor and, finally, fitted a security door that he could bolt from the inside. He had everything down here he needed. A stock of food, a fridge and, most importantly, a state-of-the-art sound system on which he could listen to the Tower series audiobooks for hours on end if he so desired.

When he'd first inherited this, his mother's ancient Victorian villa, he had made finishing the basement his first job. He had painted the walls a clean, matte white. But over time, he'd redecorated every inch of the space with his precious collection, carefully compiled over time. His secret shrine to Phillipa Roberts.

There were photographs here of every description. Phillipa at events, Phillipa arriving and leaving home. Thanks to the powerful zoom lens he had invested in, he could now sit in his padded black leather chair and enjoy the multitude of photographs he'd been able to snap covertly through the windows of her home. Phillipa in her nightwear, Phillipa on the phone, Phillipa secretly smoking, drinking far more than she ought to and, his very favourite which he'd blown up twice the size of the other prints... a magnificently naked Phillipa climbing into the bath.

No. None of her sycophants, her hangers-on, could possibly know Phillipa like Chad did. He knew every inch of her in both mind and body, and that's what set him apart from the crowd.

Eve Hewitt wasn't nearly as clever as she liked to think. It had been the easiest thing in the world to follow her when she left the shop. He'd dumped the fake clothes that he'd claimed were for his mother then, at a distance, he'd tracked her to the school. He'd watched mother and daughter from the cover of a scattering of trees at the local park and, finally, accompanied them – at a distance – back to her mother's modest terraced house.

Chad had stayed under cover there for a while, observed the

older lady puffing and panting when she put out the bins, struggling with the stiff hinges on her front gate and negotiating the broken paving slabs in the garden with obvious difficulty given her slow, laboured movements.

Over the weekend, Chad had kept busy, whipping up an eye-catching flyer in minutes. Just the one. 'No Job Too Small' screamed the banner in a rather attractive violet-blue colour he'd selected. Underneath, he'd included a laughably low hourly rate.

All ready. Now all he had to do was wait for Eve to disappear to London.

FOURTEEN

EVE

The home of Harris-Lasson Publishing is on the third floor of an impressive steel and glass office building located close to Canary Wharf.

It's been eight months since I was last in London. Even when I lived here with Hugo and Scarlet, I never felt part of the cool publishing crowd. My stomach is churning now. The way it does when you have no choice but to spend time in a place you feel like an imposter.

It's Monday morning, and I sign in at reception ten minutes early, where I'm directed to an area of casual seating. Low corner sofas with clean lines and moulded plastic coffee tables in bold primary colours dot the modern space. I haven't a clue what brand this furniture is, but its simplicity and design screams *expensive*.

Rather than take a seat right away, I walk over to the floor-to-ceiling windows that overlook the river. The Thames rolls smoothly past like a sleek, dark eel, carrying passenger boats and rowers on its back. Other steel and glass buildings glitter in the sun. Beautiful, intimidating London.

Back at the sofas, I sit opposite two other visitors. One, a man in his early thirties and wearing a well-cut navy suit. His fingers move over his phone at lightning speed as he composes a message, checking a piece of paper every few seconds for various details. I catch the tell-tale sheen of corporate stress shining on his cheeks and upper lip.

The other visitor is a woman in her mid to late twenties. She wears a fitted black shift dress with an asymmetrical neckline and a matching jacket. She's tipped her toes towards the ceiling while balancing on her heels, and exquisite red soles are revealed. She stares straight ahead and avoids meeting my eyes.

I look down at my pale hands and scratch at a tiny fleck of olive paint on my skin. You could hardly call my clothes stylish – black trousers I've had for a couple of years and a beige jacket I've paired with a white blouse and flat pumps. I don't look like I belong in a place like this. I don't feel as though I do, either.

'Eve? So lovely to see you!' Recognising the warm North-East tones of Jules, Phillipa's editor, I jump up out of my seat and we embrace. 'It's been too long.'

'Feels like an age since I've been here,' I say, taking in her fashionably slouchy linen dress and simple ponytail. I feel my shoulders relax a little. Not everyone power-dresses around here. 'If only Phillipa were here with us. I can't believe it's almost a year since she's been gone.'

Jules seems to deflate in front of me. 'Don't. I miss her so much.' She glances around cautiously. 'But we should keep it positive.'

'Agreed. It's good to be back, and I know Phillipa would be pleased we're working together again.'

Jules nods but doesn't speak. I look at her properly and see she's lost weight since we last worked together. It could be my imagination, but she looks like a faded version of the Jules I used to know.

Her eyes fix on mine before she looks away and claps her hands as if she's psyching herself up.

'OK, let's get you upstairs! The rest of the team is waiting. they're all so excited to be working with you again and I've got good news. The flatshare is ready to go today, if you want it that quickly. You'll get on so well with Nina, the other tenant. She'll introduce herself when we get up there, I'm sure.'

Relief soothes my nerves. 'That's amazing, Jules. Thanks so much, it's going to be a big help.'

Jules nods and uses her security lanyard to open the access barrier, and I follow her to the row of gleaming silver lifts.

The meeting room has an enormous desk and around twenty members of staff are sitting around it. I recognise one or two faces from when I'd visited the building before, but I mainly worked remotely in the recording studio. Harris-Lasson employs a lot of people and I imagine there have been plenty of new starters and leavers come and go in the eight months since I was last here. When Phillipa first went missing, everyone hoped she'd be back within days, that it had just been a misunderstanding of sorts. But after about a month, her absence became a bit of an elephant in the room in meetings or other gatherings. People talked around it, avoided mentioning her name altogether.

At that point, the press were printing stories daily; elaborate speculations of what might have happened to Phillipa. She'd had a breakdown and was down and out somewhere in the country, that she'd fled abroad because she had financial problems. Someone had abducted her... Someone had killed her. The press and their 'sources' – mysterious people who were never named, of course. Anything for sensationalist stories that would sell newspapers or get website hits.

I looked around the impressive foyer. Back then, I'd felt certain my career would have continued to prosper here even without Phillipa. After all, there were other authors I narrated for. But I'd under-estimated how much everything had piled up on top of me and ground me down. I kept thinking if I just ploughed on, pushed through all the heartache, I'd come out the other end. But it didn't work like that. Phillipa's disappearance on top of my marriage failing and Dad's death was just too much to bear in the end.

Jules indicates for me to take a seat and then walks up to the top end of the table and sits next to a woman who I recognise as Alicia Kent, the CEO; a slim, cool blonde in her early forties. She started at Harris-Lasson only about a month before I left. She sees me looking and trains her icy-blue eyes on mine, allowing the merest hint of a smile to settle on her lips.

The middle of the table is loaded with jugs of water and orange juice together with plates filled with different sorts of pastries. I recognise a few faces and acknowledge people.

The woman on the left of me is in conversation with her colleague, but the one on my right, a young woman with short black hair and a freckled pale face says, 'Morning! You must be Eve – Jules said she'd sit you next to me.' She offers a hand. 'I'm Nina.'

'Flatshare Nina?' I confirm the connection, and she laughs.

'The very same!'

I'm instantly relieved she seems so nice and normal, and I'm not going to have to pay over the odds for a room in a B & B. I was grateful when Jules said she might have a rental lead, but I felt a bit nervous who I'd end up sharing with.

Nina grins and leans over to scoop up an almond croissant, using a small napkin as a plate. I like her already for her lack of airs and graces. 'Jules has asked me to show you the flat after the meeting. It's tiny but quiet and in a good location.' She picks toasted almond from the top of the pastry and pops it in her mouth. 'I'm more than happy to share the rent, so if you like it, it might be my lucky day!'

There's movement at the top of the table.

'Morning, everyone,' Alicia says, her voice clear and authoritative. The room instantly falls quiet. 'I think we've got everyone here.' She checks her watch, 'It's turned ten now, so I'd like to make a start. Congratulations to everyone who's made it onto what we're calling the Tower project for obvious reasons. It was a popular one, lots of folks wanted to be a part of it.'

There's a smattering of excitable noises.

'I don't need to remind you that despite the boon of the unexpected manuscript, the situation is steeped in tragedy. It's important we all keep this in mind.' She looks to her left. 'Jules?'

'Thanks, Alicia.' Jules stands up and looks around the table. 'For those people who weren't with us last year, Phillipa Roberts, the author of our manuscript, disappeared ten months ago in, as yet, unknown circumstances. Phillipa's wife, Fleur, and Phillipa's twelve-year-old stepson, Milo, are still living with the horror of what happened. It's important we remember, in doing our job to the best of our ability, that they are yet to get the answers they need.'

Alicia nods gravely. 'I can't stress how important it is for us to treat the family's feelings with the utmost respect as we progress with this project. Phillipa's legion of fans will be watching closely, and they'll have mixed feelings about the new book.' She glances at the paperwork in front of her. 'Apparently, over the weekend, there have already been disparaging comments posted on social media following our press release about the new manuscript. Unfounded criticism that Harris-Lasson is cashing in on a tragedy. It goes without saying it's vital we quash those rumours as soon as possible.'

'The publicity department is working on a sensitive but extensive campaign to publicise the new hardback's release together with the audiobook next spring,' Jules says, glancing at me. 'Eventually, there will also be a paperback version.'

Alicia stands up and the projector springs into life. A photograph of Phillipa accepting an award lights up the screen and several people murmur sadly.

'Those of us who knew Phillipa miss her terribly,' Alicia says, looking forlornly at Phillipa's image. 'But we have been given an extraordinary opportunity in the discovery of this latest manuscript. Phillipa's wife and her literary agent are in full support of the book's release, and we are determined to do it justice. We consider it our privilege and honour to deliver this wonderful gift for her loyal fans all over the world who love her outstanding work.'

'And boost the balance sheet tenfold while we're at it,' Nina whispers from behind a hand.

'Jules, can you take us through the proposed schedule, please?' Alicia says smoothly.

The slide changes and Jules takes us through the stages.

'We've just completed the edit stage of the manuscript. We were given permission by Fleur and Phillipa's agent, Sage, to carry out any necessary editorial changes and they have kindly given us free rein to select a cover in keeping with the rest of the Tower series.'

Alicia nods. 'Everyone present here today will be required to sign confidentiality and non-disclosure agreements relating to this project specifically. Key people will be given restricted access to the manuscript beforehand to enable them to make preparations.'

I'm distracted by my phone lighting up on the table with an incoming text. I turned it to silent before the meeting, but when I see the two-line preview of the message notification it demands my attention just as if it had pinged out loud.

I called in to see your mum and I've brought Scarlet back with me to the cottage now she's broken up from school for the summer. She'll stay with us for a couple of days while you're in London. I can speak after 6 p.m. Hugo

FIFTEEN

At the end of the breakfast meeting, everyone signs the confidentiality agreement before leaving. After I've handed mine in and been given my copy, I make an excuse to visit the bathroom.

'I'll wait for you downstairs,' Nina calls.

Outside the bathroom, I call Hugo. His phone goes straight to voicemail and I leave a terse message.

'Hugo. I need to speak to you and well before six. You're completely out of order taking Scarlet without my agreement. Call me please, as soon as you get this message.'

I end the call and ring Mum. I've got no missed call from her which presumably means she made an executive decision to let Scarlet go without checking with me first. The call rings out. I try again, but no luck. A couple of women walk past me, and I shove my phone back in my bag and make my way downstairs to Nina.

We head for the Tube, and I soon discover Nina is the kind of person who constantly chatters on about nothing. I'm grateful for it. I'm furious with Hugo, but I must at least try and mask my feelings. Nina seems lovely, but it's far too soon to tell her all my problems. I'm keen to show I'm a professional and it's important my colleagues see me as someone who is capable and available, not weighed down with personal problems back home.

The flat is a tiny two-bedroom, one-bathroom affair, only about a ten-minute walk from the Tube station. It's one of four apartments in a converted Victorian villa that has a keypad on the front door. Nina opens up and we step inside. I'm expecting a musty, damp smell, but it turns out the small entrance hall has been recently decorated, and thankfully there's no sticky ancient carpet, just a modern laminate floor. Nina fishes into her handbag and hands me a key.

'This is for our flat door. This front door is keypad entry and the number is zero-one, zero-eight, four-five. The date of birth of our grumpy downstairs tenant, Joseph.' She nods to a door off the hallway bearing the number 16. 'He won't take parcels in for me while I'm at work, and he double-locks the entrance door from the inside if I'm not back home for ten o'clock at night.'

I follow her upstairs to a door marked 16A.

'What do you do if he locks you out?'

'I bang on his front window and threaten to tell the landlord.' She laughs and opens the front door. 'Here we go. Prepare to be dazzled.' We step inside a tiny, cream-painted hallway with the same wooden floor that seems to run throughout the house. Nina opens the door opposite with an estate agent's flourish. 'And here we have the impressive living room and kitchen.'

It's not a bad-sized room but a bit too small for what's in it. The seating area takes up two-thirds. It's a snug space with a two-seater sofa and a bucket chair. There's a big cream rug and a flat-screen television fixed to the wall.

Nina walks over to the miniscule kitchen and points to the fridge. 'The freezer tray at the top is broken. But we can have a shelf each and share the salad tray if you like.'

'Fine by me,' I murmur. Out of the blue, Mum's old-fashioned but homely pine kitchen flashes into my mind. Scarlet loves to sit at the table colouring while Mum makes tea. They put on the radio and if a song they like comes on, they stop what they're doing and dance around the kitchen. I feel a prickle in my eyes at what I've left behind.

'Cheer up, it's not so bad.' Nina grins, leading me back into the hallway. 'We don't get any antisocial behaviour here. Believe it or not, old Joseph downstairs doesn't throw that many parties.'

'I'm OK, just missing my daughter,' I say lightly, as she opens another door.

Nina turns around. 'How old is she?'

'She's five, and her name is Scarlet. She's staying with my mum while I'm away.'

I fight the urge to blurt out that she's *supposed* to be staying with my mum but her father has taken matters into his own hands.

'I assume you'll be going home on weekends to see her, though?'

'Yeah, course.' I don't even want to start thinking about the logistics of *that*. I'm already missing our cuddles and taking Scarlet to the park. I know she loves her dad, and it will probably be a big adventure for her, but I'm scared he'll let her down again and I'll be left to pick up the pieces.

'This is my room.' Nina opens another door and I crane my head around it. It's not a bad size, a bit messy. More surprisingly, it's full of soft toys.

'You collect teddy bears?'

She looks sheepish. 'Pathetic, isn't it? But in the absence of a decent fella, they do nicely. More importantly, they never answer back or leave the loo seat up.'

I laugh. 'Might get one myself then.'

She ushers me in another bedroom. 'This is yours. I had a set of spare bedding, so I made it up for you.'

'That's kind. Thanks, Nina.' It's a smaller room than the first one, but clean and bright thanks to a decent sized picture window. On the wall opposite the bed there's a small Ikea-style wardrobe and a narrow chest of drawers.

'No cleaner or anything, I'm afraid. Down to us to split the chores.'

I nod and walk over to the window. There's a view of a tree and a church and – I squint to see through the leaves – a small graveyard.

'Look on the bright side.' Nina laughs, watching me. 'At least the neighbours are quiet.'

* * *

Back in the living room while Nina makes coffee, I try Hugo again. His phone is still turned off. My stomach churns when I think of the apparent ease with which he has engineered this situation, no doubt to support his bid for custody. If I wasn't so determined, it might have scuppered my job opportunity. Waiting until I'm out of the way to take Scarlet to the cottage. The very thing I told him couldn't happen.

Nina brings over two mugs of coffee and puts them down on a small table.

'I overheard people at work saying you knew Phillipa Roberts quite well,' she says, sitting down.

I nod. 'My great-aunt taught her at school and we met at a family party a few years ago. Phillipa helped me a lot at the beginning of my career, and I saw quite a bit of her in London.'

'I didn't realise you had that big a connection.'

'Yeah, I've always liked her and not just because of my job – I'm a real fan of her books as a reader, too.' I take a sip of my drink, thinking back. 'She always seemed down to earth despite her success, a genuinely lovely person. I was so shocked when I heard she'd gone missing.'

Nina nods thoughtfully. 'Everyone was shocked. There were all sorts of rumours at work at the time. People saying stuff, all behind the scenes of course. Prissy Alicia would have a fit if she'd heard some of it.'

'Stuff like what?' I'd been so low after my marriage failed, then with moving back to Mum's just a couple of months after Phillipa's disappearance, I hadn't been around to hear what everyone thought. Working as a narrator is a solitary career and most of it is spent in a recording studio. It was easy to lose touch with everyone I used to see on my occasional trips into the office.

Nina looks at me doubtfully and I realise she feels a bit put on the spot.

'I won't say a word,' I tell her. 'If we're going to share a flat, we should agree now to trust one another. Deal?'

'Deal!' She grins and drains her coffee cup. 'When Phillipa first disappeared, people were surmising she'd had enough and just took off for a new life somewhere. Sounds crazy, I know, but you hear about people doing it, don't you? Everyone imagines people like Phillipa having amazing lives but, as the saying goes, nobody really knows what goes on behind closed doors.'

'And are people still saying that?'

'Well, now everyone is confused. Like, why would Phillipa secretly write and hide away a manuscript before taking off? It doesn't make sense. Have you got a theory on why she might do that?'

She looks at me expectantly, as if I might have some insider knowledge.

I think for a moment. 'Well, she might have just thought to put it away for a while. Lots of authors do that, pop a first draft in a drawer and try to forget about it. Then they read it with fresh eyes a few weeks' later.'

'I doubt that was the reason.' Nina's eyes gleam. 'I heard it was properly concealed. Up in her loft, buried under a load of old paperwork. That's where it was found, apparently.'

I pull a face. 'It does sound a bit odd.'

'Unless of course, Phillipa's editor knows more than she's letting on...'

I shake my head, sceptically. 'I've known Jules for years, and she's not the sort to keep secrets. She's loyal and honest.'

Nina sniffs. 'She's changed since the Ice Queen took over. Nobody knows Alicia that well. She doesn't let anyone close, even her own management team.' Nina finished her coffee and put down her cup with a flourish. 'I mean, why is someone so senior involving herself in every minute detail of the Tower project, huh? Ask yourself that.'

I think about Jules's hangdog demeanour, how she seemed so much more nervous than I remembered her. I could see how gossip might grow from that. But it was nonsense, it had to be.

'Has to be the business angle.' I shrug. 'Most publishers are finding it tough right now, and I suppose having a new Phillipa Roberts book is like having a licence to print money.'

SIXTEEN

She is lying on the floor, halfway between sleep and wakefulness when it comes to her. The sudden vivid recollection of drinking in a car, feeling confused and out of sorts before a struggle. She'd felt the tug of fear in her gut, a sharp pain in her arm and then nothing.

She has clearly been drugged. Possibly the drink had been laced with something and then the pain in her arm – an injection – had knocked her out. It is the obvious reason every inch of her body now throbs and aches. The reason for this overwhelming feeling of weakness in every movement, every action.

She must have then been brought here, bundled into the hellish basement she is starting to believe she might never escape from.

Noises sound up above her and then outside the door. She sits up, feeling weak and dizzy from hunger, but more than that, there's the unstoppable thirst. A terrible stench fills her nostrils and, as she shifts on the floor, she recoils, realising the smell is coming from her.

The door flings open, the bright light dazzles. The dark figure moves ominously into the basement then steps back before walking to the door and beckoning her. They come close and then take a step back, a gloved hand moving up to their face.

She almost apologises before a bolt of fury brings her to her senses.

Her throat burns in protest, but she still manages to whisper, her voice croaky and faint. 'Please... let me go.'

She braces herself for a sharp kick or, even worse, the taser again, but the figure takes several more steps back and beckons her.

Hope rises like a sunburst in her chest. She shuffles forward on her hands and knees and the figure continues to back up towards the door. Leaning heavily on the mossy wall, she somehow manages to pull herself up to standing. The figure waits, not making a sound but watching her every move. She stands and then moves unsteadily and slowly forward. She is cautious, but they beckon again, in the doorway now.

Could it be true... Is she really being set free?

The figure disappears outside the door and the momentous moment comes when she steps past the steel door and out of the foul basement. She immediately takes a deep breath in. The air is cleaner out here even if she stinks to high heaven herself. She is in a long corridor with cold tiles on the floor and plain white walls. She follows them, feeling grateful for the freezing cold floor on her bare feet.

She is still not sure of the gender of her captor. It's so hard to tell, but the clothes look as though they might be padded, shoulders wide, biceps chunky. They continue to walk and her hope rises.

Could it be... could it really be she is being set free? She'll need clothes, shoes. Her mind sifts through the haze, trying to remember anything, anything at all about how she got here but the single flashback with the drink is the only clue. Apart from that, it's still a blank canvas.

All she knows for sure is she is here now, and her only aim is to get away. If only she can escape this building, there's a chance she can find someone who will help her.

Her body feels so weak and insubstantial. She knows she won't be able to run even if she gets the opportunity. She is so weak now, she couldn't even make a dash to get away like she did when she got tasered. Her poor, shaking legs can barely carry her even to walk at this snail's pace.

At the end of the corridor, the figure stops walking and waits until she has caught up. They turn the corner, and she is helped up two small steps onto another level. Again, it's a corridor, but now there's a feeling they have definitely left the damp basement behind. A few more steps and she is led to a plain wooden door.

There are no markings on it, but she cannot fail to notice the three heavy-duty bolts spaced equally along the length of the door. A key is inserted into the door, and it is pushed open. The figure stands back and sweeps an arm before her, indicating she should enter.

She steps cautiously from the wooden floor on to carpet. Soft lamplight illuminates the space. The room is large, larger than she could have imagined after what seemed like a lifetime cooped up in the dungeon. There is no window in here, but it is decorated pleasantly and there are framed pictures of all nine published books in the Tower series dotted around the walls.

There is a formal desk with a laptop, headphones, a notebook and pens. An armchair in one corner and, next to it, a small trolley bearing mugs, cutlery and, tucked underneath, a mini-fridge.

There is a full-sized single divan bed made up neatly with pillows and a quilt. Next to the bed is a small rail with a few garments of comfy, stretchy black clothing hanging. Leggings and tops. On a shelf running along the bottom are socks, underwear. A folded blanket.

The figure walks over to a door on the far wall that bears no bolts or locks. Obediently, she moves forward when she is again beckoned, the carpet feels soft as cotton wool underfoot. The door is opened, a light switch flipped, and she is invited through. It's a bathroom. A bathroom! She feels like crying when she sees a walk-in shower. There's a toilet and a sink... but no mirror. Towels, soap, toiletries and even a toothbrush.

She feels like crying. She had hoped to be set free but knew in her heart that wouldn't happen. But this... this is nirvana compared to the damp, filthy hole she's been held captive in.

The light is turned off and she is led back into the main room and over to the desk. She stands by the chair and looks down. The MacBook is closed. A hardback Leuchtturm notebook and their brand of rollerball pens – both of which she uses when working at home – are placed to the left, and to the right of the laptop is a typed sheet.

She leans forward and squints at the words. She has no reading glasses, but she can just about discern her name at the top of the sheet in larger, bold letters.

The figure taps a gloved finger on the sheet then opens the top drawer of the old-fashioned mahogany desk. Inside are several pairs of reading glasses.

The figure walks away and wordlessly leaves the room.

She feels a jolt of panic. 'No, wait... please!' But they do not hesitate, and the door is slammed shut. The bolts are drawn on the other side and she hears the key turning in the lock. 'Please! Come back. Come... back...' She drops to her knees and begins to sob into her hands.

What's happening to her? Why is she here? She looks around the walls. The posters. The desk. What can they possibly want from her?

Eventually she pulls her aching body to standing and walks across to the desk. She opens the drawer and pulls out the spectacles. The first pair are too weak. The second pair are fine.

She will not sit in the pleasant, cushioned chair until she showers, but she pulls the letter towards her and begins to read.

After only a few lines, she closes her eyes and covers her face with her dirty hands.

'Oh no,' she whispers out loud. 'Please... no!'

SEVENTEEN

EVE

Tuesday morning, I emerge from the Barbican underground station and head directly to the Harris-Lasson recording studio.

My first night in the flat was disastrous. Mum didn't pick up my call and I sent her an email asking how Hugo had ended up taking Scarlet to his house. I wasn't too worried she hadn't answered as Mum suffers with arthritis and often takes herself off to bed early. But she really should have let me know Hugo had taken Scarlet.

I'd managed to speak to Scarlet eventually on the telephone, but Hugo had literally come to the phone for seconds to say, 'Sorry, Eve, something's come up. Let's have a chat tomorrow about Scarlet staying here.'

She was bubbling with excitement. 'I have my own room, Mummy, and there's a riding school right next door!'

I had to bite my tongue and be happy for her. At least in the interim. As a result, I barely slept a wink and now I feel tired on my first, proper working morning: my first day recording.

The fully equipped studio is located in purpose-built facilities across town.

I sign in at reception and check my emails. There's a message from Jules with an encrypted file attached.

Eve,

Manuscript attached. Please do not share or discuss as per confidentiality agreement.

Best, Jules

Another message contains instructions and passwords on how to open it. I feel like I'm working for MI5.

I follow the instructions and figure out how to access the manuscript, feeling a sense of excitement and anticipation. I start to read but within a few minutes, a thin woman in her forties in a white coat and spectacles with her hair pulled back severely into a bun comes through. I've worked with a few producers in my time, but she isn't one of them.

'Eve? Hi, I'm Deidre. I'm going to be your audiobook producer.'

We shake hands and I follow her up the steps in reception and through the security doors into the building. There are three recording booths and I've worked in all of them. Deidre leads me into the first one.

The small, soundproofed room is split into two with a glass partition separating us.

'I know you're an experienced narrator, so just shout if you've got any questions,' she says.

I look at her desk, at all the sound-recording equipment. Then I look at my seat and working area with the microphone and headphones. It feels so good to be back.

'Hope you don't mind but I've still got some setting up to do.' She glances at her watch. 'Should be ready to go in around fifteen to twenty minutes if you want to grab a coffee or something.'

'I'm fine.' I fish my phone out of my bag and hold it up. 'I've got the book on here, so I'll just run through the first chapters.'

Fifteen minutes pass in a jiffy and I've managed to speed-read the first three chapters.

'I'll be another ten minutes,' Diedre calls, breaking me out of my thoughts.

'Fine,' I say vaguely. I have a deep-seated discomfort swirling in my chest.

I haven't got time to read the three chapters again, but I know the bits that jarred. I re-read the first section I have a problem with.

> *Jane looked at her father slumped in his chair, drool dripping from the corner of his mouth. Her stomach turned as she mopped him clean. She couldn't do this anymore, couldn't look after him at home. It was time for him to go into a specialist care facility. She'd put her life on hold, spent too many years wiping up his mess and she refused to feel guilty about it.*

It's *unthinkable* DI Jane Tower could even consider doing this to Art, her beloved father. Via flashbacks through the entire Tower series, readers have seen the detective grow up, raised by her single father after the untimely death of her mother. My dad, as an avid reader of Phillipa's books, was touched by their special relationship and always said it reminded him of us.

During the series, Art's dementia has steadily worsened from the early books through to the ninth which I'd just re-read. Art had raised Jane alone after her mother was killed by a runaway train when Jane was just ten years old. She was a compassionate, caring daughter who could not even imagine putting him into a home particularly with such a cold attitude.

I scroll through and re-read a few paragraphs in chapter two. The part where Jane meets her good friend of many years, Mitzi, for coffee.

Jane stared down into the depths of her espresso before looking up into Mitzi's dark, trusting eyes.

'I've realised I don't really know you at all,' Mitzi said, holding Jane's gaze. 'Everyone thinks you're this bright, wonderful person who can't put a foot wrong. Well, your luck has just run out because they're all about to find out what a snake you are.'

Jane pushed her tiny glass cup away and reached for her handbag. 'You're twisted and you're a liar. There's no room for you in my life.' Jane stood up. 'Goodbye, Mitzi. I hope I never see your double-crossing face again.'

And with that, she walked away.

For nine whole books, retired coroner Mitzi has been devoted to Jane, occasionally helping her out with cases over the years. Mitzi even lived with Jane and her father for a while when she found herself homeless thanks to a legal property tangle. The two women had an unbreakable friendship, one that other people envied. Yet here, in book ten, in the time it takes to drink a cup of coffee, they are happy to simply walk away from each other vowing never to allow their paths to cross again.

Also, on that subject, Jane detests strong coffee, particularly espresso. Phillipa has mentioned this throughout the series as a humorous aside. It might not sound important it's part of Jane's character and any Tower reader worth their salt will notice this detail.

I leave the room to get a glass of water, and when I come back in, Deidre holds out a tablet. 'The first three chapters are on there,' she says. We've got to make sure this book is perfect so the sessions will be short and edited as we go along rather than at the end.' Pretty much as Jules had said. 'Take as much time as you need to read them through and let me know when you're ready to make a start.'

'I've just read the first three chapters on my phone so I'm ready to go.'

'Great. Ready when you are.'

I glance at my phone screen and see I have an email notification and missed call from Jules. I turn the phone face down so it's not distracting. I'll get back to her on my break.

I test my mike and Deidre counts down. 'Three... two... one,' and I start to read. After reading out the first few lines of chapter two, I stumble and stop. Deidre looks up from her controls and presses the button that enables her to speak through the glass.

'Problem, Eve?' Her voice echoes around my space.

'I... I think there might be a mistake on the manuscript. The version I just read was slightly different to the one Jules sent me via email.'

Deidre frowns and checks her paperwork before shaking her head. 'Nope. This is the latest version. Maybe yours is out of date. OK, let's take it from the top again. Three... two... one.'

By the time I've got to the end of the first three chapters we've had to stop and start again three times. Deidre is fine about it to my face, but I can sense she's a touch irritated. She's probably thinking it's going to be hard work recording with me, and the last thing I want is for her to pass on any misgivings about my ability to the management of Harris-Lasson.

'It's a wrap!' Deidre beams when she's carried out her checks. 'Well done, Eve. We had a couple of false starts but generally it was a good session. Happy?'

'Happy with the recording, yes.' I roll my shoulders, trying to shrug off the tightness.

Deidre looks at me, tipping her head to one side. 'Are you sure everything's OK?'

We don't know each other, but she's clearly spotted I'm tense. I can't help wondering if she's got instructions to report back to Alicia after our session.

'Everything's fine,' I say, forcing a little joviality into my voice. 'Just getting back into the swing of things.'

We're taking a fifteen-minute break from recording, so I look at my phone. Now I've got two missed calls from Jules, an email and a text message which I open.

Eve, I'm trying to call you. I sent the wrong version of the ms through, so sorry. Please delete immediately. I've just emailed over the correct encrypted file. Pls confirm when you've deleted and got the new one. Thanks, Jules

I open the email and the new file. I scan over the problem sections and see that this manuscript matches the one I'm reading from. This is the latest version, the edited one. So the initial file that Jules sent in error must be... Phillipa's original draft.

They've edited out the inconsistencies.

EIGHTEEN

The studio is booked up until lunchtime and the rest of the recording goes smoothly. The inconsistencies in Phillipa's initial draft bother me because I know what a perfectionist she is, always having a cast-iron grip on her character and plot development. I'd bet money Phillipa would never make mistakes like that... and yet she had.

If the errors are a reflection of her confused state of mind, then it's very sad. Now I can see why the police came to that conclusion about her possibly taking off without telling anyone.

At the end of the session, Deidre pops her head round the door of my booth.

'Got to run to my next job now. Hope everything OK with you, Eve, you seem a bit unsure. If you want a chat about—'

'Thanks, Deidre, but I'm fine. I'm missing my daughter and just getting back into the swing of things after so many months out.' I smile apologetically. 'I'll be great at our next session, promise!'

'Ahh, that's grand! You can keep the tablet to use next session. See you soon. Ta-ta!'

I feel relieved when I'm alone again. I can hardly discuss

my concerns with Deidre, a producer I don't know who's employed by Harris-Lasson. Her job is to record the book with as few errors as possible. She doesn't care about character consistency compared to previous books or wonder about why Phillipa wrote an entire book and then concealed it, prior to going missing.

After Dad died, it had felt as though something changed on a cellular level inside me. After always being a happy-go-lucky person, I can now easily get a bit hung up on things that other people seem to easily push aside. Obsessed – Mum unhelpfully calls it. I can feel the murmurings of it now, flickering inside me like a flame that's trying to ignite and take a hold.

My phone lights up and I take the call. 'Hi, Jules.'

'Did you get my message?' She sounds slightly breathless as if she's been rushing around. 'About the first encrypted file?'

'Yes, but the session has only just finished. I—'

'Have you deleted it? It's vital you delete it right away.'

'Yes,' I say without hesitation. 'I've deleted it and we're recording from the latest version. I double-checked with Deidre.'

She blows out air. 'Thank God for that. Thanks, Eve, sorry for the panicky messages.'

'I did read a few chapters of the original manuscript before I got your messages and I see you've edited out some fairly glaring inconsistencies.'

'Just a few bits that needed to be tightened up, yes,' Jules says quickly. 'Well, I can relax now. Sorry for the upset. I...' There's an awkward pause. 'I'd really appreciate it if you don't mention the mistake I made, Eve. I've just got so much on right now and—'

'Course,' I say. 'It never happened.'

'Cheers. I owe you one. Bye for now.'

When Jules ends the call, I swipe the tablet's screen to get to the new manuscript again. Obviously, things are a bit different this time, but the usual procedure for before the recording of a book used to be that Jules would forward the final typeset manuscript to me at least a couple of weeks before our scheduled recording date. This gave me a chance to read through it a couple of times and flag up any queries I had. There was never anything big or of real concern. Sometimes it might be the pronunciation of a particular word. Phillipa was fond of adding in the odd Latin phrase. Or perhaps I might wonder about the tone of something a particular character had to say.

Occasionally, Phillipa herself would get back to me. When I answered, her cultured, musical voice would say, 'Eve, darling! How are you?' When we'd got through the niceties, we'd chat about the issues I'd raised in the latest book. Then I'd say something like, 'How are the cats?' or, 'How's your dodgy discs?' That's what she used to call her frequently excruciatingly painful back pain: 'I'm fine, darling. If only I could get rid of these dodgy discs!'

Sometimes, she'd carry on talking. Everything had seemed light-hearted at the time, but on reflection, I often sensed an undercurrent of melancholy. Like the time I had to cut our conversation short because I was on my way out to another publisher's recording session. Phillipa had sounded wistful. 'It's so lovely to talk to you. I've always felt like I can tell you anything.' Had that been a signal she had a weight on her mind? If I'd have taken the time to ask her if anything was wrong, would she have opened up and shared her worries?

I recognise it now as the same feeling I've had inside me since Dad died. Yes, despite her jolly demeanour, I often got the impression something was bothering her. I never got to find out what either of them were really thinking, deep down.

I open the first encrypted manuscript on my phone and compare the differences in the first three chapters to the version I was currently recording from. Jules had skilfully edited out the inconsistencies and replaced them with dialogue and actions that matched the characters Phillipa's readers so loved.

My finger hovers above the delete file icon. Jules had asked me to get rid of it without delay and I'd lied to her and said I had. I still can't bring myself to press the delete button. Now I want to read the actual words Phillipa herself had written, not some sanitised version. These are the final words she wrote before disappearing which meant at some point, she'd wanted them out there.

I decide here and now I'll read the rest of the original manuscript and then I might think about getting rid of it. I'll let Jules continue to think I've deleted it as promised. There's no sense in worrying her further.

I'll be reading the manuscript for my own interest, but I won't get fixated on it. I'll record the book as contracted and then move on with my life and career.

That's all there is to it. That's all I need to do.

NINETEEN

TWELVE MONTHS EARLIER

She unlocked the deep desk drawer, took the laptop out and logged in. Phillipa read the email again, slower this time. Heat began to channel into her face and neck. There was no doubt the situation was getting worse. The threats. She felt it as a build-up of pressure at the back of her head and closed the email before it turned into a migraine.

A message notification popped up from her Facebook superfan group.

> *Hi Phillipa, I have a question about Book 9 in the series. When*
> *DI Jane Tower travels to the neighbouring town to question...*

She skipped the rest of the message and deleted the notification. It was that irritating guy who helped run the group. Chad something-or-other. He was a pest. Always messaging to ask some inane question or trying to get yet another signed photo to be left at the Harris-Lasson reception for him to call in and pick up. God knows what he did with them all, there had been so many. Phillipa had come to dread events because he'd always be the first one in the queue, waving his superfan pass, and she could guarantee he'd be the last to leave.

She logged out, closed the laptop. Her hands jerked and she nearly dropped it as she replaced it in the drawer.

Next, she logged into her iMac and opened her current work-in-progress, book ten in the Tower series. The document was blank. With a heavy heart she reached for her headphones and double-clicked on the hidden icon.

Her phone started to ring. She checked the screen and, reluctantly, she slipped off her headphones and answered it.

'Hi, Sage,' she greeted her agent, forcing an upbeat tone. 'How are things?'

'Well, fancy that – I was calling to ask you the same question,' Sage said drily. 'I'll cut to the chase... How's book ten coming along? You've usually sent me something to look at by now.'

Blood rushed to Phillipa's head making her feel dizzy even though she was sitting down.

'This one's proving tricky, I'm still in the planning stages,' she said quickly.

'It's just Jasmine pointed out you hadn't mentioned anything about the draft to her, either,' Sage murmured.

Phillipa bit down on her back teeth. These days, Jasmine loved to make trouble for her wherever she could and Phillipa had just about had enough of it. She cleared her throat. 'Actually, I wondered if you'd managed to speak to Jules yet about increasing the advance and extending the deadline like we discussed?'

'It's all in hand,' Sage said smoothly. 'You just worry about the writing and let me sort the rest.'

Gone are the days she'd sit for hours with Jasmine, Sage's assistant. They could work anywhere together: the agency office, a coffee shop or Phillipa's office here at home. Often Sage would join them for an hour. Phillipa had felt so supported and safe knowing the two of them had her back. But those days were long gone and her relationship with Jasmine had soured somewhat, as over time, the once shy young woman's confidence had grown in leaps and bounds and her attitude had become quite arrogant.

When Sage ended the call, Phillipa rested her elbows on the desk and held her head in her hands. She felt so incredibly low. Her life had spiralled out of control so quickly, it was hard to know the best thing to do.

The sun filtered softly through the white shutters behind her. She could hear the birds whistling outside. If someone were to have taken a snapshot of her life right at that moment, it would have seemed perfect.

The trouble was, everyone's life was so much more than you saw on paper, or online. It was more than the interviews they expected her to do in the weeks before the book signings. It was more than the pictures she would post holding a copy of her latest book with a glass of wine at the bottom of the landscaped garden, with the Thames glittering in the distance.

Readers loved to hear about her day, about her family, about how much she loved writing. They didn't want to hear she was struggling, or she was worried. Or that she was going to ditch the Tower series altogether.

There were other things in her life, too. Stuff nobody was aware of but her... and the other person. The Devil. The evil one. It might sound dramatic, but nobody could imagine the hell she was being put through.

* * *

Phillipa closed the current manuscript and took a burner phone from the same drawer as the laptop. She composed a text and re-read it several times before sending.

She grabbed her handbag and checked her regular phone was in there, the only phone Fleur thought she had. She slid the burner phone into a black fabric case before inserting it into a rip in the lining of her handbag, so it was invisible unless you knew it was there. She locked the drawer and popped the key in the clay pot on the windowsill, burying it amongst the paperclips.

Phillipa walked along the long landing, enjoying the feel of the plush cream carpet under her bare feet.

She passed their master suite and then the nursery, next door. When they first bought the house, they'd had builders knock through two bedrooms to create a super-size nursery and playroom. The twins were to have had their own rooms eventually, but for starters, this had been the most practical option.

The surrogate had been selected very carefully. A professional woman and her academic partner. It was the perfect solution. Fleur was thirty-five and suffered from polycystic ovary syndrome. She and Simon had conceived Milo through IVF treatment. Phillipa was in her early fifties now, and with her career at its peak, the surrogate option had ticked every box on a number of fronts. It had also meant they'd been able to just get on with it and, thank goodness, hadn't had to embark on a raft of invasive tests.

Simon, Fleur's ex, had been dead set against the surrogacy, claiming Milo would be traumatised, that it was an unnatural procedure... all manner of ridiculous opinions that he had no right to even utter out loud. Phillipa had taken great pleasure in watching his discomfort when Milo had excitedly showed his father the finished nursery he had helped design.

The nursery door was ajar now and Phillipa slowed, catching a glimpse of the vivid jungle mural that had been her stepson's idea. Fleur had commissioned a locally famous artist to create it on the longest plain wall of the room.

Back then, Phillipa had enjoyed imagining their soon-to-be-born babies – a boy and a girl, the last scan had revealed – squealing and clapping their chubby little hands, grasping at the dark green foliage and hot pink flowers with their fat little fingers. The five of them would play 'spot the animal' for hours, spying the cunningly hidden monkeys, tigers and parrots amongst a whole menagerie of jungle creatures the artist had so skilfully created.

But the surrogate mother had changed her mind late on into the pregnancy and decided she'd be keeping the twins.

The grief she and Fleur had felt had been staggering. Far beyond what she'd imagined possible. The prospect of having the twins had forged them together as a couple, strengthened them on all sides, and the tragic outcome had had the exact opposite effect. The glue that had held them together had seemed to dissolve overnight. When Simon had called in to see Milo, Fleur had tearfully told him the news. He'd turned to look at Phillipa, and the slightest smirk had twitched at the corners of his mouth. Phillipa had felt a flare of anger she could barely harness and had to restrain herself from going for him. This cruel, heartless man.

Fleur had fallen into a melancholic state, had lain in bed for more than two weeks. The doctor had visited twice, and a local lady who offered natural therapies such as reiki and crystal work, came in each morning. Then one day, Fleur had got up, showered and dressed and told Phillipa she wanted to start the surrogacy process again. She'd found another agency with a 'perfect couple' who were willing to carry their children. There had been only one hang-up – it would be twice as expensive as before.

With other problems building that Fleur knew nothing about, Phillipa had felt trapped and afraid. But she had taken Fleur in her arms and kissed her wife. 'Of course we can try again, if that's what you want,' she'd said gently.

How she was going to get the money together this time, she

didn't know. It was another problem that felt completely insurmountable.

* * *

Downstairs, Phillipa headed into the enormous kitchen, the family hub of their home. She lingered in the doorway, watching her stepson, Milo, sketching at the industrial-style wooden table they had specially made to seat up to fifteen people. She couldn't remember the last time they had hosted a dinner party here.

The housekeeper stood at the counter chopping a rainbow of vegetables, probably for Milo's lunch. Fleur was dressed in white, loose, linen trousers and a slouchy top that slipped off the shoulder. She was sitting on one of the squashy oversized sofas by the bifold doors. She was drinking coffee and leafing through what was almost certainly a lifestyle or high-fashion magazine.

Phillipa walked into the kitchen. The sun streamed in through the wall of glass, but the air-conditioning was on, and the room remained pleasantly cool. Nobody looked up when Phillipa entered the room. She walked over to Fleur but didn't sit down.

Her wife looked up and smiled at Phillipa. 'This is a nice surprise – I thought you were going to be holed up in your office until at least mid-afternoon.'

'That was the plan.' Phillipa sighed. 'But I've decided to pop over to the library instead. Some research books have just come in that I ordered a while ago.'

Fleur put down her magazine and sat up. 'Well, I'm glad you're having a break because it means I can tell you the good news.'

'Oh? What's that?'

'The agency has called.' Fleur beamed, excitement dancing in her eyes. 'The surrogate couple have agreed to meet with us.

We can fly over to Austin as early as next week if we like! As soon as your work schedule allows it, really.'

Fleur reached up to squeeze her hand, and Phillipa forced a smile so wide it felt as if it might split her face. 'Wow, that's... amazing! Unexpected, too. I thought they said it would be months before anything could move on this.'

'I know. Isn't it great? Apparently, the guy had a work contract to fulfil on the East Coast but that's fallen through now. So the couple are free to start the process much earlier!'

Phillipa found herself wondering cynically if the couple had prioritised the lucrative surrogacy deal above any other obstacles. Flying to Texas with what was happening elsewhere in her life felt an impossibility at the moment. After meeting the couple, there would be hefty fees and deposits becoming due immediately if they decided to go ahead with this new, exclusive agency. Tens of thousands of pounds. Medical tests, travel and accommodation costs, consultants to cover every medical speciality under the sun... The mere thought of it made Phillipa want to throw up.

'It's great news,' she told her wife, keeping her voice as upbeat as possible. 'I'm so sorry, darling, I have to run now. The head librarian is expecting me. We'll talk when I get back, OK?'

Fleur jumped up, practically bouncing off the walls now. 'I could walk over there with you! We hardly ever go for a walk these days and it'll be nice to get some fresh air. We can start to think about when we might book the flights. I'm keen to let the agency know, so they can tell—'

'I'm just going to scoot over there in the car, Fleur. I'll probably be there a while. No sense in you hanging around on my account.'

Fleur's smile faded. 'It was just a thought.'

Phillipa bent forward to kiss her on the mouth, but at the last second, Fleur turned away, so it landed on her cheek.

'See you all later,' Phillipa said, taking in everyone,

including the housekeeper, with a wave. On the way out, she ruffled Milo's hair, but he was in his drawing zone and shrugged her off.

Phillipa walked into the hallway and slipped one long riding boot on over her jeans. Stumbling, she grasped the banister rail before she lost her balance. Her heart hammered so hard it felt like it might burst out of her chest. As she reached for the other boot, she heard footsteps behind her.

'Hey,' Fleur said softly, sliding her arms around Phillipa's neck. 'I'll miss you.' It was an unusually affectionate reaction from her wife. A guilty discomfort twitched inside her.

'Sorry I have to rush off.'

Fleur looked up into Phillipa's eyes. 'It's you I'm worried about.'

'Me?' Her chest tightened. 'No need to worry about me.'

'You just seem... I don't know... a bit off, lately. Just recently, like something's really bugging you.'

'Well, you'd be right there,' Phillipa said lightly, bending to put on her other boot. Fleur's arms slipped from her. 'It feels like I'm banging my head against a brick wall trying to get the outline together for the new book.'

'What are you going to do?' Fleur said.

'What can I do?' Phillipa pulled a face and reached for her jacket. 'That's what I'm trying to work out! Might as well do something useful while I wait for inspiration.'

Fleur nodded but didn't comment.

Phillipa was painfully aware of the reason the new draft was stalling, and she was not going to the library that afternoon. But Fleur didn't need to know any of that.

Phillipa's only job, right then, was to make sure her wife did not find out the truth.

At least not until she was ready to tell her everything and face the consequences.

TWENTY

It's a relief to be out of that stinking basement with its damp, mouldy air that invades her throat and chest like a toxic fog.

But despite the improved conditions, she is in denial when she reads the letter on the desk again and again. She can't stop reading it. She's unable to shake the enormity of the task she must complete if she is to be a free woman again.

Finally, she moves away from the desk and into the bathroom where she showers and washes her hair. The soft white towels and the use of the toiletries and hairdryer feel like pure luxury after the horror of the dungeon.

She dresses in a pair of leggings and a soft tunic top. Curiously, everything fits perfectly. She drinks only water and eats only a little fruit. She has discovered the mini-fridge contains milk, fresh juice, cheese and chocolate, but she gives all of this a miss, aware of the effect it will have on her starved stomach and digestive system.

She has already opened the laptop, just in case there's an internet connection, which of course, there is not. There is no clock. There is nothing installed on there at all apart from

Microsoft Word and nine audiobooks: each one of the nine published titles of the Tower series.

She ignores the desk and its contents and lies on the bed staring up at the white ceiling. She is physically shattered but too wired to rest. The words of the letter are whirring round and round inside her head. After a few restless minutes she sits up again and looks around the room. There is a small round camera in the corner, its flashing red light winking infuriatingly at her. She's already checked the bathroom and, thank goodness, there is no camera in there.

The letter does not contain a friendly or reasonable request. It is an order to write the tenth book in the Tower series.

She refuses to write on demand. She will certainly not be writing the tenth eighty-thousand-word novel in the Tower series.

Oddly, the letter has given her hope. She has clearly not been brought here to be tortured and killed. She has been brought here to *work*.

There's still that missing part of the puzzle to solve: the blocked memories from just before the awards ceremony until waking up in the basement. She's had a couple of flashbacks, and she feels sure that's a sign the memories will return.

There has to be a way out of this. There just has to be.

Now she knows why she's been brought here, and she knows exactly what she is required to do, she needs to get her thoughts in line. And quick.

Suddenly it comes to her. She needs to stop playing the helpless victim and take control. Her captor is desperate for her to write the tenth book. So desperate they have resorted to this. She looks around the pleasant room... her new prison.

But here's the thing. Nobody can write the Tower books but her. *She* is the voice of the characters, *she* is the heartbeat that threads through the narrative keeping the stories alive. If she dies, then DI Jane Tower dies with her.

That fact gives her the power of negotiation, surely? She's been feeling so weak, but this realisation gives her strength. She stands up and walks over to the desk again. She picks up the letter and, holding it up to the camera in the corner, she screws it up and tosses it in the wastepaper basket. It misses, but her captor will get the message.

She is not going to play ball.

'You can't make me do this,' she screeches up at the blinking red light in her hoarse voice. 'I won't do it. You hear me? It's not going to happen so you might as well let me go.'

Despite her exhaustion, she feels a steely resolve inside. She remembers snatches of a conversation in what feels like the recent past in which she is telling someone she will not continue writing the Tower series.

'Nine books is enough,' she recalls herself saying. 'I want some time off, and then I want to work on something else. Something I feel passionate about.'

She had been such a fool. Wasted so many years churning out a stagnant series her heart was no longer in. She'd done it for the money and that had been enough at first. But then it wasn't nearly enough. She wanted more from it... more than she could possibly get because other people were controlling her.

The publisher and the readers demanding the next instalment almost the instant she'd delivered the current title. Writing on demand was stunting her creative juices. Stuck with the same tired old characters and setting. Increasingly, she'd had to curb new plot ideas, avoid bringing in fresh modern characters in major roles. She was constantly expected to give the readers more of the same because that's what the publisher thought they wanted.

Ironically, she'd been a prisoner back then, too. That's why she'd decided to take control and *just stop writing*.

It was becoming very clear to her that the reason she is here is because of her insistence she wanted out. It would be laughable, if it wasn't so serious and real. But the publishing world doesn't pull stunts like this. They don't hold people hostage until they toe the line.

* * *

Each book in the series was between seventy and eighty thousand words. Enough to give the readers a good story, but a quick enough read to leave them wanting more.

It is a process that cannot be rushed. Anyone who thought they could hold someone hostage to write a novel had to be crazy. Pure and simple.

That's when it occurs to her that her abductor could well be crazy. Someone with insider knowledge, who knew her plans. But it is no use trying to second-guess until her memory has returned and she can remember the days before she ended up here.

A shock jolts through her body. There is someone on the other side of the door. As she'd hoped, her defiant treatment of the letter has provoked a reaction. It's time for her to show some mettle.

She hears keys rattling and the bolts begin to slide back. She sits up and swings her legs over the side of the bed before standing up. Her legs still feel wobbly but they're getting stronger. She can do this. She can start to change the balance of power.

The door opens and the figure stands there, masked, gloved and suited, just like before.

'Why are you wearing a disguise?' she says, unable to keep the vitriol out of her husky, sore voice. 'Are you too much of a coward to face me?'

It feels good, to answer back. It feels good to assert herself again.

The figure walks briskly over to the desk, plucks the letter off the floor next to the bin and flattens it out. It is placed back on the desk and tapped with a finger before the figure points to the laptop. 'Write!' The word is snapped loudly, the distorted tone echoing around the walls.

'No!' She folds her arms. 'I can't write on demand. You can't force me.'

The figure moves quickly, striding across the room and snatching something out of a pocket. Too late she realises what it is.

'No! Please, I—'

The needle of the syringe is plunged into her upper arm. She screams out before her body flops involuntarily, as if her bones have turned to powder.

'Please don't, I'm sorry... I...' She hears herself protest softly and then the room starts fading out.

When she wakes up shivering, she has no idea how much time has passed.

Her clothes are gone. She is back in the filthy cotton shroud with bare feet and lying on the floor in the damp, dark, cold basement.

Her fingers flutter as she grasps a handful of the torn pages. The hundreds of thousands of words she has written are scattered around her like rotting leaves.

She no longer feels in control.

TWENTY-ONE

EVE

When I leave the recording studio at lunchtime, my heart feels heavy.

Deidre left when our session had finished but I went to the staff area, made myself a drink and caught up reading Phillipa's unedited manuscript – the one Jules thinks I've now deleted. I now have the overview of Phillipa's original story and Jules's edited version and the comparison is worrying.

Jules is an experienced editor and Phillipa's only editor for the Tower series, so it's no surprise she spotted the anomalies. She would have quickly realised that Phillipa's superfans like Chad Belton would be up in arms if the inconsistencies had made it into the published book.

I'm not a copy editor or a proofreader. It isn't my job to pick up on character inconsistencies or flag innocuous dialogue, and I'm sure Jules might be annoyed if I try to talk to her about it. Plus, she'll know, if I'd deleted the email when I claimed to have done, I wouldn't have had time to read so much of it. Harris-Lasson are paying me a substantial fee to just record what is in front of me, and I certainly don't want to annoy them.

Despite trying to put my concerns behind me and just focus

on recording the book, the fact remains that, after only a few chapters of the original story, I don't recognise DI Jane Tower, the character I feel I know so well.

I'm already wondering if I've imagined it. But after narrating and reading nine books, the last one fairly recently, I ought to know.

Like any loyal series reader, I feel like I know these people in the real world. Jane, with her unique way of looking at cases; Marlon Jones, her psychologist partner who, unbeknown to his colleagues, is a functioning alcoholic.

I decide the best thing to do is to speak to Jules, after all. I felt a little distance between us now, but we used to be really close. I considered her a friend as well as a colleague. Maybe there's a way I can get her to open up without confessing I'm still reading the original story I was meant to delete.

I sit on a low wall just down from the studio and call Jules's direct number, intending to leave a message. I'm surprised when she answers almost immediately.

'Eve! Glad you called. How did it go at the studio?'

'Went well,' I say cautiously. 'We recorded the first six chapters.'

'Good, good. I'm glad you rang because I managed to get us a meeting with Alicia in the morning. Nine thirty, is that OK with you?'

'That's fine. I... I wondered if you had time just to chat for five minutes, now?'

I hear the shuffling of papers on her desk. 'Course, go ahead.'

'It's Phillipa's book, Jules. It feels... odd.'

The shuffling stops. 'What do you mean, odd?'

'In places, it doesn't feel like Phillipa's work at all. I know that sounds mad. I read the first few chapters before you asked me to delete it, and I saw the places you've edited it.'

She keeps her voice light, but I can tell she's taken aback by my comments. 'Can you give me an example?'

'It's mainly Jane Tower. She's just... different. The way she speaks, her inner thoughts – it doesn't ring true. It's hard to pinpoint it exactly, when I've seen so little of the book.'

'It was a rough draft. Phillipa probably wasn't feeling her best at the time she wrote it, Eve.' Her easy manner seems to have turned slightly more formal. She's in the office, I can hear the buzz of voices around her.

'But I thought you said Phillipa always wrote amazing first drafts?'

'Well, yes, she does. Mostly. But everyone has their off days. Nothing for you to worry about, Eve.'

I get the distinct feeling Jules wants to move on from this conversation. Then, 'Look, do you want to drop by this afternoon? You and I need a catch-up, it's been so long.'

'That sounds good,' I say, thinking about all the listening to the Tower series I've done since being offered this job and how fresh the characters' voices feel in my mind.

'No harm done,' she says briskly, and I hear the shuffle of papers again. 'See you soon, I'm free after three.'

I'm sliding my phone back in my bag when it rings again. It's Nina.

'Where are you?' Her bright voice cheers me instantly. 'I've got some paperwork to deliver so I'm out and about. We could grab a sneaky coffee if you're around?'

We meet at a tiny beans-to-cup coffee shop in Clerkenwell. Nina is already there when I arrive.

'That looks heavy,' I remark, nodding to her big bag of paperwork by the chair.

'All in a day's work for a publishing exec,' she says sourly. 'They call it "learning the ropes". Sadly, it must be done before I can take a step up to a better salary. I'm never going to get on the housing ladder until that happens.'

Our coffees arrive and she takes a sip.

'Anyway,' she says, a line of froth above her top lip. 'How'd it go this morning? How was the sparkling, secret book that must not be discussed?'

I laugh. 'It went OK. And I can't comment on the book, not least because I only read six chapters of it.'

She pulls a face. 'Thought you'd be bouncing with enthusiasm, but you're a bit like a wet sock.'

I smile and sip my coffee. She has such a way with words. 'Sorry. I suppose I am, a bit. It's probably just the anticlimax after all the hype.'

Her eyes widen. 'It wasn't any good?'

'No, no. It's not that. It's... never mind.'

'Oh, come on! You can't leave me in suspense like this, Eve. Spill the beans.'

'Honestly, it's nothing.' I look out of the small window at the people rushing past. On their phones, drinking takeout coffee, eating... everybody so busy. So indifferent to each other. 'As you said, I've been told very clearly that I'm not to discuss any part of the book with anyone.'

'I'm only teasing.' She grins. 'I know you can't talk about it. Just like I shouldn't talk about a conversation I shouldn't have heard today in the café. About Phillipa.'

'Oh?' She has my attention.

'Two women, one whose husband works for the bank Phillipa used. She said something quite strange.'

I sip my coffee and look around the shop at the shelves stacked with rows of brown bags filled with different types of coffee beans. I'm trying to pretend I'm cool about this conversation when really, I want to shake the gossip out of Nina.

'She said her husband had been shocked that Phillipa was basically on her uppers when she went missing.' She leans in closer. 'Apparently, she badly needed a cash injection to avoid defaulting on her mortgage and other commitments. I mean, she was probably Harris-Lasson's best-paid author, so I can't really believe that would be the case.'

I frown. 'Anyone can get into money difficulties though. Bigger incomes usually have bigger houses and fancier lifestyles that need paying for. But I agree it's a very strange thing for him to say for another reason altogether.'

'Go on.'

'Well, Phillipa had written the next book and instead of submitting it to her editor and thereby releasing her next chunk of advance payment from the publisher, she decided to hide it instead. That's the thing that makes no sense at all.'

The empty table next to us is taken by three students and I signal for Nina to be careful. 'Time to change the subject.'

Nina nods. 'How's your daughter? It must be tough for you two being apart. I'd love kids one day; despite being nowhere near that point yet, I can visualise myself as a mum.'

'You'll make a lovely mum,' I say, feeling touched at her words. 'And yes, I'm finding it really tough. Although... Scarlet probably isn't missing me as much as I am her.'

'Why's that, is she with her dad?' Nina says easily.

'Yes. Her dad and his new pregnant girlfriend.'

Nina's cheeks flush. 'Gosh, sorry. They said not to ask you about that stuff... I mean because of it being Saskia and all. I honestly didn't mean to pry.'

I wonder who 'they' are. Obviously Harris-Lasson staff.

'Nice to see the gossip-mongers are as active as ever,' I say drily. 'But don't worry, it's fine. I wobbled for a few months when I found out before I managed to feel like myself again.'

'We've all had low times,' Nina says, and I feel grateful she's not making a big deal of it, even though she hasn't got a clue how bad it got. 'Life can easily get on top of you. Maybe that's what happened to Phillipa – who knows. There were rumours she'd fallen out with her literary agent and she had problems at home. Maybe everything just got on top of her.'

Fleur had mentioned Phillipa acting distracted and going out of the house more. But I didn't know she'd had problems with Sage, her agent.

'The police knew all about this, did they?'

'I don't know. It could just be water-cooler gossip for all I know. Sometimes I wonder if we'll ever find out.'

TWENTY-TWO

When we've finished our chat, Nina heads off for a meeting across town and I go back into the office. Before I get on the Tube, I try Mum's phone again to see exactly what's happened with Scarlet. She must have her voicemail turned off because it rings and rings. I leave her another message before heading back to Harris-Lasson to meet with Jules.

Her desk is at the far end of the building. I walk past open-plan offices full of white furniture and publishing staff. Lots wear headphones and each person works at a computer in their own little pod consisting of low desk dividers. Barely anyone looks up as I pass and there are no signs of seniority here; not even managers get a private office.

Alongside the office space, assorted sizes of meeting rooms line the wall opposite the floor-to-ceiling windows. All the rooms have glass walls, so you can clearly see who's in there at any one time. It's an efficient, modern way of working, but there's something about it that strips every one of their individuality and rank.

Right at the other end, there's a final open-plan working

space, and I spot Jules right away, sitting at one of the work-stations.

She removes her headphones and stands up. 'Eve! Let's go up to the café and get a drink. It's a lovely day; we can sit out on the rooftop terrace.' We head over to the lifts. 'Is the flat OK? Bit basic probably, but at least you get a cheap rental.'

'It's brilliant, honestly,' I say, genuinely grateful for the accommodation. 'Nina is lovely, too. We get on well.'

We step out into a bustling café at rooftop level. 'Go and find somewhere for us to sit outside,' says Jules. 'I'll get the drinks. Latte OK for you?'

'Lovely, thanks.' I find a table amongst potted topiary trees and wooden raised beds that house colourful plants.

I sit, entranced, the buzz of conversation all around me. It's just the start of my journey back into publishing, but it's hard not to feel like I've made it, sat here with the Thames glittering close by.

I'd love Scarlet to see this. I smile, imagine her saying something like, 'It feels like we're on top of the world, Mummy!' I'd love her to experience this place, to see what's available and achievable out there in the wider world. My chest cramps when I think about Hugo whisking her away after I'd explained at length she'd be staying with Mum and attending local summer clubs with the kids she knows.

Jules arrives with drinks within minutes.

'Thanks for bringing me up here.' I take a sip of the frothy latte. 'And thanks for giving me the chance to narrate the new book. I can't tell you how grateful I am.'

'Not at all. Thank you for coming back. It means we have that crucial continuity between the titles. As I told Alicia, Phillipa's fans would hate it if this book had a different voice to the others. Readers can have very strong opinions about that sort of thing.'

'I bumped into one of Phillipa's superfans the other day.

Chad Belton. Bit of a strange guy, I thought. He had strong opinions on my take on one of the characters.'

She thinks for a moment. 'Ah yes, I know him. He can be quite... *enthusiastic* about the Tower series once he gets started.' Jules grins. 'He's odd but quite harmless, and he does a tremendous amount of unpaid promotional work for Phillipa's books.'

'Oh really? Like what?'

'Well, for starters, he runs her street team. That's a group of her most loyal fans who promote her stuff online in return for advanced reading copies and tickets to her meet-the-author type of events. He's also the main administrator on the biggest Phillipa Roberts online fan forum. He started that himself six years ago.'

I sip my coffee, surprised. I'll check out Chad's stuff online soon as I can. Jules seems relaxed and it strikes me as a good opportunity to dig a bit deeper. 'I've been wondering... did you know Phillipa was writing this book?'

Jules picks up a sugar sachet and tears off the corner. She considers it a moment before looking up at me. 'Why do you ask that?'

'Nothing... I mean, no reason,' I stammer defensively. 'I just wondered because it would be unusual for an author to write the next instalment in a series without her editor knowing about it.'

The ghost of a smile passes over Jules's lips. 'That's true,' she says, non-committal. I feel suddenly awkward, the easy manner we used to enjoy straining a little. Jules had called me a couple of times when I first went back to Nottingham, but I'd found stuff that reminded me of work just increased my anxiety, so our conversations were a bit stilted and one-sided. After a while, she stopped contacting me.

'Jules, I... I just want to say, I really appreciated your efforts to keep in touch when I went back to Nottingham. I was in a bad way, what with Dad's death then Hugo having an—'

'You don't have to explain, Eve,' she says kindly. 'I under-stood completely at the time, and I understand now.'

I nod. 'I know, but I want to let you know that I really valued the close relationship we used to have, and I hope we can rekindle that. I give you my word I'll never breathe a word of anything we talk about. So I hope you feel we can speak openly to each other.'

'I miss our chats, too.' Jules puts the sugar down without using it. 'Look, Phillipa was under contract to write the next instalment and she'd asked for an extension which was unusual for her. But...' She pauses. 'Her agent had confided she was having some difficulties getting the story down. Phillipa and I often chatted over aspects of the story when she was writing a new one, just general aspects like theme and plot. There had been none of that for book ten. I admit it was a surprise when an entire book was discovered, particularly as...'

She hesitated and I waited.

'Particularly as there had been rumours – and that's all they were – rumours that Phillipa had had enough of writing the Tower series and wanted to move on to pastures new.'

I made a noise of surprise.

'Phillipa never said that to me but I heard the leak had come from someone at her literary agency. I haven't got any answers, but I hope to God she's OK, wherever she is,' Jules continued. 'I hope she comes back very soon.'

I feel like nobody wants to talk about the possibility some-thing awful has happened to Phillipa. Something unspeakable like if she's taken her own life, or if she's been... I don't know... abducted or something. It sounds a bit far-fetched, I know. Also, after ten months you'd expect there to be developments if it was either of those things. The fact she might have had enough of writing opens up the possibility again of her just taking off, running away from what she perceived to be too much respon-sibility.

'One last thing,' I say, throwing caution to the wind now. 'This is awkward, I know, but have you, personally, got any theories, any clues why she just disappeared like that?'

Jules straightens the paperwork in front of her before looking straight at me. 'I don't know, Eve. I tortured myself for those first few weeks she was gone, wondering if she'd tried to give me a clue or some kind of sign. Had she tried to reach out and I hadn't been listening? But my conscience is clear because there was honestly nothing, apart from the deadline extension she'd requested. Plenty of authors ask for one, although it was unusual for Phillipa to do so. But like the police said at the time, people often act out of character if they're planning to just take off and run away from it all.'

'That's the conclusion the police came to in the end?'

Jules nodded. 'I think so, yes. Even though they didn't say so publicly. I noticed a definite drop-off in interest after a few weeks when their best leads came to nothing. Officially, they maintain the case is still very much open, but nobody has asked us anything for months now.'

'I wonder what they make of the new book discovery,' I say.

Jules shrugs. 'Apparently Fleur contacted the senior investigating officer right away, and his reaction was to take it as more evidence Phillipa was clearly confused and acting strangely. That she couldn't seem to face things or function normally.'

'Sounds like lazy policing to me.' I frown. 'It usually takes more than an impending deadline to make someone take off and leave everything behind.'

Jules stirs her latte with a long spoon and regards me thoughtfully before speaking. 'Look, this stays between us, but six months before her disappearance, Phillipa and Fleur were meant to be having kids. They suffered a major upset when their surrogate changed her mind and kept the twins they were expecting. They'd seen the scans, decorated the nursery... It was devastating to them both, as you can imagine.'

My eyes widen with horror. 'Oh, my goodness... that's terrible!'

Jules nods sadly. 'I saw Phillipa start to fade in front of my eyes, but she wouldn't talk about it. She's always been the sort who ploughs through problems, the quintessential British "keep calm and carry on" type of person. But I honestly think losing the twins rocked her to her core.'

I shake my head and finish my coffee. 'I can't imagine how she and Fleur must have felt.'

'Agreed. I know Fleur suffered terribly, too, and now she's had Phillipa's disappearance to cope with on top of it all. She told me she gets through by hoping and praying Phillipa will just appear at the door one day. I think we're all hoping that because there's nothing else to go on. All we can do is carry on, as I know she'd want us to do.' She nibbles on a fingernail before looking at me. 'Thank you for deleting the original manuscript. I made a stupid mistake, and I'm grateful for your discretion, Eve.'

'No worries at all,' I say. 'I was surprised at the inconsistencies I spotted in the first few chapters though. Phillipa was always so particular about her character development.'

'I think this book gave her some trouble, and she might have been struggling a bit for the reasons we've just discussed. It was just those first few chapters, and they were easily rectified so no harm done.'

'That's a relief to hear. I'll email you what I found anyway, just so you have it,' I say. Jules doesn't reply, and I leave it at that. I'll judge the extent of Phillipa's errors for myself, soon enough, because unbeknown to Jules, I'll be reading the entire original manuscript as Phillipa intended it to be read.

TWENTY-THREE

CHAD

The call, in response to his flyer, had come in by the end of Monday, Eve's first day in London.

Over the phone, Chad had told Mrs Hewitt the sorts of things he'd be able to help her with – based on his observations on the jobs she needed doing – and she'd agreed, far quicker than he'd dared imagine, for him to call round and have a chat the following morning.

Chad considered his first visit to Mrs Viv Hewitt's house on Tuesday morning an irrefutable success. He had made a good first impression, and there and then, Viv had asked him to stay and do some jobs. He'd spent three hours there.

He'd surveyed the outside of the property for starters, making notes of what needed doing in the coming weeks. Never one to slack, he also carried out several overdue jobs for Viv. This included a creaky gate repair and the replacement of several long-expired light bulbs, and he also cleared her front garden of dangerous obstacles such as a disintegrating pile of old firewood that had started tumbling down onto the path and some broken roof tiles that had been left lying around after a bad storm the previous winter.

It was a most unexpected bonus when Viv asked him to take a look at her laptop.

'My daughter used it before she went back to work in London. Now, every time I go on, I get a list of her emails, not mine!'

Excitement warmed Chad's blood. 'I can sort that out for you in a jiffy, Mrs Hewitt. Let's have a look.'

Viv had logged him into the laptop, a simple numerical code that Chad could easily remember. She then pottered off to get him a cup of tea and a slice of her homemade cake.

Chad couldn't believe his luck when he double-clicked on the email icon on the desktop and Eve's live Yahoo email account loaded. After a few clicks, he established that Eve had set up the emails to toggle between her own and Viv's without the need for passwords.

'Sugar and milk?' Viv called from the kitchen, humming along to the radio.

'Just milk please, Mrs Hewitt,' he'd replied, barely able to string the words together when he spotted several emails from Phillipa's publisher, Harris-Lasson.

Quickly and without hesitation, Chad forwarded several emails to his own account and then immediately deleted them out of Eve's 'sent' box so that no trace of his actions remained.

Viv carried in their tea and cake on a tray and was delighted when Chad presented her emails ready for her to read. He showed her how she could easily switch back to her own emails if it defaulted back to Eve's again.

'You're a genius!' She beamed. 'I really am very grateful, Chad.'

'It's no trouble, Mrs Hewitt. I can check over the laptop each time I come if you like, to make sure everything is running smoothly.'

His offer was readily accepted. 'That's very kind of you, thank you.'

Over tea and cake – possibly the best Victoria sponge Chad had ever tasted – they'd had a good old chat about everything under the sun.

When Chad left three hours later, with cash payment in his pocket, the house had benefited from several much-needed improvements, and Chad not only had access details to Phillipa Roberts's secret book, but he also had the address of the flat in London where Eve was staying. As a bonus, he knew where her daughter was staying, too, and that there was a problematic relationship between Eve and Hugo, her ex-husband.

TWENTY-FOUR

EVE

Finally, my phone rings. It's only 4 p.m. so I'm expecting Mum, but when I snatch it up and answer without looking at the screen, it's Hugo's voice I hear. My heart sinks. I haven't had time to get my thoughts in order about what I'm going to say to him.

'Hugo? What's happening?'

'As I said, we've got Scarlet here at Oakham, Eve,' he says smoothly. 'She's here with Saskia and I, and she's absolutely fine. So please don't worry about—'

'Back up a bit. We already had a discussion, and I told you it was all arranged that Scarlet would stay with Mum while I'm in London.'

He sighs. It's the sigh he started using about a year before we broke up. The sigh that says, 'Why are you being so difficult?' Stupid and difficult.

'I've brought her here to give your mum a couple of days' rest. Viv isn't coping too well which is no surprise. Scarlet is too much for her, Eve. She should never have been left there.'

'I've only been gone two days!' I say indignantly.

'I think your mum puts on a brave face for you,' Hugo says, as if I haven't spoken. 'When I called in on my way back from a conference last night, Scarlet looked like a wild child. Food all over her face and stained clothes. She said she hadn't had a bath-time for two days, so I asked her if she'd like to come back to the cottage with me. She jumped at the chance.' He gave a moment's pause. Then he said, 'I don't know if you've noticed, but your mum looks a bit dishevelled herself these days.'

I can't speak. There have been a few times recently when I've felt moved to ask Mum if she feels OK, because she's looked a bit off. Why haven't I made more of that? At one time I'd have questioned her, kept more of an eye on her. Instead, I've left my daughter in her gran's care without a second thought, when Mum is probably already feeling a bit under the weather.

'Eve, are you still there?'

'Yes,' I say, wrestling with the guilt but not wanting him to get one up on me. 'I didn't realise Mum was struggling.'

'Well, you had to rush off, didn't you? The job was looming large in your mind.'

I want to snap at him, to defend myself. But he's right. I've been blindsided by the opportunity at Harris-Lasson.

'Mum's not answering her phone,' I say instead.

'She's probably just resting. That's what I told her to do, at any rate.' He hesitates. 'Say, what are you doing this weekend?'

'Going back to Mum's house on Friday afternoon.' I sniff. 'My plan is to spend all weekend with Scarlet there, so you'll need to have her back in Nottingham for then.'

'Thing is, I told your mum I'd keep Scarlet over the weekend,' he says. 'To give her a chance to recuperate.'

'What? You said just a couple of days before, and it's only Tuesday. There should be no problem getting her back for Friday afternoon.'

'Don't split hairs Eve. She's going to be here with us at the weekend; it's all arranged now. Why don't you come here Friday evening? You can get the train from St Pancras to Peterborough, and I can pick you up from there, bring you to the cottage.'

Indignation burns at my throat. 'By the time I get there, it'll hardly be worth it, if I'm going to get up to Mum's at a decent time.'

'Nonsense, you can stay here, at Bee Cottage. We've got plenty of bedrooms,' Hugo says, clearly warming to the idea. 'You can spend the day with Scarlet, then I'll drop you back at the station to carry on up to your mum's on Saturday evening. What do you say?'

I'm mute with frustration. Hugo is clearly taking the mickey while I'm working away. Organising everyone else's lives, just the way he likes to. I've agreed Scarlet's care with Mum, but now Hugo is suddenly running the show. Mum is no match for him, particularly if she's feeling off-colour, but I can't help feeling miffed with her, too. I wish she'd at least called me before allowing Hugo to ride roughshod over our plans.

'So, Eve? Are you going to come over Friday?'

I search for a reason why I can't go. Nina has told me she has her birthday party arranged for Friday night. She's got a couple of friends coming over straight from work to decorate the flat and sort out the party food. I can't bear the thought of all the twenty-something noise and energy levels, and besides, I'm missing Scarlet like crazy.

'OK,' I say. 'But I don't want to make a habit of this, Hugo. I've already arranged Scarlet's summer arrangements, and now you've thrown everything up in the air again.'

He laughs disparagingly. 'So funny you seem to have forgotten Scarlet has two parents, not just the one.'

'I'll call Scarlet in the morning,' I say shortly. 'And then again tomorrow night.'

A pause, then Hugo says smoothly, 'I don't know what Saskia has arranged for tomorrow. I'll have to speak to her, see if those times are convenient. Ta-ta for now.'

Before I can argue, he ends the call.

TWENTY-FIVE

Upstairs, I sit on my bed and look at the bags I still haven't fully unpacked. There's not much in there so not that big a job, but there's something more pressing I want to do while Nina is still at work and it's nice and quiet.

I make a coffee and sit down in the small lounge with my phone and the tablet Deidre gave me. I open the first and second manuscripts on my respective devices and carry out a reading comparison of the next few chapters. I find the irritating inconsistencies continue, disproving Jules's claim that it's only a problem at the very beginning of the story.

DI Jane Tower is recalling her many seaside visits to Sheringham in Norfolk as a child when, for the last nine books, her family is documented as holidaying year after year at Salcombe in South Devon. The main suspect's name changes halfway through a police investigation. All fairly minor and annoying but not seeming to really add up to anything.

I check each mistake against the latest version of the manuscript and find, unsurprisingly, Jules has airbrushed the prose to reflect the correct details.

I'm getting a feeling – a feeling I can't ignore – that these small details perhaps *do* mean something. As if they might be building up to something else. Maybe something Phillipa couldn't bring herself to say to anyone, just like Dad couldn't find it in himself to talk to me, or to Mum. Trauma has a way of hiding away, building up and then bursting out in the most unexpected of ways.

I'm disrupted by a text message from Nina to say she's been delayed in a meeting and won't be home until seven, giving me more time to work through the manuscripts. I make a sandwich and continue reading. When I get to chapter ten, there's a section that makes me sit up straighter in my chair. I read it again, out loud.

Back at the station and after speaking to the desk clerk, DI Jane Tower went through to the interview room where Jason Bates waited like a coiled spring. He looked up when she entered, his eyes like black holes that sucked up the light. Jane couldn't help but think about his victims, the terrible end the innocent women had met while those eyes hovered above them during their final breath.

'I've read Mr Bates his rights,' DS Joe Marsh said. 'I'm sure he's raring to go.'

Bates narrowed his eyes but said nothing. Marsh turned on the tape.

'So, Mr Bates.' Jane kicked off the interview. 'We were wondering how a supposedly upstanding member of society, a bank manager no less, came to be implicated in the deaths of three young women, all of whom have worked for you at one time or another.'

He glared at her but did not answer.

'We'll get to the evidence very soon, I promise you. I'm just curious as to how your transformation took place. From a

person who ran marathons to raise money for charity, to a
serial killer who indulged in the very worst depravity.'

    A smile played at the corners of his lips.

    'It's very simple, DI Tower. People can have two sides to
them. A person respected by many can also be a monster in
plain sight. It's just that most people don't want to see it, so
they don't look in the right places. Sometimes, the person who
will destroy you has been right there in front of you all along,
and you've never even noticed.' He hesitated. 'And here's the
key detail... neither does anyone else.'

This passage is powerful. It stands out, says something, and I feel as though Phillipa is speaking to me, the reader. It's a slightly darker turn than usual in Phillipa's narrative style.

I turn to the edited version, find chapter ten and there it is. Word for word. Jules has not touched it, hasn't amended it, because she's just focused on correcting error in detail. Could Phillipa be telling us something here about someone close to her? She talks about danger being in plain sight and yet nobody sees it... like a cry for help.

What I cannot understand is why so many of the people closest to Phillipa – her wife, her editor and her agent – were under the impression she was struggling to get the first draft of book ten written. Phillipa must have virtually finished the draft at the exact time she was leading everyone to believe she had stalled and needed her deadline extending. Why would she do that? Why would she write an entire book in secret and then hide it away?

I haven't got the answers yet, but I am determined to find them.

I refuse to ignore the signs and remain blind like I did with Dad. This time, I'll follow my instincts – using the original, unedited manuscript as a guide.

I'm going to try and piece together the clues to find out exactly what happened to Phillipa Roberts and if there really was a monster in plain sight in her life.

Maybe, just maybe, that person holds the key to her disappearance.

TWENTY-SIX

It's pitch-black and very cold. She's back in the basement and no longer needs to imagine how it looks in here now because she has seen it. In some ways, it's worse knowing just how bad it is. In breathing the poisonous black mould and the damp, she can feel the stirrings of childhood asthma prickling in her chest.

But now she also knows the reason she feels so bad is, as she'd suspected, due to the drugs she's been injected with. It's likely what's caused her short-term memory loss.

She feels sick and sleepy. The aching in her body penetrates through her flesh to her bones.

It's now apparent things are not quite as simple as she'd hoped. Her attempt at clawing back a little power and respect has gone badly wrong. She needs another plan. A better one.

She drifts off again into a troubled slumber until banging and rattling outside the door bring her to the surface once more.

'Hello?' she calls out, her voice thin and weak in the darkness.

The door opens and the figure stands there in the gap, weak light filtering through from what she now knows are the bright lights in the corridor that leads to the wonderful facilities she'd so quickly taken for granted.

The figure does not move. They do not speak, but something glints in a gloved hand. She rubs her sore, crusted eyes and squints as the other person draws closer. Something is held up in front of her face as her right hand is grabbed so hard she cries out in pain.

Twisting, squeezing... acute pain shudders through her hand into her finger like it's about to snap off. She struggles, tries to get out of the iron-like grasp but then, in an explosion of terror, she recognises the flash of metal heading for her fingers.

'No! Please! Please don't. I'll do anything. I'll do it; I'll write the book.' She retches, but there's nothing in her stomach to come up. She doesn't know how many days have passed again.

She feels the figure hesitate. This could be the last chance to plead her case.

'Please, I want to go back to the other room. I promise I won't do anything silly. I'll do what you want.'

They both remain still and silent. She senses her captor wants more from her.

'I'm sorry I screwed up the letter, I was confused. Tired. Please, take me back there, and I'll do better. I will.'

A few agonising seconds. Then her finger is released.

She collapses down, holding her throbbing hand. 'Thank you,' she whispers.

The figure walks to the door, steps back into the corridor and, to her relief, beckons to her. With difficulty, her joints protesting, she manages to push against the damp, slimy wall and get herself to a standing position. She coughs and groans. She feels so weak, like she just ran a marathon.

She takes faltering steps towards the light, willing herself not to collapse. Just put one foot in front of the other. The figure walks back a few more steps further into the corridor, watching her. Her heart begins to hammer. She feels dizzy and sick. She stumbles.

She is observed impassively until she is able to gather herself and struggle to her feet.

The long, painful journey begins again. Down the long corridor with the freezing floor. She is helped up the two small steps into the corridor with the wooden floor, and then there it is. The door.

A small sound of relief escapes her lips as the figure stops abruptly, causing her to stumble again.

The door is opened, and there is the wonderful room with the desk displaying the laptop, the headphones, the notebook and pens. And there, to the right-hand side of it, is a fresh letter. Newly printed, not crumpled.

She looks around at the bed, the armchair. The door to the bathroom is open. The lights are on in there, and she can see the towels, the sparkling white sink with its hot water and fresh-smelling soap.

Next to the bed, the clothing has been laundered and replaced on the rail. The table, the little fridge... it's all there. It's all waiting for her.

The figure walks over to the desk and taps the letter with a finger.

'Last chance. Write.' The stark disembodied instruction is issued with staccato precision, and she can hear the certain threat contained within it.

She is left alone again. The door is locked and bolted.

Tears fall unbidden down her cheeks. She's not crying with fury like before but because she is grateful and glad to be here. In the nice room where she feels like a human being again and not a neglected animal.

This time, she doesn't care about putting up a fight or asserting herself. She will do what she needs to do. She cannot afford to be drugged and forced to breathe in black mould for a third time. She doesn't think her body can take it again.

Pride is out the window. She has no choice but to play the game or she will die here. She knows it to be the truth now, despite her earlier optimism.

Even though she hasn't been told as much, she gets the impression, if she plays ball, life will be much easier. She now believes it's the only way she's ever going to get out of here in one piece with all her fingers intact. Giving in is the only way to get back to freedom and her life.

This time, she decides, she will write.

TWENTY-SEVEN

EVE

I arrive ten minutes early at Harris-Lasson for my meeting with Jules and Alicia. I emailed Jules last night and listed the differences I'd found up to chapter ten in the original encrypted file she'd sent me. I think I can get away with saying I read the first ten chapters before deleting the document.

I take out some paperwork, happy to wait, when one of the interns approaches me nervously. She points to an open-plan meeting area. 'Jules said to tell you to go straight over when you arrive.'

I walk across the office floor and Jules immediately stands up. She always dresses down, but she looks smarter today: skirt, blouse and she's had a blow-dry. Then I see the possible reason for her image upgrade. Alicia is also present, her white-blonde hair brushed smoothly away from her face and clipped into a neat chignon.

I look down at my faded canvas trousers and T-shirt that features a square of floral pattern, tiny parts of it peeling now because it's a few years' old. My hair could do with a wash, so I have just brushed it back behind a fabric band for convenience.

I take out my phone for something to do, and the picture of

Scarlet lights up on the screen. My gorgeous girl – I miss her so much. It feels like forever since I saw her last and yet it's only been three days. I took this picture last year on a trip to the coast at about four in the afternoon. It had been such a beautifully warm day, and time had seemed to stretch on and on like some magical summer days do. We'd laughed so much – chasing each other, building sand sculptures, holding hands while we paddled and splashed. We'd finally flopped down on the sand with ice-creams where I'd nearly dozed off.

'Eve, lovely to see you,' Jules said. 'Alicia's joined us for a chat.'

Alicia absently touches what looks like a Hermès silk scarf knotted elegantly at her neck. 'Deidre kindly sent me over the audio file for the first few chapters you've recorded. She peers down at her laptop screen. 'I haven't had time to listen to all of it, but Jules and I have just played a few minutes' worth. It seems to be going very well.'

I nod, relieved, although it feels like there might be a but coming.

'But... Jules mentioned you have one or two concerns about the script. The characterisation in particular, I understand?'

I glance over at Jules who has suddenly become transfixed on pushing back her cuticles. She has clearly shared the contents of my email with Alicia.

'Not *concerns* exactly. It's just I did notice one or two—'

'Honesty and transparency are the building blocks of Harris-Lasson, Eve.' Alicia interrupted. 'Jules has told me you've had sight of Phillipa's first draft, and you have some concerns. I'd like for you to share those with me, if you can.'

I take a breath. I can feel my cheeks burning.

'I felt the story read a little oddly in places. There are sentences and dialogue where DI Jane Tower is acting altogether out of character. She comes over in parts as a completely different person to who she was in the last nine books.'

Alicia nods. 'I see. Could it be the author wanted to develop and change the character, do you think? Perhaps she was guarding against the series becoming stale, as so many do.'

'I think it's more likely Phillipa wasn't feeling herself when she wrote it, or... her heart wasn't in it,' I say. 'The awful circumstances... with her just disappearing like that. I wonder if she was trying to tell us something through the medium of writing a story. Maybe she felt as if she couldn't turn to anyone in the real world.' I'm encouraged when she nods and seems to understand what I'm getting at. But I'm reading her wrong.

'Eve, it's imperative you keep focused on the task in hand. That is, recording the story from the edited version of the book. As you know, Jules has been Phillipa's editor for nine previous books. She knows what she's doing.'

Jules gives me a weak smile. 'You usually don't have sight of the manuscript until the final editing stage has been completed, Eve. There have been lots of bits corrected like this in the previous books, too. You've just not been aware of them.'

Alicia nods smugly, and Jules refuses to meet my eyes. Why do I get the feeling they're lying? One minute, Jules is telling me Phillipa's drafts were usually pristine; the next, she's saying she's always had to edit out sloppy errors. It doesn't add up.

Surely I can't be the only person at Harris-Lasson who finds all this baffling. I try again. 'I just think, if we could take a look at her original script with fresh eyes, we might be able to find a clue as to what really happened to her. Perhaps that's what she was hoping for.'

Alicia's mouth bends into the rough shape of a smile, but her eyes remain icy cool. 'I think, if that were the case, she would not have hidden the book away in her attic!'

She has a point. That's the bit that scuppers my theory.

'At any rate, I'd appreciate it if you keep your concerns to yourself,' Alicia says firmly. 'If junior staff members hear your concerns about the new book, the press could get wind of it and start blowing this out of all proportion. Do you understand what I'm saying, Eve?'

'Yes.'

'Look, I'm not without sympathy. Phillipa's disappearance has been hard on all of us here. It's natural to look for signs of what might have gone wrong, but we must leave that to the police. There's really no room for amateur sleuths here at Harris-Lasson. I hope I'm making myself clear.'

I'm receiving her message loud and clear. *Button it or you're out.*

She pushes back her chair and stands up. 'In that case, I think we're done. Thank you for what you've done so far. For what it's worth, I think the audiobook is going to be super... so long as you keep focused on the job in hand.'

'Thank you, Alicia,' I manage to utter, as she sweeps by me and leaves the meeting area. 'I think it's going to be a big success.'

'Sorry, Eve, I didn't mean to drop you in it.' Jules looks contrite as soon as Alicia has left. 'I mentioned your email by mistake when we were talking. Alicia is so good at picking up on even the briefest wrong word.'

I shrug. 'It's fine.'

'It's not really, because you and I have always had a close working relationship. I want us to be able to trust each other.'

'I want that, too, but it's better Alicia knows how I feel, because the more I read of the book, the more I'm convinced something's not right with it.'

Jules crosses her legs and straightens the notebook on her lap. 'Look, this is hard for me because I've spent the last few weeks pushing away concerns about the book.'

I'm surprised at her change of heart. I say nothing because I don't want to pressure her, but I do want to hear what she's got to say.

'It's a hard one. When I first read it, I felt so confused. It's as if the character development has imploded in places.'

I feel vindicated. 'Exactly! DI Jane Tower is behaving the opposite to how she has in every one of the nine other books in the series,' I say. 'Like when she has to face putting her father into care and has no guilt about it.'

Jules nods. 'And she's said for nine books she'd never do that. I know.'

'OK,' I say. 'So you didn't have to change stuff like that in the other nine books then?'

Jules shakes her head.

'Be honest with me,' I say. 'Do you think the errors were intentional? That Phillipa might have been trying to tell us something?'

'I doubt it, Eve.'

'Well, you can't be sure of that. Surely, it's worth a closer look. I mean, do the police know about the inconsistencies?'

'Yes, they do.' For the first time I see a frisson of irritation in Jules. Her eyes flit around again, and I realise she's nervous. 'We ought not to be discussing it here. But for the record, it made no difference to their investigation or their opinion.'

'I find that hard to believe. If they're seriously looking for clues still, this has got to be—'

'There's stuff you don't know about, Eve. Stuff only a handful of people know about.'

'Stuff other than the surrogacy?' I push. I might never get a better chance than this.

'Yes. I'm telling you this to put your mind at rest about Phillipa's confusion,' she says, dropping her voice so I have to lean forward to hear better. 'A month before she went missing, Fleur found her comatose in bed. She'd taken an overdose of sleeping tablets.'

'Oh no!' I'd always known Phillipa as such a strong,

generous woman. It is so sad to hear she'd reached such a desperately low point.

'Fleur said she'd taken the loss of the twins really badly.' Jules's eyes lower as she rubs her index finger back and forth over her notepad. 'Sounds like she was in a bad way. So you see, her getting a little muddled in her characterisation isn't as significant as you might think.'

'Did you notice she was suffering?' I ask her.

'No,' Jules says sadly. 'But I hadn't had much contact with her. I see and hear from authors the most during the editing stage of their books, after the first draft is submitted. I had no idea Phillipa had already written the next book. The last I heard, her agent had emailed to say she required an extension to the deadline because the story wasn't coming together.'

One of my big regrets when Dad went missing is that we let the police fob us off with assurances that they were doing all they could. They'd made their minds up early on, that Dad had taken himself off somewhere. They must see so much of these things that, to the ordinary person, are so shocking. I'd been unaware of the background knowledge the police had about Phillipa: the surrogacy issue and the overdose.

Jules looked at me for a few moments before shaking her head. 'It all makes no sense whatsoever, I know. But my advice to you is this: if you want your career to prosper at Harris-Lasson, I wouldn't keep asking questions. Alicia's made her position clear.'

Far from placating me, I feel my curiosity swell again, and I can't help wondering: What the hell is Phillipa's publisher so scared of?

TWENTY-EIGHT

That morning, Phillipa and Fleur had had a massive row and still weren't speaking. It had started over something silly. Phillipa seemed to remember it had begun as a spirited debate about whether Milo should be allowed to join a local summer art school, with the attendance commitments that would bring. Tempers had become frayed quickly and Phillipa knew that, even though Fleur appeared to be a calm, measured person to outsiders, privately, she could soar effortlessly from cool to boiling point within seconds.

Fleur and her ex, Simon, both shared a helicopter-parent ethic, relentlessly pushing the lad to achieve academically. He went to a staunch private school that valued maths and English lessons and sport – particularly rugby – way above the arts. Yet Milo was a talented artist. Yes, he loved his PlayStation and TV as much as the next kid, but he'd often find a quiet spot and sketch his mother, one of their cats or a delicate flower in the garden.

Fleur constantly urged him to put down his sketch pad and

pick up a textbook – in keeping with the school's punishing homework regime. So when Milo came home and announced he wanted to take part in a painting-and-sketching summer school at the local comprehensive, Fleur had turned almost apoplectic.

'Not a chance in hell.' She had waved Milo away as if he were nothing more than an irritating fly. She constantly blew hot and cold with the kid. It was confusing for him and caused unnecessary emotional distance. Phillipa should know. 'Your father will never agree to it. He's paying a fortune for you to attend one of the best schools in the country, and here you are, wanting to mix with the local wildlife.'

'Fleur! Please don't speak to him like that.' Phillipa had intervened. Sometimes she detested her wife's snobbish attitude. Phillipa herself had come from that 'wildlife' pool, and at times like this, she wondered why Fleur had found her so attractive. Simon had had his own theories. When he'd turned up at one of Phillipa's signings to confront her after Fleur told him the two women were now a couple, he'd spat out the vicious words. 'She's a gold-digger, you foolish woman. Fleur just wants the lifestyle you can give her. She's after your money, not your company.' The readers who'd been waiting in the queue for her to sign their hardback books had fallen silent, glancing at each other in quiet alarm. Simon's voice had dropped to a menacing whisper. 'You'll see. Mark my words. She'll end up breaking you.'

Phillipa had dismissed his words as pure jealousy and resentment, but she'd never quite been able to forget them. It was painfully clear to her that Simon was still in love with Fleur. Any opportunity to have a dig or to undermine Phillipa in some way was always seized with both hands. Sometimes it felt like Simon was always watching and waiting for the moment he could win Fleur back.

'I wish you wouldn't encourage Milo like this,' Fleur had

hissed. 'His time needs to be spent wisely and in the protective environment of his own school.'

'It will do Milo good to mix with people from other walks of life,' Phillipa had insisted, trying to reason with her wife.

'You're being obstructive again,' Fleur had raged, her eyes wide and sparking. 'Milo's education is everything, and his school already has a full summer programme of extra studying. Doodling on a pad won't bring him a career at Canary Wharf! You can come with me to the parents' summer activities meeting at school this morning.'

'This morning isn't a good time. I'm trying to break through this block.' Phillipa had tried to reason with her, explain how she was feeling about her work. But she cared about Milo's education and wanted to support Fleur too, so Phillipa had acquiesced. 'Look, if you don't mind waiting an hour or so, I'll come in with you.'

It had clearly not been the answer her increasingly volatile wife had been hoping for. She took a saucepan out of the dishwasher and threw it into a deep drawer. The clatter set Phillipa's teeth on edge.

'How could I forget that nothing must ever stop the writing!' Fleur had shrieked. 'Can you not, just once, put your family first?'

'Not if you want to carry on living this very nice lifestyle,' Phillipa had shot back in the calm, reasonable tone she knew Fleur found infuriating.

Still, what she said was true enough. The writing had bought the house and, two years ago, the seafront apartment in Brighton. It had paid for Fleur's designer wardrobe and maintained her membership at a very exclusive gym frequented by celebrities. The writing funded regular meals out in top-class restaurants and exotic holidays abroad several times a year. Simon, with his successful IT consulting business was wealthy but not to the extent Phillipa was.

Without the writing, they could kiss their lifestyle goodbye, and Fleur detested Phillipa reminding her of that. *Fleur just wants the lifestyle you can give her.* Simon's words wormed their way into her head again.

Phillipa was so taken up with her own thoughts, she didn't notice Fleur move swiftly across the kitchen to get right in Phillipa's face where her voice changed to resemble a threat.

'I live my life keeping quiet so as not to disrupt your precious writing,' she hissed.

'Let's just calm down, shall we?' Phillipa tried to walk away from the confrontation but was forced to stop when Fleur refused to move. 'Don't let's do this in front of Milo, Fleur.'

The next thing Phillipa knew, her mug of black coffee was knocked from her hand and close-to-boiling water cascaded over her fingers. She let out a howl of pain and saw Fleur fly towards her, and then... then everything was just a blur. A horrible blur.

That night, Phillipa slept in a spare bedroom, nursing her burnt hand, and watching as her forearms gradually patterned with blue-black bruises over the coming hours.

But the worst thing of all, by far, was knowing that Milo had seen everything.

She knew then that she couldn't confide her worries in Fleur. She had no choice but to continue to shoulder the ever-increasing burden on her own.

Where was the funny, loving woman she had married in their glorious Maldives wedding six years earlier? Increasingly, Phillipa found herself in situations where she didn't recognise her wife anymore.

Sometimes, it seemed Fleur was turning into someone else altogether.

TWENTY-NINE

EVE

I've got an early start on Thursday, so I call Hugo's phone about seven forty-five, just as I'm about to leave the flat. The call goes straight to voicemail. I call again. And again.

The third time, he answers. 'Eve, hi. I'm in the car.'

'I told you I was going to ring to speak to Scarlet this morning.'

'Sorry, it slipped my mind, I've been busy.' *Haven't we all*, I think but manage to bite my tongue. 'Could you call her tonight?' Hugo adds, impatiently.

'I'd like to speak to her now, just quickly. Can you give me Saskia's number? I'll call Scarlet on that in future, so there's no need to bother you.'

'I don't know Saskia's number without looking and I'm driving. I'm running late, actually.' He sounds hassled. Fraught. I remember those days, when I found myself walking on eggshells and overcompensating in an effort to appease him. 'We're going to have to leave it until tonight this time, I'm afraid.'

I could scream with frustration. How on earth has it got to

this? A situation where Hugo has full control of when I speak to my daughter?

'I'll call at five then,' I say irritably.

'I won't be back then. Can you make it seven?'

'Seven is too late, Hugo! She's usually had her bath and in bed for seven thirty at home.'

'What? That's a bit early, isn't it?'

I make a noise of incredulity. 'Not if you're five, it isn't!'

'Well, she's almost six, but we won't split hairs. Seven it is. Speak soon.' And then he does that infuriating thing again – he cuts off the call before I have a chance to respond.

I swallow the last of my lukewarm coffee. I've been speaking to Hugo just a couple of minutes and I'm full of niggles. Not a great way to start the day. I grab my bag and phone and leave the flat.

It's a bright morning, and I start to feel a little better, out in the fresh air. Last night when I came off the phone with Hugo, I had rung Mum straightaway. This time, she had answered.

'I'm ringing to see how you're feeling, Mum?'

'I'm fine!' Then, 'Well, I've felt a little bit under the weather. In fact, I was going to call you because Hugo—'

'He's taken Scarlet to his house. I know.'

'It's probably for the best, Eve, love. Hugo explained she'll be in her element down in Oakham with the horse-riding and their lovely big garden. She'll have a far better summer than being stuck here with me and my arthritic knees. He's going to take me to the cottage to stay overnight one day soon, too.'

I wrestle with a bitter retort. Hugo's always known how to get around her, easy as pie. But he's also managed to make Mum feel inadequate. 'That will be nice,' I say. 'But you really should have called me, Mum. Before he took her, I mean.'

'Yes, I did think that afterwards, but then, as Hugo said, he's her father, isn't he? He has a right to see her.'

'When it suits,' I mutter. I can't remember the last time he looked after her, and he's only just started paying me regular child maintenance. Hugo and Saskia seem to be flying high right now financially, and I wonder whether one of his business ideas has finally come good. 'I have full custody of Scarlet, Mum, and it's vital I know where she is at all times.'

'Well, I shall make sure I check in with you and ask for permission next time,' she says frostily.

'It's going well in my new job.' I don't know why I bother mentioning it – she's never had any interest in what I do. Dad loved to hear about my day. He revelled in it and wanted to know every detail, particularly if I was working on a Phillipa book, as he called the Tower series.

'Oh good. Hugo was saying his business is flourishing, and his new lady, Saskia, she used to work in publishing. Do you know that?'

'I do, Mum, yes.' Since we split, I've told her a bunch of times how Hugo and Saskia had met at a publishing event, and that rather hilariously (not), I'd introduced them myself. Maybe Hugo was right, and Mum was getting a tad confused.

'It'll do me good to have a couple of days at their cottage,' Mum continued. 'Hugo says I deserve to be spoiled.'

'Well, I just wanted to check you were OK. Hugo said you were finding it difficult to cope with Scarlet.'

'Not really, but he worries about me, doesn't he? Sometimes things get on top of me, and even with the day-to-day stuff, there seems so much to remember and get right, but I'm ticking along.'

'This weekend we can sit down and go through anything that's bothering you, Mum,' I say gently. 'Maybe I can help out, get some jobs done for—'

'I've got some help now,' she says brightly, as if it's only just occurred to her. 'A nice young man who's going to come in a couple of times a week and do a few hours. A bit of weeding, odd jobs that sort of thing.'

Relief softens my taut neck muscles a little. It's a good sign she's organised some help for herself. 'That's great, Mum. And you'll soon have Scarlet back in the house, nattering in your ear. She's good company at least!'

'It'll be so nice for Scarlet to spend some time with her daddy.' A tinge of sadness has entered her tone. 'You and your father were so close, Eve. I worry she hasn't got that same bond with Hugo.'

Something in the way she says it makes me feel like she thinks I'm to blame for keeping Scarlet and her father apart. I dread to think what Hugo has been telling her. I'd rather not know.

'I worry about it, too. That's why I've tried so hard to come to an access arrangement with Hugo since we parted.'

Mum's voice drops to a whisper. 'I miss your dad, Eve. I miss him so much. I'm tortured that he went without saying goodbye. That he was so unhappy but didn't feel he could share it with me.'

I swallow a lump in my throat. She hardly ever mentions her feelings about Dad. She must be really suffering to do so now.

'I know, Mum. I miss him, too. Every single day.' I feel a wave of hopelessness wash over me. There's nothing I can do to ease her pain and being away just makes me wretched with guilt. 'I'll be back with Scarlet at the weekend, and perhaps we can look at some old photos of the good times, eh? Scarlet will love hearing about her grandad.' Mum stays quiet. She can't handle the memories, even with the time that has passed. 'Scarlet can still start her holiday activity club next week.'

'I thought she was staying with Hugo for longer than that,' Mum says vaguely. 'I've probably got it wrong. It sounds like I'll see you both soon.'

I had fallen asleep last night turning her last comments over in my mind, wondering if Mum was party to other arrangements Hugo had in mind that I didn't know about yet.

I check my phone for emails. There's a Twitter notification informing me I have a new follower. I click on it and see my new follower is @ChadBSuperfan.

I know Jules considers this guy harmless, but he gives me the creeps. I click on the three dots to the right and my finger hovers over the block user option. Then I decide, before doing anything rash, I'll scroll down his posts. His timeline is full of mainly book review retweets and, further back, links from the Phillipa Roberts fan forum. I click on one such link and it takes me to a forum discussion entitled: *Where is Phillipa Roberts?*

When I try to read the thread, a message box pops up.

Oops, looks like you're not a member! We want to put that right. Click here to join Phillipa Roberts Fan Forum...

I glance at my watch. I haven't got time to do this now – I can look at it later. I close Twitter. I don't block @ChadBSuperfan for now, but I certainly don't follow him back.

THIRTY

Later that afternoon when I get back to the flat, I find Nina sitting at the breakfast bar eating Ben and Jerry's straight from the tub. Nina is short and diminutive with a freckly face and upturned nose. I don't know how she can eat so much and keep so slim.

'So, how did your meeting with Jules go?' She eyes me cautiously. I'd told her I had some concerns about the manuscript but not the detail. She knows something is wrong but doesn't want to push me, and I appreciate it.

'It went OK,' I say. 'Alicia was there, too. She made it clear I should stop griping and just get on with the job.'

'Anytime you want to talk, I'm here,' she says. 'I won't repeat a word, just so you know.'

'Thanks, Nina.'

'Want some?' Nina pushes the ice-cream tub towards me.

'No thanks.' I wave a hand and walk over to the kettle. 'I'm making coffee, want one?'

Nina shakes her head and scrapes another frozen curl of cookie dough from the pot. 'There's a letter for you on there.' She nods to the worktop. 'It was in the downstairs letterbox.'

Frowning, I pick up the white envelope. There's no stamp, so it wasn't that the postie had delivered it to the wrong flat. Handwritten in green ink:

Eve Hewitt. The Narrator.

'It must be a message from Harris-Lasson,' I murmur. 'Nobody else knows I live here.' Chad Belton's face drifts through my mind for some reason. But he has no idea where I'm living.

I hook a finger under the flap, rip it open and pull out a single sheet of lined paper which I unfold. My eyes travel down the page quickly. Once, twice, three times, and then I perch on a tall stool, my heartbeat quickening.

'Is everything OK?' Nina puts down her ice-cream. 'You've gone really pale.'

I look up. 'What?' I'd almost forgotten Nina is here.

'The letter,' Nina says. 'Is it bad news?'

'No, no. It's fine.' I fold up the paper and slipped it back into the envelope. The kettle clicks off. 'You know, I think I'm just going to go for a lie-down. I won't bother with coffee, after all.'

Nina's eyes follow me as I walk quickly to my bedroom and close the door behind me. At Mum's house, my room looked out over the rose garden Dad had planted from scratch and so lovingly tended. I sit on the edge of the bed with my face in my hands.

This was supposed to be the restart of a successful career, and yet it's starting to feel like a punishment. I take out the letter again and study the five words that have been neatly printed in green ink.

STOP ASKING QUESTIONS. FINAL WARNING.

That's it. Five words that don't sound all that threatening

the first couple of times you read them. But then the phrase seems to twist and take on a whole new meaning. *You need to stop asking questions. Final warning...* and then what? Well, then something bad will happen. That is what's meant here.

When I hear Nina turn the television on in the other room, I lie back on my bed and stare at the ceiling. But a couple of minutes later there's a tap on my door.

'Eve? Can I come in?' I half sit up, startled as the door starts to open and Nina's concerned face appears. 'Look, I don't want to pry but... I know something's wrong. Your face... it suddenly went really pale.'

'It's that letter.' I say, sitting up. 'Whoever sent it knows exactly where I'm living.'

'OK,' Nina says, unruffled. 'What does the letter say?'

'It says: "Stop asking questions. Final warning."'

'Stop asking questions about what?' She frowns.

'About Phillipa Roberts. I've been... asking around a bit.'

'Asking what exactly?'

'I don't know, just general stuff. Asking Jules and Alicia about things this morning. How she seemed in herself before she went missing. That sort of thing. The note feels like a threat.'

'I suppose it depends how much you read into it. It doesn't actually make any threats but...' She shudders. 'I agree it's not a very nice tone. At least whoever it was didn't come inside the building. Now that *would* be creepy.'

'To me it implies something bad will happen if I keep asking questions,' I say. 'And whoever brought it, hand-delivered it, which means they could be still hanging around here.'

'Jeez, you're making me nervous now.' Nina walks over to my window. 'Well, there's nobody hanging around the grave-yard, so that's a good start. Radical thought, but maybe you should just get on with the job and stop asking questions.'

'This sort of thing happening just makes me more determined,' I say, folding the letter back up. 'If there was nothing to find out about Phillipa's disappearance, nobody would care. Maybe I'm on to something.'

'Perhaps I should start calling you Miss Marple,' Nina teases. 'Let's just try and forget about that silly note. We don't want anything making us feel uncomfortable here at the flat.'

I nod, but inside, I feel determined. I've always worried I backed off too early when Dad went missing. Mum hated me trying to talk about it, and I hadn't wanted to upset her. I'd tried respecting the police opinion on the matter and pushed aside my own discomfort. Now it feels like the same thing is happening with Phillipa, a person who always treated me well and who I liked very much.

They say you learn most about yourself when you're under stress, and I'm beginning to realise something important. Rather than lose interest and back off the way everyone is trying to get me to do, I have become more resolved than ever to find out exactly what it is some people clearly want left undisturbed.

Perhaps it's time to widen my net.

THIRTY-ONE

It feels like I've reached the end of the road with Jules in terms of finding out information about Phillipa. She's clearly too frightened of Alicia finding out she's been talking to really relax and fully discuss what happened back then.

Phillipa's wife, Fleur, found the hidden manuscript and immediately contacted Sage, Phillipa's agent. Sage then involved Harris-Lasson. These people all know each other; they were all closely linked to Phillipa.

I decide the only chance I have of getting any more information, is by contacting Fleur and bringing the conversation round to Phillipa's state of mind. Fleur is the only person who could really know if the overdose was deliberate or accidental, although I'm not supposed to know about that or the surrogacy disappointment.

I decide to extend a friendly invite to meet up for a coffee. It won't seem amiss because I'm narrating Phillipa's book. Hopefully it will simply appear a polite and appropriate thing to do.

* * *

The house is big and white with a pillared entrance and a double-wide oak door. A small woman wearing a plain black dress with a white apron appears as I get out of the car. Her black hair is slicked into a neat bun, and she has a pleasant, smiling face. The housekeeper, I presume.

'Ms Hewitt?' she says before I can speak. 'Miss Fleur is taking her walk. She said to send you down there. Or I could accompany you, if you'd prefer?'

'No, no, just point me in the right direction,' I say. 'I'll be fine.'

'Very well. Walk out to the front and around the side of the house to the back garden,' she says. 'You'll see Miss Fleur down by the trees at the bottom.'

I thank her and turn around, walking past the ornamental fountains across the front of the house, my feet crunching on the perfectly round, white, marble pebbles. Walking close to the house and its regal floor-to-ceiling windows affords me a glimpse into their life. Minimalist rooms with white carpets and walls and the odd piece of glossy black furniture or modern sculpture on a plinth. This place is straight out of a magazine.

Fleur's son is a bit older, but I know Scarlet would wreck the look of a room like that within minutes. Minimalist designs don't tend to do well under piles of Lego bricks and discarded Disney dresses with masses of tulle froth.

My stomach feels fluttery – I hope I've done the right thing in contacting Fleur. I still have Phillipa's landline number in my phone, so it was easy enough to get in touch. When Phillipa disappeared, it had seemed wrong to delete it at the time. For a long while, I thought about her a lot and hoped she'd suddenly turn up. Maybe she'd had an accident and lost her memory had been one of my thoughts. It didn't seem very likely. I knew that, even back then.

As instructed by the housekeeper, I take a sharp right turn to cut down the side of the house. A full border of slender-stemmed French lavender with fat heads of purple flowers accompanies me all the way around to the back garden. I enjoy breathing in the heady fragrance before emerging onto a slabbed area, that gives the impression of breadth and space, framed by flowering bushes. I gasp as I emerge from it into an enormous back garden that is perfectly manicured to within an inch of its life.

The phone call had gone well, despite me nervously blurting out my intentions in one breath. 'Fleur, it's Eve Hewitt here. I'm narrating Phillipa's new book. I hope you don't mind me calling; I just wanted to touch base as I haven't been around since Phillipa... went away.'

Fleur had been gracious and friendly in her reply. 'I think Phillipa would like the idea of us discussing her genius stories.' She'd sounded upbeat, but I could sense an air of sadness behind her words. I'd suggested meeting at a coffee shop, but Fleur had had a better idea. 'Why don't you come over to the house? I can show you Phillipa's writing room and her awards.'

It was a better outcome than I could have ever imagined.

As I walk, I notice the perfectly sculpted topiary hedges that sit around the edges of the lawn, a vast emerald velveteen blanket.

I think about Fleur's son, Milo, again. I'd bet my bottom dollar he never plays ball games out here. I certainly can't imagine how they were intending on dealing with unleashing two bouncing twin babies on such perfection. Although sadly, that never came to pass, of course.

The garden slopes gently down to the small cluster of beech trees that the housekeeper mentioned. I can see the Thames undulating at the edge of the land. It seems dark and foreboding today with the covering of pale grey clouds diminishing the light above it.

Gingerly, I follow another white-pebbled path, careful not to kick a stone out of place or stray onto the spotless oasis beyond it. About the halfway point, I hear someone call, 'Down here!' A woman dressed in white stands at the edge of the trees, waving her arms in the air like an air traffic controller.

Fleur de Bois walks a little way uphill to meet me. She is a short, slim woman, with smooth brown skin and short blonde hair with fashionable dark roots. I've met her a couple of times over the years but she's more diminutive than I remember. The sides of her hair are slicked back with product and the top is left long and backcombed into a high quiff.

'Hello, Eve,' she says in a clear, confident voice. 'Nice to see you again.'

'It's good to catch up. Thanks so much for seeing me.'

We shake hands and Fleur begins to walk. 'We can sit down here for a while. Milo has gone out with his friend and their family for the day.' She leads me through the trees and out the other side to reveal two enormous carved root benches that look down on to the river. We sit down, leaving space between us. 'Phillipa loved it here; it was her favourite spot. The view was the reason we bought the house, really. Soon as she saw it, she was sold on the idea of living here.'

There's an air of sadness about her as she reminisces. I'm pleased she's mentioned Phillipa so openly early on in our conversation.

'I just wanted to say how very sorry I am about what happened,' I say, careful to avoid saying anything too bluntly. 'I sent a card ten months ago, but I'm sure you had so many. It's not the same as saying it in person. I can't imagine how you're coping.'

She nods and looks down at her hands. 'Thank you, Eve. Every day is so hard, and it never ever gets any easier. Seeing Milo growing so fast and knowing Phillipa is missing it all – they were very close – I can't explain how that feels. He calls me "Mama", and Phillipa is "Mummy", you know. Adores his father of course, but loves Phillipa, too.'

'That's heartbreaking,' I say sadly.

'This probably sounds strange, but finding the book was like scratching at the open wound. It didn't make any sense that she'd done it, and yet, on that day, I felt she was with us again.'

'You had no idea she'd been writing the tenth book?'

'No. I mean, since I've known her, she's always been writing something. Tinkering, or working on outlines and ideas. She didn't talk much about her writing – I confess I'm not a big reader. But she'd been more restless about work in those last few months.'

'Restless?'

'She used to spend hours in her office. Great swathes of time without breaks. But she'd not been like that for a while. She seemed to be spending less and less time in there. She was constantly popping out 'on an errand', as she put it.'

'What sort of places?'

Fleur shrugged. 'I don't know, some area of interest she wanted to look at for a book location, or... the library. She liked going there. She ordered reference books in, and she'd go and pick them up. That sort of thing. It was always book-related.'

'I suppose the police asked the sorts of things she'd done prior to that day,' I said.

'Oh yes. They asked lots of questions, but I never felt they were pulling out all the stops, you know? Sounds awful, but with the absence of a body, or evidence suggesting foul play – of which there was none – they swiftly concluded she'd just got sick of her life and took off.' She made a sound of derision in her throat. 'Apparently, it's more common than you think. Especially when people have had... problems.'

Jules had sworn me to secrecy about Phillipa's attempted overdose, so I said nothing, and Fleur continued.

'Course, nobody admitted that's what had happened, but I'm no fool. I saw their interest waning, and the senior officer –

he kept gently dropping it in that, sometimes, people just take off if life becomes overwhelming.'

I squirm a little inside. When they found Dad's body, I'd felt a compulsion to run away, to be on my own, to reach out to strangers. It didn't make any sense, but at the time, it had seemed the best thing to do. I had felt myself slipping, losing my grip. I'd been lucky enough to ask for and get help from my GP, but it sounds like things hadn't been so simple for Phillipa.

'I know you were quite open about your feelings back then,' I said, referring to the news reports around the time of Phillipa's disappearance. 'I remember being touched by an interview in a magazine where you spoke candidly about the grief you continue to feel.'

'Yes. Phillipa's publisher didn't like that. They said it was best to say nothing because the press would twist my words. But I found them generally quite supportive. More so than Phillipa's agent at least.' She didn't elaborate, but a flash of something dark moved across her face. 'My motive for speaking out was in the hope that if Phillipa was out there somewhere, if she had left us as the police kept hinting, there was a chance she'd read the interviews and realise how much we were suffering and missed her.'

I stared down at the dark endlessly flowing water. It was all so unbearably sad. After Dad went missing, it had been a week before they found his body in the river. During that week, Mum and I had had real hope he'd be found safe and well. If there had been some public platform I could have reached out to him on, like Fleur, I would have done so in a heartbeat, no matter what anyone else said.

'You stressed in all the interviews that you knew Phillipa had some problems, but you hadn't realised just how unhappy she was.'

'And that was the truth. At the time. But after ten months of thinking about little else, there *were* signs. Strange things that didn't mean anything back then, but now... well, I can't help but wonder.'

'Like what?'

Fleur stares forlornly into the middle distance. She looks as though she should be frowning, but her forehead remains unlined. 'It's hard to give precise details, because a lot of what I'd thought relied on my feelings at the time. Feelings I pushed away.'

I stay quiet.

'She was struggling with her mental health, I think, but – and I have no solid evidence for this – I believe Phillipa was having trouble with someone.' I stare at the moody scene in front of us. The dark water and the solid grey, scudded clouds that prohibit any peek from the sun.

'When you say "trouble", what do you mean exactly?'

Fleur bit her lip. 'I don't know. I mean, sometimes you just get a feeling, don't you? That your loved one might be... distracted by someone.'

She's talking around the issue, but I think I know what she's referring to. 'Did anyone else notice this about her?'

'Nobody saw it but me, I suppose.' She hesitated before continuing. 'I did discuss my concerns with a friend at the time, and she asked me if there was any chance Phillipa might be having an affair.'

I cringe at her candour, not sure what to say.

'At the time I thought absolutely not, but... with hindsight, I sometimes wonder. She seemed so restless. If she was going out, and I asked where to, she'd give me a vague answer which was unlike her. It was stuff that couldn't really be checked like, "into town", or "I have a few errands to run". That sort of thing.'

'And that was unusual?'

Fleur nods, and her eyes cloud over again. 'We always used to go everywhere together. Writers often say they become hermits, and it was true in her case. It was hell getting Phillipa out of the house and I think sometimes she resented me going on at her, but she needed a break from her imaginary world every now and then.'

'But she'd started going out more, and alone?'

'Exactly that!' Fleur's green eyes spark. 'The last few months, she'd just announce she was off out as she picked up her car keys from the side, even if we had a call arranged with the—' She stops. Looks at me before lowering her eyes. 'With the surrogacy agency. But I'd rather not talk about that. Suffice to say, it went terribly wrong and added even more pressure and stress to the situation.'

'Did you try and discuss how you felt with Phillipa?' I say, feeling guilty that, thanks to Jules, I know all about the surrogacy issue.

'Oh yes. I made it very clear I wasn't happy.' A muscle in her razor-sharp jaw clenches hard. 'But whatever she was doing, whoever she was seeing, that was clearly a stronger pull, in the end, and she'd just go anyway.'

'How long were things like this before she went missing?'

Fleur looks up at the sky, thinking. 'I'd say maybe about six to eight weeks, maybe a bit longer. I wasn't really tracking the time. But I remember the feeling she was up to something grew stronger. I pleaded with her, begged her to tell me if she was unhappy. I...' She hesitates. 'I'm not proud of telling you I got really angry at times. Threw stuff around. I was so frustrated, you know? I felt our relationship wasn't that close anymore, but all I got from Phillipa was denial that anything was wrong. But there *was* someone I know she was very close to. Too close in my opinion.'

I feel a bit awkward. I don't know Fleur that well, and what I'm about to say next requires her to trust in my discretion. But I gain confidence from the fact she's being so open with me.

'Did you know this person?'

Eve nodded. 'Her name was Jasmine, and she worked at

Phillipa's literary agency. She turned nasty after she overheard Phillipa trashing her to Sage, her literary agent and Jasmine's employer. She maintains Phillipa got her fired on purpose which is utter nonsense. Anyway, before they fell out, they were really close. Phillipa claimed it was just a professional relationship, of course. She's done this periodically. There was someone else she used to be very friendly with, too. Someone you know, I believe.'

I frown. 'I don't think I've ever met any of Phillipa's friends.'

'But you know people at Harris-Lasson, right?' Immediately, Jules's face jumps into my head. 'Does the name Saskia Peterson ring any bells? I think you have first-hand experience of *her* underhanded activities.'

My eyes widen. 'Saskia was Phillipa's PR manager,' I say faintly.

'Yes, I know. Look, it's probably just me imagining stuff. Anyone Phillipa was friendly with is fair game for me to start wondering.' She shakes her head and looks away. 'The only thing I'm bothered about is getting Phillipa back home. I don't know if she purposely took off somewhere because she became so confused and upset she couldn't think straight, but one thing I do know is that she had every intention of attending the awards ceremony that night. She was all dressed up and ready to go.'

I nod, but I'm distracted. I wonder if Hugo knows about Saskia and Phillipa being so close. He's certainly never mentioned their connection to me.

Fleur sighs. 'There's something else. One thing that keeps coming back to me. It's something Simon, my ex-husband, said, just few weeks before Phillipa went missing. He and I were bickering on the phone about a property we still jointly own, and I said Phillipa felt strongly that we should sell it.' She bites her lip and stares into space, thinking back. 'He just reacted so crazily, started yelling down the phone that it was nothing at all to do with Phillipa, and if she knew what was good for her, she'd keep her nose out of his business.' Fleur sighs. 'I knew there was no love lost between Phillipa and Simon – of course I did. He blamed her for our marriage break-up. But after years of them managing to be civil to each other on the odd occasion they met, I was shocked into silence when he said how much he despised her. His actual words were, "I hate that woman so much. I wish she'd just disappear off the face of the earth."' She looks at me. 'And then, of course, she did.'

THIRTY-TWO

We walk up to the house and sit in the supersized airy kitchen and chat while Fleur prepares us some cool drinks.

'It must have been a shock, finding the manuscript hidden in the attic,' I say as ice cubes rattle into our glasses. 'It sounds like Phillipa told everyone around her she was having problems getting to grips with this instalment of the series.'

'That's true and so it was a surprise, but... I never really knew what Phillipa was up to, writing-wise at least. She'd mope about not seeming to do much at all for a few months, and then one day she'd emerge from her office suddenly with a big smile and there it was. A new draft.' Fleur wiggled her fingers in the air to signify magic. She looks at my perplexed expression. 'Tell you what. I have something you might be interested in. Wait here.'

She brings my lemonade over then pops out for a few minutes. When she comes back, her arms are full.

'I put together two files after she went missing. I've never told anyone else because I thought they might think... well, I don't know. It just seemed a bit amateurish at a time when there was a full-scale police investigation happening,' Fleur says. 'The files don't amount to much, but you're welcome to have a look through if it helps.'

My heart rate picks up. 'Those could be really useful. Thank you.'

She shrugs. 'Back then I felt pretty hopeless. Useless, in fact. I found myself just sitting here, waiting for news, day after day. When Milo was in bed, I couldn't focus on TV or anything like that. I decided I'd gather what evidence I could while it was still readily available. It felt like I was doing something useful.'

She pushes a bulging buff-coloured foolscap folder across the kitchen table. 'I printed off all the newspaper and magazine cuttings I could find. Kept any email communications I had from the police and Phillipa's publisher. It's not an organised file, it's more like a set of jigsaw pieces that don't make up a coherent picture. It might be no good to you whatsoever.' She stares at the thin light filtering through the featherweight voile at the floor-to-ceiling windows. 'At the time, I imagined it wouldn't be long before Phillipa and I would be sifting through it together. After she came back, I mean, and explained what had happened to her.'

'Well, I'm sure I'll find it very useful,' I say, laying my hand flat on the folder.

She pushes a MacBook Air across the counter. 'The other file is on here. Soundbites of news reports, personal home videos and family photographs taken in the weeks before she disappeared. I just wanted to keep it all together.' She hesitates. 'There's another thing, too. Something the police were aware of, but information that wasn't generally released.'

I wait for her to elaborate and sip my drink. The sour-sweet taste makes me wince, but it's delicious.

'I only found out when Phillipa had disappeared that we had some financial problems.' So, the gossip Nina had over-heard about Phillipa's bank details had been correct. 'Substantial problems. God knows how with the amount she earned. But

Phillipa had always dealt with our finances, so I wasn't aware. Fortunately, I was able to speak to the accountant who had been trying to convince Phillipa to take remedial action. He advised me to sell the Brighton flat to stabilise the situation and that's what I did. But...' Her teeth scraped her lower lip. 'It's a problem that will raise its head again before too long without any new income. So you can imagine, when the book was found and the publisher told me about their plans for it, it was a big relief.'

'Thank you for trusting me with that information,' I say. 'Has anyone else seen your files?'

'The police had them for a while, but they came up with nothing new. They said it looked as though she'd covered all her bases, and it seemed to them like she didn't want to be found.' She closes the lid of the MacBook. 'There's no expectation,' Fleur says, placing her elbows on the table and steepling her fingers in front of her. 'I know you're not a police officer, Eve. But just the fact someone else is going to cast their eyes over this stuff, someone who knew and liked Phillipa. You've no idea how much better that makes me feel.'

I have an odd sense I'm getting into something I might regret. But after chatting with Fleur, it seems to me Phillipa had a lot to stick around for, even if she was going through tough times for whatever reason. She had people who loved her – who would have willingly helped get her through it.

For some reason, she kept them all shut out of her life.

THIRTY-THREE

On Friday afternoon, I get the 16:01 train from Kings Cross to Peterborough. Before I left, I gave Nina a birthday card and a bottle of fizz for her twenty-sixth birthday.

'It's such a shame you can't stay for the party,' Nina said. 'It would've been nice for you to meet my friends.'

'Next time,' I'd said, warming to her kindness, even though I couldn't imagine anything worse. 'I just really need to see Scarlet and get this thing sorted out with Hugo, once and for all.'

'Yep. Totally get that,' Nina said, making a strong-arm gesture. 'Make sure you show him who's boss, yeah?'

The train journey takes fifty-five minutes. When it leaves the station and emerges from the initial tunnels, I stare out of the window at the grey, rundown areas of London, desperate to see Scarlet and hold her in my arms again. This week has been a good one workwise, but it's felt like I was doing everything with chronic toothache the last couple of days. I've missed her so badly.

I imagine her little face lighting up when I arrive at the station, running to the car with her arms out wanting a hug.

Mummy Bear and Baby Bear, back together again. Nothing can shake us; nothing can ever come between us.

The link between Saskia and Phillipa has darted in and out of my mind since my conversation with Fleur yesterday. I know Saskia accompanied Phillipa on her last UK book tour. When you spend a lot of time with someone like that, you usually get a bit closer to them, and I find myself wondering if Saskia and Phillipa had developed a strong friendship as a result of it.

Despite my reticence about visiting Hugo's new house, one benefit from being at Bee Cottage: I might get the chance to speak to Saskia about Phillipa's disappearance and perhaps ask her a few questions.

The train journey drags on, and I wish I was heading back to Mum's house to see Scarlet, instead. I'd be looking forward to just chilling together for the evening, now. Everything nice and familiar, Mum relaxed and the three of us effortlessly comfortable together.

Now I can only look forward to spending the whole evening under Hugo's scrutiny, feeling like an imposter as his and Saskia's guest. More than likely, I won't get any quality time on my own with Scarlet. Instead of talking about the new friends she's made at the holiday activity club, it'll be one long brag fest for Hugo about where he's taken her and what he's bought for her.

Surely, I can think of a good excuse why I can't stay over... good enough to be able to gather Scarlet's stuff together, have Hugo run us back to the station and get the train up to Mum's tonight. It's probably just wishful thinking.

I half doze during the second half of the journey but perk up when we're ten minutes away from Peterborough station.

I've arranged to meet Hugo on a side street. His text had been clear:

Come out of the station, turn left, and left again. I'll be waiting on Cornell Street in my new motor. Black Mercedes S-Class.

Hugo was never one to miss the chance for a quick boast. I'm surprised there isn't even more detail: surely leather seats, alloy wheels and a private number plate as the bare minimum. I allow myself a small peevish grin, exit through the ticket turnstile and walk across the station concourse.

I follow his instructions, and sure enough, when I turn left onto Cornell Street, I spot what can only be described as a gleaming black limousine. I get closer and see Hugo is sitting in the driver's seat. Alone.

Disappointed, I open the passenger door. 'Didn't you bring Scarlet with you?'

'Hi to you, too, Eve,' he says drily. 'Boot's open if you want to pop your case in.'

I've only got a small hard case with wheels and a big shoulder bag, so it's not too cumbersome. Did I really expect Hugo to jump out and do the honours? I've clearly forgotten how quickly his 'old-fashioned gentleman' act grew tired once we were married.

I'm gutted he's not brought Scarlet with him to greet me, but the traffic on the side street is very busy, and knowing Hugo, he'll be itching to get back home. Irritation swirls in my stomach that I don't get to see Scarlet for another thirty minutes though.

I get in the car and promptly have a coughing fit. Hugo's aftershave is overwhelming.

'Sorry,' I say. 'OK if I have the window open a touch? I'm a bit sensitive to strong smells.'

'I remember,' he says, pressing a button his side which takes my window down half an inch. 'That time at the theatre when you wanted to leave because of a bit of smoke. You've always been flaky like that.'

'You've gone a bit mad with the aftershave,' I say spitefully. If we're trading insults, then I'm happy to give him a run for his money. 'It smells like you've washed your hair in it.'

'That's what two hundred and forty quid a bottle smells

like,' he says in a pinched voice. 'A birthday gift from Saskia, but I suppose you've got to be accustomed to the finer things in life to appreciate it.'

We fall quiet, both realising we've slipped into our old snappy ways. After a few minutes, I say, 'How's Scarlet? I've missed her so much. I wish you'd have brought her to meet me.'

'Scarlet's fine. She's better off in the garden than stuck in a stuffy car at the station.' He stops at lights and looks at me, his face brightening. 'She loves our new place, Eve. It's a kid's paradise, you'll see.'

'That's good,' I say, thinking about Mum's small Victorian terrace on the wrong side of town. Still, kids aren't bothered about houses or 'things'. Kids want love and attention, and Scarlet gets both those things in abundance from me and Mum. 'I don't want to argue about this now, Hugo, but I don't like what you've done.'

'What do you mean?' He looks at me, looks back at the road, as if he can't imagine what I'm talking about.

'Taking Scarlet from Mum's without asking me. You wanted her at your house for the summer, I said no, so you just took her anyway.'

'Now hang on a minute, it wasn't like that. I told you, your mum wasn't feeling well.'

'Well, I've spoken to Mum, and she says it was just a sniffle, that she was managing fine.'

He shakes his head and kisses his teeth. 'She's seventy-two years old, Eve. It's wrong to leave her with sole responsibility of a five-year-old. It's not good for her – or for Scarlet, for that matter.'

I don't reply, but my face feels suddenly hot. He's touched a nerve.

'How's work going?' I say. 'You seem to be very busy.'

'Business has never been better.' He brightens. 'The balance sheet is looking very healthy indeed.'

I wonder about his meteoric rise in assets since we split only two years ago. He got a small amount of equity out of the house just like I did. Not enough to buy a house like Bee Cottage or drive a fancy car, and Saskia had been working full-time in publishing, so I assume she can't be awash with spare funds. 'What is it you actually do these days?'

Hugo looks at me before turning back to the road. 'Storage. All the smart business people are getting into storage.'

'Storage of what?'

'Anything. Everybody at some time in their life needs space for storage, right? Tell me about this job you've taken on in London.'

I really don't want to discuss my career with Hugo. 'Maybe later. I'm tired from the journey. Does Saskia miss working at Harris-Lasson?'

'Frankly I'm surprised you've taken on such a big commitment, what with your mum struggling and Scarlet starting her new class in September,' he says, completely disregarding my reference to Saskia.

OK for him to build a career without a thought for anyone else. But I'm a bad mum and daughter for doing the same. I stay silent.

Soon, the built-up areas on the outskirts of Peterborough give way to semi-rural surroundings, and twenty minutes later, we pass a sign bearing a crest and signalling we're entering the county of Rutland. After that, I'm looking out at full-blown leafy lanes, verdant fields and stone-built farmhouses.

'It's very lovely out here.' I feel bound to comment.

'It's gorgeous,' Hugo agrees for once. 'Smallest county in England, Rutland, you know. I regularly have to pinch myself I'm living here.'

I'd like to feel more pleased for him, but one glance at that smug face and I discover I can't find it in me. We enter the village of Oakham five minutes later.

'Very nice,' I murmur as we pass a traditional old coaching house replete with dazzling hanging baskets and flower troughs stuffed to the brim with summer colour. A small primary school displays a sign that says SUCCEEDING TOGETHER and next to that, a village green complete with flower barrels and a maypole.

'Oakham was voted the best place to live in the Midlands by the *Sunday Times*. It really is very desirable.' Hugo sounds like an estate agent. 'As they say around here, it's as charming as the Cotswolds without the extortionate price tag. So, here we are. Home sweet home. Welcome to Bee Cottage, Eve.'

We turn into a tiny lane and bear immediate left into an open driveway lined with blossom trees that leads up to a cottage so chocolate-box pretty I have to force myself to stifle a gasp.

THIRTY-FOUR

The first thing she does now she is free of the vile, damp basement is take a long shower. She has to wash every trace of that filthy dungeon and her own stink from her body.

The needles of hot water feel like the definition of heaven against her clammy, cold skin. She dries herself on a fluffy white towel, cleans her teeth – her gums bleeding – and combs her wet hair back from her face but doesn't bother using the hairdryer.

She sprays deodorant and puts on a fleecy bathrobe that's hanging on the back of the bathroom door. It feels so soft against her skin, and she wonders at how it's the small pleasures she's missed the most.

She had been so focused on making money, yearning for attention and recognition. She'd been prepared to risk everything to get it, but what did it all mean, really? Nothing, if she didn't have her freedom.

The fridge contains a carton of fresh orange juice, two large bottles of water, yogurt, cheese and fruit.

She pours herself a small glass of juice which she mixes

with water so it's gentler on her stomach. She walks over to the desk and sits down, opens the laptop. There's no password. The only items on the desktop are the nine Tower audio files and a Microsoft Word icon.

She clicks on book three, *Death at the Tower*, pops on the headphones and presses play.

After listening for five minutes, she takes off the headphones. This narrator is perfect for the Tower series. She brings the characters to life and the readers love her.

She'd adored writing the series back in the early books. She'd thanked her lucky stars on a daily basis that she was doing what she loved for a living, even if it hadn't turned out to be quite the glamorous career she'd once hoped for. It hadn't felt like work at all. But then the pressure had started. The demands, the attempts to dictate what happened in her plots. The more popular the books became, the worse the interference from various quarters. And the more she felt resentful she wasn't getting the money and recognition she alone deserved.

The pressure had increased until she'd found it unbearable. She wanted to show *she* was in charge of her own words and she could not be forced to write to order.

In the end, she'd been worried for her own safety and that's why she'd had to make a stand... a decision that had gone horribly wrong.

The precise details of the who, where and when of her predicament were tantalisingly close now. She could feel them almost within grasp but, like trying to recollect a dream, the harder she tried to reach for them, the more the details drifted away. So she let it be for now.

A complete book would usually take her months to write, but under this kind of pressure and strain, it could be longer. She had better get started.

She works for three hours solid, until an all-consuming

tiredness envelops her. She saves her work and walks across the room. She doesn't see the slipper she's left lying on the floor. She trips over it and falls, banging her head on the wall.

She stands up, dazed, and staggers over to the bed. She lies down, and within minutes, she falls into a deep sleep.

THIRTY-FIVE

EVE

The white-painted cottage itself looks old, maybe even seventeenth century, and reminds me of Winnie the Pooh's house. Its thatched roof looks like it's been lifted above the building and artfully draped on top of it. Parts of it seem to drip down over the eaves like golden honey from a jar.

My only thought is: How on earth can Hugo afford to live somewhere like this?

The car creeps across the gravel frontage and comes to a stop slightly past the cottage. I spot a large, tasteful extension at the back with what looks like the top of a glass orangery poking above the top of building.

Hugo looks at my expression and laughs. 'It's fantastic, isn't it? You look like us when we first lay eyes on the place.' Then, 'Uh-oh, here comes trouble!'

The front door opens and Saskia waves. From under her arm, Scarlet ducks and runs outside.

'Mummy!' she cries out, and bolts forward.

I jump out of the car and run to greet her, scooping her up into my open arms. 'I've missed you so much, sweetie,' I whisper into her ear, inhaling the fresh apple smell of her hair. 'Let me look at you.'

She's beaming. She looks so well! A ruddy complexion on her usually pasty cheeks. And something else is different... her clothes. They're brand=new.

I run my fingers over the soft, fine fabric. Just a simple T-shirt and shorts but they scream understated designer quality.

'You look beautiful, darling. I love your outfit.'

'Saskia bought them for me,' Scarlet says breathlessly, squeezing me again in her little arms. 'She let me choose everything myself.'

I look over at Saskia in the doorway. She smiles and waves, and I wave back. She's wearing a pair of small white shorts with white leather sliders on her feet – at the end of very long, very slim, brown legs. A white square-necked, broderie anglaise smock sits prettily atop a barely visible bump. Hugo hasn't mentioned how many months pregnant Saskia is. I wonder again about her close friendship with Phillipa. Somehow, I need to bring the conversation around to their connection.

'Welcome, Eve!' she calls. 'I'll make us a drink and take it out back.'

Hugo opens the boot and pulls out my case. 'I'll take this up to your room,' he says. 'Scarlet, darling, why don't you show Mummy the garden?'

I open my mouth to say we're not going to be able to stay over after all and perhaps we can arrange something later in the year, but Scarlet pulls at my arm.

'Mummy, come on! I'll show you the secret garden where the fairies live!'

She skips ahead and I follow. I admire the large front garden as we walk. There's a gravelled area where Hugo parked, but beyond that, it's classic cottage planting. A myriad of colours and textures skilfully planted so everything looks completely natural, as if there's been no human input at all.

It's so peaceful here. The air seems so much fresher, and I'm struck by the absence of traffic noise. A scattering of tiny wrens dart back and forth in the blossom tree above us, and the exquisite birdsong is almost ear-piercing. Scarlet creeps forward on tiptoes. 'See the bees, Mummy?' She points to a fragrant drift of lavender. 'They're collecting pollen to take back to the hive. They stuff it into little pockets on their legs, so small you can't see.

'That bird sitting on top of the red robin bush is a thrush. Sometimes she sits outside my bedroom window in the morning. She has a speckled breast, and I think her whistling is the prettiest!'

My bedroom window.

We turn down the side of the house. It's cooler here, in the shadow of the cottage. A neat gravel border is dotted periodically with potted topiary trees. I slow my walking.

'So, have you had a good week here with Daddy and Saskia?' I reach for Scarlet's hand.

She nods, pausing to rub a sprig of rosemary between her fingers. She sniffs her hand and smiles, holding it up for me to try.

'Lovely!' I say. 'What sort of things have you been doing with Daddy and Saskia?'

'We play games in the garden all the time! I helped Saskia plant some herbs for cooking. When they've grown, we're going to make some pea and mint soup and...' She frowns as she thinks hard. 'Oh, Saskia's made my bedroom sooo pretty, and Daddy reads me lots of stories every night. He never says *just one*.' A wide smile blooms on her face as I recognise my own bedtime story rule. 'And best thing ever is, on Monday, I'm having my first horse-riding lesson!'

My heart sinks. I'm planning on taking Scarlet back to Mum's with me tomorrow. I'd made that clear to Hugo.

'Are you looking forward to seeing Gran tomorrow? She says she's really missed you...'

Before I can finish my sentence, Scarlet runs around the corner and out of sight. As I round the end of the extension, I follow the path and I'm suddenly in another beautiful garden. It must be around a half acre with an expanse of perfect emerald lawn and more wild flowers all around it. At the bottom of the garden is a pergola covered in white roses. It's a very different – more informal, smaller – garden than Fleur's yesterday, but it's just as beautiful in its own way.

'Come and sit down, Eve,' Saskia calls out. She's sitting in one of two dark-green Adirondack chairs on the patio. 'I made us a Pimm's.'

Perfect. A chance to speak with Saskia alone.

While Scarlet skips around the garden, singing to herself, I slip off my lightweight jacket and ease myself into the chair. I'm uncomfortably hot in my jeans and long-sleeved top, and I feel like a big overheating blob next to Saskia's cool perfection. I jut out my bottom lip and blow my fringe off my sticky face.

'You must be tired after your journey,' Saskia says, pouring me a drink from a glass jug full of Pimm's with chopped fruit and cucumber. She's calm and collected, and although her hair and make-up are done, she looks perfectly understated. This whole scene – apart from me, who looks like the gardener – is like the quintessential shot in a *Country Homes* magazine.

'How's the job going in London?'

'It's going well. Strange, recording the words Phillipa wrote but without her around to be part of it all.' I take a sip of the icy, refreshing drink, and it's predictably delicious. 'I'd almost forgotten how well you knew her until her wife mentioned you the other day.'

Saskia's smile falters slightly. 'You've seen Fleur?'

'Yes, I called for a chat. She gave me some stuff she'd put

together when Phillipa went missing. Photos, newspaper reports, things like that.'

'Gosh, it sounds like you're properly investigating what happened!'

'Not really. I'm not, it's just... recording the new book has brought it all back. About Dad. I really like Phillipa, and I'm just interested in finding out what I can about her disappearance.'

'And Fleur mentioned me?'

'She just said you and Phillipa were very close at one time.' I fix my eyes on hers, but she doesn't look away.

'That's true. We spent a lot of time together on the book tour, of course.' She raises a hand to shield the sun and looks down the garden to watch Scarlet running around. 'We grew apart a bit when I met Hugo. He's keen I spend as much time with him as possible.'

Keen. That was one word for it. I remember coming home from after-work drinks to his thunderous face on several occasions. 'What time do you call this?' Never any mention of the regular late nights caused by his own work and the stony silence that could last for days if I dared to bring it up.

'Did you and Phillipa part on good terms?'

'We didn't part as such – we just saw less and less of each other. She'd ask me to accompany her to various things, and I'd say no to avoid Hugo's wrath.' She shifts in her seat. 'One day she came over to our old house and she seemed really low, looked as if she'd lost weight. I wondered if she had something on her mind she wanted to talk about, but we never got chance. Hugo had a go at her. I was so embarrassed. Turns out he'd been out for a drink with Simon, Fleur's ex-husband, and they'd been whipping each other up about her.'

'Oh, I didn't know Hugo and Simon knew each other.'

'Back then, they were both members of some kind of business networking group, apparently.'

'I assume Simon doesn't like her, either?' I don't mention Fleur has already confirmed that.

Saskia shakes her head. 'Phillipa told me he totally blamed her for the failure of his marriage to Fleur. And Hugo mentioned that Simon was delighted when Phillipa disappeared. Simon said he hoped she'd gone for good.' She bites her lip and then says, 'How was your journey over here?'

'It wasn't a bad journey, thanks,' I say, looking around the garden. 'Your home is so beautiful. I can tell Scarlet has had a wonderful time here. She's been telling me how the bees gather honey and all about the thrush that sings outside the window. You mustn't miss publishing one iota, living here.'

'I've got mixed feelings about it, really. I did enjoy my job, but Hugo hated the long hours and the national book tours where I had no choice but to stay away from home.'

I take a sip of the Pimm's. 'What do *you* think happened to Phillipa?'

She frowns and looks at the wall for a few seconds before replying. 'I've thought a lot about this, and honestly, I haven't got a clue. I know about the rumours, people saying Phillipa ran away to make a new life. But when I worked with her on her last book tour, she seemed so happy and well adjusted. She could have been putting on an act, I suppose, but I spent a month travelling the UK with her, and in my experience, you usually get a sense of when someone is down. I never got that feeling with Phillipa.'

'Mummy, look!' Scarlet swings on a low tree branch, and I wave, blow her a kiss.

We both watch as she bends to gently cup and smell a flower. Saskia says, 'Scarlet really loves nature. I think if children can experience it first hand, they learn and appreciate it far more. If it's fine weather, she asks to come outside. Does she love the garden at home?'

I put down my glass. 'Mum's only got a small garden,' I say.

'Mostly roses, so there's nowhere to run around. But we do go to the park regularly and she enjoys that.'

Saskia nods and lays a hand on her stomach. 'She's been asking lots of questions about the baby.'

'Has she really?' She hadn't shown much interest when I told her that Daddy and Saskia were having a baby and that it would be her brother or sister.

'Oh yes, she's going to help me decorate the nursery, and she's painted a picture for him already.'

'Him?'

'Yes.' Saskia beams. 'Hugo is absolutely convinced it's a boy.'

Hugo would be. He'd been hoping for a boy when I was pregnant. When we found out I was having a girl, I saw the disappointment flash across his face before he could gather himself to assume a false, ecstatic expression instead.

'Can I ask why you left Harris-Lasson?'

Saskia looks down at her stomach, but I know she left her job way before she got pregnant. 'Hugo wanted me to. His business had picked up and me working full-time with all the extracurricular activities like book tours and organising events just got in the way.' That figures. Nothing is ever as important as Hugo's career. 'But anyway, on to more interesting topics. Give me the lowdown on this secret book!'

'If I told you, I'd have to kill you.' I grin.

'What do the Harris-Lasson staff think of it? Has it been positively received?'

'Yes, I mean, they're going full steam ahead to publish it.'

She gives an impish smile. 'I feel like there's a but coming! What do you think of it?'

'It's... different. That's all I'll say.'

Saskia frowns. 'Different how?'

'Oh, I don't know. Different in tone, people in the story acting out of character.' I'm feeling really uncomfortable. 'I'm really sorry, Saskia, but I've been told in no uncertain terms not to discuss the book with anyone. I hope you don't mind, but—'

She holds up her hands. 'I understand completely. I shouldn't have questioned you. But now I see why you're so interested in finding out more about Phillipa's disappearance... because you think there's something strange about the new book.'

She watches me and I turn to look down the garden. 'I love Scarlet's little outfit. You must let me know what I owe you.'

'Don't be silly! It's from a gorgeous little shop that's just opened in the village. They've got some amazing stuff in there. Scarlet's outfit is Kenzo Kids, but they stock Hucklebones and Molo, too. We can pop into the village for breakfast tomorrow and take a look, if you'd like.'

I stare at her a moment or two. It's as if she's speaking in another language. I get Scarlet's clothes from a variety of places. Supermarkets have great value clothing ranges for kids, obviously Primark and for that special occasion, the odd party outfit from Next. I've never heard of the brands she just mentioned.

'Actually, I think there's been a bit of a mix-up,' I say regretfully. 'I'm going to be taking Scarlet back with me tomorrow when I go to Mum's.'

'Oh!' Her eyes widen. 'Have you told Hugo about this development?'

'I thought he knew. I said I'd stay over tonight and then we'd get the train to Mum's tomorrow afternoon.'

She shifts in her seat but does not respond.

'Top up?' She picks up the jug again. I notice she's already halfway down her own tall glass. 'It's really weak,' she says, when she sees me looking. 'Hardly any alcohol in there.'

'I'm fine, thanks.' I take another small sip before steering the conversation back to tomorrow's journey. 'Mum's feeling fine in herself, so there's no reason Scarlet can't go back.'

'I really think you need to tell Hugo,' Saskia says nervously.

'Tell Hugo what?' We both turn as the man himself walks out of the French doors and on to the patio. He's changed into shorts and a Ralph Lauren striped polo shirt and sliders.

'I'm taking Scarlet back with me to Mum's tomorrow,' I say lightly.

'Oh, no, that's not happening,' he says easily, perching on the low stone wall in front of us.

My face burns. 'It's what we agreed, Hugo. Scarlet's missing out on her new holiday club and—'

'Scarlet, honey,' Hugo calls, beckoning her. 'Come over here.'

'There's no need to involve Scarlet in this,' I say tightly.

Scarlet runs up breathlessly. 'Yes, Daddy?'

He pats his knee, and she climbs on. 'So, you've got a decision to make. Do you want to go back to Gran's house with Mummy tomorrow, or do you want to stay here with us, at Bee Cottage?'

'It's not Scarlet's decision, Hugo,' I say from behind clenched teeth.

'Bee Cottage!' She declares, pumping her fist into the air.

Saskia gets up out of her chair and walks into the house.

'We have to go back to Gran's, sweetie,' I say gently. I'm churning inside, questioning if I'm being selfish or sensible in taking her away. 'You were looking forward to making friends at your new holiday club remember? And we—'

'I've got a horse-riding lesson!' Scarlet says crossly, folding her arms. 'And I've promised to help Saskia decorate Arthur's room.'

'Arthur?'

'My new baby brother!' She rolls her eyes as if I'm a hopeless case.

'This is not the way to do things.' I glare at Hugo. 'You know I'm in an impossible situation and—'

'This isn't about you, Eve,' Hugo says pleasantly. 'It's about

Scarlet and what's best for her. She's very happy here, right, honey?'

'Yes, Daddy.' She smiles up at him adoringly. 'I love Bee Cottage and Mrs Thrush.'

'She's so excited about her horse-riding lesson and... tell Mummy what's happening next week.' Scarlet looks puzzled, and he whispers something in her ear.

'Hens!' She jumps off his knee and begins jumping around the patio. 'We're getting two hens, so we have fresh eggs for breakfast, and guess what, Mummy? I get to name them!'

She runs back onto the grass, waving her lightly tanned arms in the air and shouting, 'The hen house is going to be down here!'

I push my hand through my hair. 'Look, Hugo, this is all getting out of hand. It's not fair what you've done, it's—'

'I've made us a nice cup of tea, Eve.' Saskia reappears, carrying a tray.

'We're talking,' Hugo tells her tightly, his eyes dark.

'Sorry.' She puts down the tray and goes back inside the house.

'Thanks, Saskia,' I call after her.

'What's not fair about it?' Hugo continues. 'It's you who's being selfish. Look at this place.' He sweeps his arm around the cottage and garden. 'What's best for Scarlet? Ask yourself that. Suffocating in your mother's dank, poky garden or the chance to enjoy all this?'

My mouth feels dry, and I take a gulp of tea. I feel so out of place here, I just want to get away. I'm going to take Scarlet and travel to Mum's tonight. He can't stop me.

'Scarlet,' Hugo calls to her again. 'Why don't you show Mummy your bedroom?'

'Yes!' She runs up and dances around me. 'Come on, Mummy, it's the best bedroom in the whole world!'

I take her hand, and she leads me into the house.

Saskia is perched quietly on a stool in the kitchen as Scarlet runs ahead.

It's a large, airy space fitted with cream hand-painted Shaker units. It's been designed to fit in with the age of the cottage, but on closer inspection, it includes every mod con. A nickel hot water tap, Miele appliances, an olive-coloured Aga range cooker.

'Scarlet wants to show me her bedroom if that's alright,' I say to Saskia.

'Of course it is,' she says. Then, 'I wanted to ask you, Eve, is everything OK in London? It's just that you're asking a lot of questions about Phillipa.'

'Yes! Everything is fine – it's just recording the new book has brought it all back, you know? How lovely she is and how we're no further forward finding out what happened.'

I can hardly confide my concerns about the anomalies in the hidden manuscript.

I nod towards the kitchen door. 'I'd better go upstairs, or Scarlet will be calling for me.'

'I'll come up with you,' she says.

The inner hallway has a polished wooden floor, and the stairs feature a Berber runner with a narrow black border, and features an antique brass rod across the bottom of each stair riser. The walls are quirkily uneven and painted an eggshell off-white. Professionally shot 'couple' photographs of Saskia and Hugo dressed in white linen trace our journey to the upstairs.

'My room is here, Mummy!' Scarlet charges up the landing and back again, through an open door to her bedroom. 'Look!'

I follow her inside and stand for a few moments, taking it all in. The room is large and mostly decorated in white. A life-size unicorn with glittering silver horn and rainbow wings stands across one corner, front leg bent and forelock lowered. The bedding is white, with a unicorn-print throw and a white canopy that frames the plush pink headboard. Soft toys are dotted around the decorative cushions placed in front of her pillows.

'My goodness,' I gasp, looking round. 'It's... it's incredible, Saskia. Just incredible.'

'I had to guess what Scarlet would like,' Saskia says, almost apologetically. 'I knew I was probably on to a good thing with the unicorn theme. But Scarlet was able to choose the soft toys herself, yesterday in the village.'

'I'm speechless,' I say. 'It looks like a kid's room from a magazine.'

I walk over to the window. It's made up of tiny individual panes of glass, in keeping with the exterior. She has a fabulous view of the garden from here.

'This is the tree Mrs Thrush sits in and sings to me when I wake up each morning, Mummy.' Scarlet points to an ancient-looking oak tree straight out of the Hundred Acre Wood, its gnarled branches spilling in front of the window.

'Thank you for making such an effort for her, Saskia,' I say. I'm genuinely touched she's gone to so much trouble to make Scarlet feel at home here.

'We want her to feel part of the family, particularly when baby Arthur arrives,' Saskia says, smiling affectionately at Scarlet.

'She's already part of the family.' I whip round to see Hugo has joined us, the beginnings of a smirk on his mouth. 'That's why you need to leave her here with us while you're working away, Eve. Look how happy she is. You know it's the right thing to do.'

I turn around and look at Scarlet. She rushes over and regards me pleadingly. '*Please*, Mummy,' she says, clasping her hands together while Saskia throws me an apologetic look. '*Please* can I stay at Bee Cottage with Daddy and Saskia while you're working in London?'

THIRTY-SIX

CHAD

Armed with the information he'd garnered from the loquacious Mrs Hewitt, Chad jumped in the car on Wednesday morning and headed to his destination.

After hours reading the new Phillipa Roberts book, he'd barely been able to eat anything. His stomach churned; his heartbeat felt strange. Palpitations, that was the word. That's what he was having.

He'd part-read both the original and the edited version of the script that the Harris-Lasson editor had sent to Eve. People were going to start asking questions about Phillipa's disappearance, that much was certain. The police were going to get involved and the truth would be discovered.

Chad was a planner. He'd always understood that when an important job was planned down to the smallest details, the chances of success were increased tenfold.

The drive to his destination was uneventful. Chad listened to a true crime podcast on the way there to take his mind off his worries. He'd studied Google Earth the night before and planned out exactly the best spot for his surveillance. Somewhere that afforded a clear view for himself but was also screened from several angles.

When he arrived, he parked the car, wound down the windows and organised everything he'd need around him.

His cool box containing his sandwich lunch, fruit and water in the footwell. Check.

A flask of English breakfast tea. Check.

A foil wrap of two digestive biscuits for his mid-morning break. Check.

Binoculars and camera sat on the passenger seat completing his arsenal of tools.

He had to speak to Eve Hewitt. He had to make her listen to him.

THIRTY-SEVEN

EVE

Scarlet wins out and I decide to let her stay on at Bee Cottage with Hugo and Saskia for a few more days. She pleads for me to stay the night and, as it's my only chance to spend some quality time with her before I go back to London, I give in.

Saskia shows me to my bedroom and leaves me to get settled.

I sit on the edge of the bed, rubbing my hand over the silky smooth, high-thread-count sheets. The room they've given me is small but perfect. As with the rest of the place, it features the classic cottage look with beams and quirky uneven walls. The wooden floor has a soft white rug thrown down, and there's a tiny en-suite containing a sink, a loo and a shower.

The window is slightly open, and the birdsong is incredible.

I'd felt pressured downstairs. Scarlet, Hugo and Saskia, all staring, waiting for my answer. And of course, I'd agreed. I'd said Scarlet could stay at Bee Cottage for the duration of me working in London. My head said I had no choice, that it was essential for me to do my job effectively and also to give me time to find out more about the circumstances of Phillipa's disappearance. But as Scarlet's mummy, my heart bucked against it.

Jealousy, concern, worry... I try to pinpoint the source of my discomfort and fail. I'm backed into a corner and feel bound to accept Hugo and Saskia's offer.

Regardless of my troubled feelings, Scarlet does seem very content here. I'm surprised that she's already built a bond with Saskia who, despite having no children of her own yet, seems to know exactly what to do to keep Scarlet entertained. She's obviously a natural mother.

Before I had Scarlet, I was clueless with kids. I'd go over to Mum and Dad's house most days when she was very young rather than sit on my own in the house while Hugo constantly worked away.

Dad and I would take Scarlet and Benjy – the family's Jack Russell – out for long walks in the woods and countryside. Dad was in his element, showing Scarlet the different plants, birds, wildlife... It didn't seem to matter to him she could barely talk yet. I'd laugh, and he'd say, 'She's taking it all in, Eve. Children are like sponges. One day when she's five, she'll just know all the names of the birds.' My heart squeezed, and I blinked quickly to clear my eyes.

I longed to have her back in our room at Mum's house. For us to cuddle up in bed together and watch television. We can't be ourselves here at the cottage. Scarlet has already changed... not in any profound way but changed because she's been here almost a week and learned new routines and ways of living.

I rack my brain for a way I can retract my permission for her to stay. I long to be on the train with her, travelling up to Mum's. I don't want to stay here longer than I need to, however beautiful it is.

This picture perfect, middle-class existence isn't my life.

It will never be my life.

* * *

Saskia calls me down for dinner. I'm relieved it's a simple meal: quiche and salad with some tasty accompaniments – artichokes in oil, pesto pasta and sundried tomatoes.

'Eve's doing a bit of sleuthing about Phillipa's disappearance,' Saskia tells Hugo when he comes into the kitchen for glasses. 'Fleur's given her a folder of evidence! It all sounds very cloak and dagger.'

Hugo makes a disparaging noise. 'Good riddance to Phillipa Roberts, I say. Never liked the woman. She broke up Simon and Fleur's marriage – there's no doubt in my mind about that – and she thought Saskia was her own private assistant.'

'I'm not investigating as such,' I say quickly. 'Just trying to understand what happened.' I glance at Hugo. 'My own life was a bit of a state back then, and a lot of it went over my head.'

Saskia has the grace to look uncomfortable, but Hugo merely smirks and walks outside with the glasses.

We eat on the patio. I cover my glass with my hand when Hugo opens a bottle of white wine, the bottle frosted and perfectly cooled.

'I'll stick with iced water, thanks,' I say. 'I shouldn't really have drunk all that Pimm's earlier.'

'Oh, come on, Eve,' he says. 'Just have one glass, for goodness sake. I'm even pouring Saskia a tiny measure. We must toast our new home.'

Saskia says. 'No wine for me, darling. I'll stick with water, too.'

'Nonsense.' He pours the wine into three glasses. 'You two are killjoys, and tonight, it's not allowed. I have my beautiful daughter with me, my gorgeous partner and my bossy ex-wife. All together for the first time.'

'Cheers!' Scarlet holds up her Fruit Shoot bottle and we all laugh. She's obviously learned that from her daddy. He's always been a big wine drinker.

Despite my misgivings, the meal is pleasant. Relaxing with

a glass of wine or two, we chat about lots of different things. Life in the village, the manic pace of London and mainly, the stuff Scarlet has been doing since she got here. It's a relief to stay on safe ground.

Later, lying in my bed, unable to sleep and listening to the hoot of a distant owl, I revisit my concerns about Scarlet staying here with Hugo who I know can be unreliable and moody. I feel better knowing Saskia is with her. I can see she's a steadying influence in the house, and she seems to genuinely enjoy having Scarlet around.

Saskia is clearly a quieter person than I am, but she's no less adept at handling Hugo. I've noticed she has a clever way of making him feel as if he's in the driving seat while, at the same time, wheedling her own way with things.

I wait and wait for sleep to come, but it's a fruitless exercise. I get out of bed, slip on the white waffle robe hanging on the door and go downstairs to the kitchen. It's softly illuminated as the under-cupboard lights have been left on. I make a cup of tea and sit by the French doors looking out to the garden.

There are solar lamps glowing all the way down to the bottom of the lawn. It's so pretty, no wonder Scarlet adores being here. The tea helps to relax me, and I decide to go back up. I wash my cup and pad down the hallway. Hugo's office door is open, and the desk lamp is still on, highlighting the paperwork spread out. He has a couple of framed photos on there, and I walk into the room to have a peek if one of them is of Scarlet. It is, and I pick it up. A picture of Hugo with her at her first birthday party in our old family home.

I feel sadness for what we had together, sadness for my unrealised hopes and dreams back then, when I didn't know the extent of Hugo's disloyalty and deceit. I replace the photograph, and I'm about to leave when the edge of some paperwork catches my eye.

I take a sharp breath in at the handwritten note and slide the piece of paper fully out so I can see it.

Hugo, I have today transferred the money over as agreed. P.

Those elaborate capital letters. That beautifully scripted 'P' that I would recognise anywhere. This note is from Phillipa.

Back in my room, I'm more awake than ever, turning the contents of Phillipa's note over and over in my mind. Phillipa was paying Hugo for something, but what? He disliked her, never had any business contact with her, I'm certain of that.

* * *

At some point, I must have somehow managed to drop into a deep sleep because the sound of my phone ringing – I forgot to turn it to silent when I came to bed – jolts me awake. I grab it from the bedside table and sit bolt upright in shock. It's Nina, ringing at 2:08.

I answer the phone straightaway, worried it will wake the house. 'Hello?' I hiss.

'Eve? It's me, Nina! Oh God, something awful has happened. I'm so sorry... I feel terrible. The party was—'

'What's happened?' I say, my voice still thick with sleep.

'I don't know exactly what... The party got a bit out of hand and... I didn't realise until they'd all gone. It's terrible, I—'

'Just tell me, Nina. What's happened?'

'It's your bedroom; it's been ransacked.'

'What?' I sit bolt upright. I only drank two glasses of wine with dinner, but I have a banging headache and feel disorientated.

'Someone got in there and trashed the place. It's a mess, Eve. I'm so, so sorry.'

'Who?'

'That's just it, I don't know. I invited a bunch of people from work, and then throughout the night, others turned up – people I didn't recognise. I'd had so much to drink and... It wasn't until everyone had gone I saw your bedroom door was open.'

'What do you mean by ransacked? They stole my stuff?'

'I'm not sure because I don't know what you had in there. I mean, it looks like the aftermath of a police search. Your drawers are emptied, the wardrobe... even the drawers under the bed! It's as though someone was looking for something, but that can't be right, can it?'

I close my eyes, thinking about the note I received. STOP ASKING QUESTIONS.

'I can report it to the police, but you'll need to tell me what's missing,' she adds. 'You ought to be here, really.'

'I'll come back this morning,' I say. 'Hugo will run me to the station, and I'll get an early train back to London.'

'I'm so sorry, Eve. This has ruined your weekend.'

'No, I'm glad you called. I was going to travel to Nottingham to see Mum next, but I can give that a miss and go next week instead. I'll text you when I set off, let you know timings.'

Nina makes a noise of relief. 'I haven't touched anything, so be warned, you'll be seeing the room how it was left. Again, I can't apologise enough. Let me know if there's anything you need.'

'There is one thing you can do.'

'Anything.'

'Make a list of everyone who came. Everyone you knew and then contact them and ask them to write down everyone they knew who was there, too. Hopefully, that way we'll be able to get a full list of guests to give to the police.'

'Good idea, I'll do that now. See you in a few hours' time.'

When we ended the call, I threw the phone on my bed and

sat staring out at the night sky. I hadn't bothered closing the curtains when I crashed out last night, and now I feel glad for that. The sky is inky black with what looks like a million tiny stars peppering the night. A cool crescent moon dangles as if someone has hung it there. There is so little light pollution out here. For a few seconds I almost don't want to leave it myself.

But reality has kicked in, and now I have no choice. I must leave this leafy oasis and head back to the flat in London to hopefully find out who wanted information so badly, they tore my bedroom apart.

THIRTY-EIGHT

ELEVEN MONTHS EARLIER

Phillipa took a cab to her literary agency. She paid the driver, got out and looked up at the second floor, the office of Sage Heathfield, her agent of many years now. She said a silent prayer that Jasmine Sanderson, Sage's aloof assistant, wouldn't be in today. She was *not* in the mood for her.

She pressed the intercom, and one of the office staff buzzed her in. The entrance to her agent's eponymous office was a door at the top of the stairs that bore a simple black sign with gold lettering: THE SAGE HEATHFIELD LITERARY AGENCY.

Phillipa's heart sank when Jasmine came to the door. Slim and petite, she was dressed in a pale-blue linen shift dress paired with tan leather Birkenstocks. She was in her late thirties but looked ten years younger. Sage had once intimated that when Jasmine wasn't at work, she was in the gym. She'd never mentioned if Jasmine had anyone else in her life.

'Phillipa, how nice to see you,' Jasmine said in the voice she always used with Phillipa: sour, with an acerbic edge. No one else seemed to notice. 'I sent you two emails last week which you haven't replied to yet.'

Sage waved from across the other side of the office.

'Well, I get *a lot* of emails, Jasmine, as you can probably imagine. I'm sure you understand that the writing has to come first,' Phillipa said with a disingenuous smile. 'I'll get around to them, don't worry.'

'Everything alright?' Sage queried, looking from one woman to the other.

'Everything's fine, Sage,' Phillipa said lightly. 'I was just explaining to Jasmine that, sadly, the books don't write themselves.'

Jasmine's eyes narrowed and she turned away without replying.

'Phil, darling!' Sage air-kissed both sides of Phillipa's face. 'How's the new book coming along?'

'You asked me that the other day and the answer's still the same, I'm afraid,' she replied bluntly, following Sage as she led her through to her office. 'I seem to be stuck on go-slow.'

Sage turned around quickly and followed Phillipa's gaze out of the office window. 'What is it, Phil? You seem... stressed and you look as if you've lost weight. Are you fretting about the book?'

Fretting was an understatement, Phillipa thought. But it wasn't just the book.

Sage narrowed her eyes. 'Everything OK with you and Fleur? I mean... I know it's going to take you an age to get over what happened with the babies, but—'

'Everything's fine,' Phillipa said shortly. 'Thank you.'

Phillipa sat down heavily on the comfy chairs and Sage did the same, following her gaze out of the window again. 'Are you bickering with Jasmine again? What is it with you two? You used to get on so well.'

'That seems like a *very* long time ago now.' Phillipa sniffed.

'I find her rude and unhelpful these days, Sage. Maybe it's me, I don't know.'

'Hmm. I confess I've noticed a change in her attitude these past few months. She's gained a new kind of confidence. I've been wondering if she's got a new man in her life.' The women watched as Jasmine moved dreamily around the office. She stood at the window that overlooked the street. She slipped her phone out of a pocket and began scrolling through it with a smirk. 'Just between you and me – she might not be around much longer.'

Phillipa sat up straighter. 'How come?'

'Jasmine told one of the office juniors that, soon, she'll have saved enough to ditch this job and take herself off to save the animals in some far-flung place.'

Phillipa shook her head in disbelief. 'So when's she planning to leave?'

Sage shrugged her shoulders. 'Don't know, but put it this way... if she doesn't buck her ideas up, she'll find herself ready to leave for pastures new far earlier than she might have planned.'

Phillipa grinned, but deep down a sense of unrest began to brew. Jasmine was vindictive and quick to blame. She'd bet her bottom dollar if Sage fired her, Jasmine wouldn't go quietly. She'd cause casualties where she could, and the stuff she knew... it made Phillipa's blood run cold.

'So then, down to business,' Sage said crisply. 'I've spoken to Jules and Alicia, and they've agreed to extend your current deadline by another two months.'

Phillipa let out an audible breath. 'Thank you, Sage. You're a miracle worker.'

Sage watched her carefully. 'You've got the two-month extension period and the additional advance we asked for, but they've made it clear that's as much as they can do. No more negotiations.'

'Right-o,' Phillipa said. 'Well, at least that gives me a bit of breathing space for getting the first draft done.'

'You said it was coming along very slowly when I asked you earlier. Can you be more specific? Exactly how slow do you mean?' Sage ventured.

Phillipa's heart was pumping faster now. It felt stuffy in the office and there was no ventilation. Sage wanted to tie her down, and she couldn't afford to let that happen.

'I'm on track, don't worry. It's just... well, some books seem to write themselves, and this isn't one of them. That's all I meant by "slowly".'

Sage smiled, relieved. 'Well then, I can relax.'

There was a tap at the door before Jasmine's head appeared.

'Sorry to interrupt. Sage, just to let you know Harris-Lasson have sent an email through, detailing the amendment to the contract and the nice increase in Phillipa's advance.'

'Excellent. Thank you, Jasmine,' Sage said, walking over to her desktop computer.

Jasmine looked directly at Phillipa and smiled before closing the door.

Phillipa's stomach twisted. The woman was really getting on her nerves. It was wrong she knew everything about Phillipa's private business through her job at the agency. God knew who she was gossiping to.

'Call me paranoid,' she told Sage. 'But I'd like someone else to deal with my contracts. Someone other than Jasmine.'

THIRTY-NINE

EVE

I sit on the train on my way back to London, reliving my tearful goodbye with Scarlet.

Before I left Bee Cottage for the station, she wrapped her little arms around my waist and buried her face in my stomach. 'Love you, Mummy.'

When I say 'tearful' goodbye, I'm referring to my reaction. Scarlet was loving and tactile, blowing me kisses as Hugo pulled the car off the drive, but I could tell she had one eye on Saskia who was heading to the back garden with two little trowels and a pot full of seedlings.

The air in the car was frosty as we made the journey back to the station. I texted Nina with my approximate ETA.

'I don't understand why you've had to leave so early.' Hugo frowned. 'It's more upheaval for Scarlet. You were supposed to be going into the village for breakfast with her and Saskia this morning.'

'I told you, my flatmate has a problem. Things don't always work out according to plan in the real world, Hugo.'

He laughed. 'I live a very real life, thank you very much. I work hard for what I've got, and I make no apologies for it. Too many people want the spoils of success but aren't willing to work their socks off.'

'You shouldn't generalise like that. Not everyone who hasn't got your success is lazy. We didn't have much when we were still together and that was only a couple of years ago. It wasn't through lack of trying. You only went up in the world when you met Saskia.'

Quick as a flash he shot back. 'Saskia had nothing to do with it. I've got what I have through my own efforts. Nobody else's.'

I rolled my eyes. God forbid a woman might have contributed in some way. He was so pleased with himself – it would be nice to wipe the smile off his face.

'As Saskia mentioned, I had a conversation with Fleur, Phillipa's wife. She'd invited me over to the house.'

'Why did you go and see her?' He frowned, pinning his eyes to the road.

'Phillipa's still missing if you hadn't noticed. Recording her new book has brought it all back into sharp focus. Plus, I wanted to let Fleur know how the recording was going.'

'And did she have anything interesting to say? Anything interesting in her so-called "file"?' he said dismissively.

'She said some really interesting things, actually,' I replied, ignoring his jibe. 'What's your take on what happened to Phillipa?'

He shrugged. 'Dunno. Haven't given it a thought for ages.'

The note in his office had been undated, so there was no way of knowing how old it was. But it was amongst his current paperwork which seemed odd.

'You must have some kind of theory. You know Simon, don't you?'

He looked at me sharply. 'You know, you sound far too interested in Phillipa's disappearance. You haven't got her locked up anywhere, have you?' He laughed, and it sounded hollow and misplaced. 'For what it's worth, I think she just moved on. She probably moved on to wreck another new conquest's marriage.'

'If that was the case, you'd have thought someone would have recognised her by now,' I said. 'Equally, if she'd been taken, presumably for money, someone would've got around to demanding a ransom.'

'Maybe she did away with herself,' he remarked dispassionately.

'Like Dad, you mean?'

'Eve, I... I didn't mean that at all!' he protested. 'You always manage to twist things.'

'As you know, they found Dad's body within a week, so if Phillipa had taken her own life, you'd expect they'd know about it fairly soon after she'd gone.'

He seemed relieved to change the subject.

'I did want a private word before you go back to London,' he said, tapping the steering wheel. 'Now I'm properly settled with Saskia, I want joint custody of Scarlet.'

My breath caught in my throat. I hadn't seen *that* coming.

'Now, just hang on a minute—'

'No, you hang on! My circumstances have changed for the better. I know I've not always been a brilliant dad, but I want to put that right. Saskia is going to be the best mum; you must have noticed what a natural she is with Scarlet.'

It stung like personal criticism, but I acknowledged Saskia was doing a great job looking after our daughter. 'I'm not denying Scarlet is having a wonderful time at Bee Cottage, but why the rush?'

I'm not worried about Saskia, but Hugo is another matter. He has always had a problem sustaining the energy and enthusiasm to carry out his elaborate plans. So often, real life doesn't match up to the ideas in his head, and his reaction is always to lose interest. I can't let Scarlet be a victim of that. 'I'm happy to be flexible about her visiting, and you're going to have your hands full with the new baby soon. This has to be right for Scarlet, Hugo.'

He looked at me and then back at the road. 'You know, the irony of what you're saying is staggering. Are you aware of that? You took off to London without a second thought. I wonder, were you questioning whether that decision was right for our daughter? It's simple really. If you want to avoid custody problems, then you need to be present for our daughter.'

I swallowed down a snappy response and answered him calmly.

'Don't you dare dictate to me what I can and cannot do. As a single mother, I need to support myself and my daughter. Rebuilding my career is how I'm going to do that. I'm not going to end up like my mother. She never had the means to support herself and ended up nearly destitute when Dad died. No court is going to rule against me for that.'

'No. But they might be concerned when they hear about your *problems*.'

I glare at him. 'That's out of order and you know it. Mental health isn't a taboo subject anymore, Hugo. I had some problems and now I'm recovered. Just like if I'd had a physical disease and got better.'

'Of course, and I'd never want to have to use something like that in court.'

The implication being he could if he so wanted. The king of manipulation...

'Dad dying hit me hard. I'm not sure I'll ever get over it, but I got through and that's what matters.'

'The least said about your dad and how he hurt you and your mum, the better.' Hugo sniffed. 'Not all men are like him, unable to cope. I don't mean to sound harsh, but I don't want you letting Scarlet think he was a role model in any way.'

His words stung, but I wasn't going to start an argument about Dad. My memories of him were worth more than that, and if Hugo really held that view then nothing I could say would change his mind. He had been there in the middle of the fallout when Dad died. He'd seen our devastation. So I felt sad and gullible to hear how he had really felt about the tragedy.

The car approached the train station drop-off point. Hugo slowed and applied the handbrake, turning towards me in his seat.

'Anyway, I've told you about the custody issue as a courtesy, Eve, that's all. I've already got my solicitor on the case, so you can expect a letter soon. Hopefully we can keep it civil for Scarlet's sake.' He paused and the corners of his mouth twitched. 'And the family court takes the child's wishes into consideration these days, even very young children like Scarlet. Did you know that?'

Scarlet's pleading to stay at the idyllic Bee Cottage filled my head, and I shook it loose.

'Thanks for the lift, Hugo.'

I got out of the car, grabbed my suitcase out of the boot and slammed it down harder than necessary. I headed for the station entrance, and I didn't look back.

* * *

Back at the flat, Nina rushes to the door as soon as she hears my key in the lock.

'I'm so, so sorry about your room, Eve,' she splutters, grabbing my case and carrying it inside. 'I'll never forgive myself for what's happened. I'm terrified they've taken some irreplaceable family heirloom or something.'

I can't help but smile. 'There's nothing like that in there, Nina,' I say. 'I brought the bare minimum to London with me. Anything dear to me is still safely at my mum's house.'

She lets out a dramatic sigh. 'Oh, thank God. Still, it's a very unpleasant mess.' She beckons me through. 'I've got all the cleaning stuff out and fresh bedding. I just wanted you to see it in case you recognise anything as being missing.'

She wasn't exaggerating when she compared the fallout to a police search. Someone has all but ripped the place apart. My underwear spills out of dislodged drawers. Perfume and toiletry bottles – some of them smashed – lie on the wooden floor. Even the bed has been stripped of its covers, and the pictures – hung as soon as I unpacked – have been torn from the walls.

'Either someone was very drunk and very aggressive, or they were looking for something specific,' I say.

'Like what though?' Nina frowns, looking around the room. 'What could possibly warrant this?'

'Who knows?' I say, turning my suitcase around on the bed so the lid acts as a barrier to Nina's view. 'Probably just opportunists. Drunken ones.'

I open my suitcase and lift up the corner of the clothes to check the laptop and files are still concealed under there. If someone had been looking for these items then they must have followed me to my meeting with Fleur at the house, and to take that theory one step further, they would have to have known what Fleur entrusted me with.

I close the suitcase and shiver, although the air in the room is warm and stuffy.

It was a valuable lesson. I now knew I had to cover my tracks more carefully. Someone out there has been watching my every move.

FORTY

After we've cleaned up my bedroom, I take out my notes on the hidden manuscript and find passages in Phillipa's backlist titles that demonstrate the stark contradictions. I bookmark the sections to save the audio clips.

The more I think about it, the more I realise this book contains none of the magic of her previous titles. If the rumours were true and Phillipa had intimated to some people that she didn't want to write any more of the Tower series, maybe her heart simply hadn't been in it and that's why it read so flat. Perhaps she'd purposely had characters acting inconsistently because she didn't care enough to think it through.

It doesn't make any sense at all, but then, nothing makes sense about her disappearance. No clues, no ransom demand, no body... The only answer that makes any sense is that Phillipa had left of her own accord, and yet there have been no sightings at all. All this has been debated on her reader forums for months and is still going round in circles.

Writing a book and hiding it scuppers the new-life theory. If she'd written the tenth book, then why wouldn't she publish it and pocket the funds before going off to start again?

Obviously, Jules, her editor, had spotted the consistency issues, and she'd put them down to Phillipa being in a confused state of mind. Harris-Lasson had rectified the problems without a second thought after sinking hundreds of thousands of pounds into advertising, PR and hardback editions of the book. As soon as that manuscript was discovered, Alicia Kent would have known the stratospheric financial possibilities of releasing a hidden book with the dramatic 'missing author' story behind it.

I know of several online forums for the Tower series where people discuss the titles and characters and are generally obsessed with the plots and the lives of the regular characters in the books. Negative views travel fast and it would be disastrous for the publication if readers feel their beloved characters have changed in some way or are acting strangely.

I work methodically, transcribing both excerpts and setting them side by side on a clean page for ease of reference.

NEW BOOK

Jane surveyed her mother-in-law's buffet. She detested vegetables of any kind. Some salads she could deal with, but she was a fussy eater and had been ever since childhood. Olga knew this and yet, every plate Jane set eyes on had some kind of vegetable on it.

BOOK 5

Jane had prepared a meal for their guests based on the food she liked to eat. She adored any kind of vegetable and that was reflected in her choices of butternut squash soup, mushroom and chickpea curry, and even the carrot cake she'd made for dessert.

I also clip the sections in the new book that don't contradict an earlier character trait but are ones I think are trying to tell the reader something.

> *He was pure evil, disguised as an ordinary man. Only Jane knew his terrible depths, but she was trapped. She could tell no one. How must it feel, for the world to see you as one thing and to know in your heart you were the opposite? A monster.*
>
> *She was trying her hardest to find a way out of the problem. As time went on, she began to realise that drastic measures would be her only way to escape.*

Could this reflect how Phillipa herself felt? Had she been in the clutches of someone the rest of the world saw as good, when only she knew the truth?

Perhaps I am clutching at straws, but this is a new theme. DI Jane Tower is being controlled by a man who appears to be likeable to everyone else.

Maybe Phillipa concealed it out of doubt and fear over what her fans might make of it. Or perhaps someone forced her to hide it because it was so different to her other books? So many possibilities.

If only I'd done the same before Dad got so low. If only I'd taken the time to look for the signs.

FORTY-ONE

The second she opens her eyes after her nap, she knows something is different. Her head is thumping from where she fell.

Her surroundings are the same – the nice room that's still a prison, the desk, the part-written manuscript that is finally taking shape. But her mind and what is within it have changed.

She can remember certain things. The literary agency, talking to Sage... it's still cloudy, but it's closer than ever.

She turns onto her stomach and buries her face in the pillow. She swings her legs out of bed and sits upright, covering her ears with her hands.

Images, words, people rush at her like a tornado. Her cocktail dress hanging on the wardrobe, the limousine pulling over so she could climb in.

She lurches forward and vomits all over the carpet.

She's sick of writing this book, sick of being here... she can feel herself starting to fade away.

Next time her captor shows up, what has she got to lose? She might as well make a break for freedom. It might be the last chance she has.

FORTY-TWO

EVE

I'm deep in an anxiety dream. Scarlet and I are at the coast, walking along the beach and watching the waves, crashing and bursting. I point out a big one thundering our way, so big, it will reach us, even at our safe distance. Scarlet doesn't answer me and when I turn to grab her, I find she's gone. She's disappeared into thin air.

I'm rushing to the promenade to look for her when there's a big bang and light floods into my face startling me awake.

'Eve!' hisses Nina. She's in my bedroom; the lights are on. 'There's someone at the door.'

I look at her, disorientated. 'What time is—'

'It's one thirty in the morning!'

I rub my eyes, slip my legs out of bed and stand up.

Bang, bang, bang. Hammering on the door.

'Have you looked through the spyhole?' I say as I grab my dressing gown and pull it on.

'No! I just came straight into your room. I thought we should both go to the door.' She follows me out of the bedroom and holds up her phone. 'I've got 999 ready to go on here; I just need to press the button.'

I belt up my dressing gown as I rush down the short hall-way. We get to the door just as the banging starts up again. I can hear crying, sobbing. I look through the spyhole and reach for the latch. 'It's Saskia,' I say, my hand flying to my throat. 'My ex-husband's partner.'

Nina clasps her chest. 'Maybe she can give you some notice next time and make it a more decent time.' She puts her eye to the door. 'Jeez. It gets worse... old Joseph's out there, too, he's had to let her in. I'll have to grovel so he doesn't complain to the landlord.'

'Saskia looks really upset,' I say, my voice wobbly as I think about Scarlet again. 'Somethings definitely wrong.'

I open the door and Saskia stumbles in. 'Eve! I'm sorry, I...'

'Come in,' I say, and Nina dashes out on to the landing to apologise to Joseph. 'Let's get you inside.' I take her gently by the arm and guide her through the tiny hallway towards the sofa. 'Are you hurt, Saskia?' Her face is red, and her eyes are swollen as if she's been crying for hours.

'I'm OK,' she whispers. 'I'll be fine.'

'I'll make some tea,' murmurs Nina, throwing me a concerned glance.

I have no problems listing Hugo's bad points. I know them by rote. He's a natural bully, he has no problem intimidating women, gaslighting, his words can be cutting, and he has the ability to zero in on a person's weak spot, no problem. But in all the years I was with Hugo, he never laid a finger on me. He was never physically violent.

That's not to say he hasn't hurt Saskia. People change and not always for the good. Something or someone has really upset her.

Saskia sits down and wraps her arms around herself. I reach for the folded blanket we keep on the back of the sofa. 'Here.' I drape it around her shoulders. 'Saskia, what's happened? You were fine when I left Bee Cottage.'

She starts to shiver, her eyes wide and staring at the floor.

'I'm worried about Scarlet. Is Hugo at home with her?'

She nods. 'She's fast asleep, they both are. Hugo doesn't know there's anything wrong,' Saskia says. 'I waited until he was asleep to come over here. I've been sleeping in the other room as I've had insomnia the last few weeks. I've driven over, I'm in a parking-permit-only spot outside.'

Her voice sounds hoarse, as if she's been shouting. Every so often she makes an involuntary sobbing noise that sounds like a little inward shiver. I'm guessing she's been crying in the car all the way here.

I'm getting an uncomfortable feeling. I hate the thought of Scarlet being away from me. She's bound to sense if there's upset in the house between Hugo and Saskia.

Nina brings a tray over, bearing three mugs of strong tea. 'No sugar in any of them, but I can get you some if you take it.'

Saskia shakes her head. 'I'm OK, thanks,' she says, but doesn't take a drink.

She's so upset, and of course, I want to help her. But I don't know Saskia that well. It begs the question of why she's come to me, and the answers that start to present themselves make me more nervous still. Is she here to tell me something about Scarlet... about Hugo's plans to get custody, perhaps?

'Saskia, you can stay here as long as you like, and you can tell me what's wrong in your own time.'

She wipes her eyes with the back of her hand. I reach down to the side of the sofa and grab a box of tissues. She shifts in her seat and grimaces. 'Can I use your bathroom?'

'I'll show you where it is,' Nina says, and directs her to our tiny shower room. I think about the beautiful marble bathroom at Bee Cottage with its freestanding bath and nickel taps in front of the big picture window that overlooks the apple orchard in the garden. But what does all that matter if you're living with constant intimidation?

'She's in a bad way,' Nina hisses when she comes back in. 'Do you think she's scared of your ex?'

I shake my head. 'Not in that way. He was a lot of things, but he was never violent to me. That's not to say he can't be intimidating and controlling at times.'

'Well, someone's upset her, that's for sure.'

We both look up as Saskia returns to the room. She stands in the doorway wringing her hands.

'I'm so sorry to wake you both... and your neighbour, too,' she says in a small voice. 'I came here because... I just need ten minutes to speak to you, Eve.'

'I'll go back to my room,' Nina says.

'Sorry, Nina, I...' Saskia falters.

'No worries at all,' Nina says, walking out of the lounge. 'Give me a shout if either of you need anything.'

'Thanks, Nina,' I call to her.

'Sorry,' Saskia says again to me.

'No need for apologies,' I say. 'But it's the early hours of the morning, you're obviously upset you've driven all this way. What happened?'

'We had an argument earlier. Hugo, he's out nearly all the time. He's leaving me to care for Scarlet which – and please do believe me – I do not mind. I love Scarlet; we have lots of fun together.'

'But that's not the point, I know,' I say tightly. 'I used to try and make him see how it felt, but...'

'I've tried to talk to Hugo about it, but he's on edge all the time like something is bothering him. I can't say anything without him snapping my head off and I'm obviously more emotional at this time.' She touches her stomach.

This is a side to Hugo I've seen and can identify with. Especially during our last year together – it was as if he had zero ability to empathise with anyone else's pain or problems.

'Anyway, I started feeling a bit unwell around midday

yesterday. I texted him several times and called, too. His phone went straight to voicemail, so I left a few messages.' She sighs. 'Scarlet was a dream. I took a couple of paracetamols and managed to get comfortable on the sofa, and she was a darling. Brought me a glass of water and a magazine to read.' Her eyes glistened, and I could see she'd been genuinely touched by Scarlet's concern. 'There was no contact from Hugo. I assumed he must be in a low signal area and unable to access his phone. The discomfort was getting worse, but I wasn't in pain. Calling an ambulance felt too dramatic especially with having Scarlet with me. I knew Hugo kept all my maternity paperwork upstairs in his office. So I managed to get up there to find the details for the helpline, but his desk was all locked up.'

'Why had Hugo locked away documents about your pregnancy?' I say. 'You should have kept those papers yourself, surely?'

'You know what he's like.' She shrugs. 'He's got a bit of a thing about organising paperwork.'

I nod. He used to obsessively file and categorise paperwork. Each day when he opened the mail, it had to be either discarded, dealt with or filed away. If a document was needed, such as the logbook for the car, or an insurance policy, he'd take great pleasure in darting to his home office to put his hand straight on it. I can recall the smug pleasure on his face even now.

'I looked around for the keys and couldn't find them. Then I saw the filing cabinet. That was also locked, but I remembered when I walked by his office one day, I saw him dropping keys in a little vase on the bookshelf.' She pauses to take some breaths and a sip of her tea. 'I opened the filing cabinet and looked through the hanging file tabs until I came to "Baby". You know the way those hanging files are organised?' She wiggles her fingers. 'Sometimes you're not sure if the file you need is in front of, or behind the tab?'

I nod. 'Can be confusing,' I say, wondering where this story is going to end.

'Well, I guessed wrong, and I pulled out the wrong folder.'

She stares at me. Falls silent.

'And... then what?'

'I found some things I was never meant to see. Paperwork concerning your dad, Eve.'

'My dad?' I swallow. 'What kind of paperwork?'

Saskia looks pale and wretched. 'I know your dad went missing, right?'

I nod. 'They found his body a week after he disappeared. But Dad took his own life. We'll probably never know exactly what happened.'

She shakes her head and covers her face with her hands. 'I'm so sorry, Eve, but...' Her hands drop away, and she fixes me with a frightened stare. 'I think Hugo might know more than you think about what happened to your dad.'

FORTY-THREE

'I love Hugo, I do. But I'm feeling increasingly uncomfortable with the way he's behaving. You've been so nice to me, and I know how your dad's death affected you and your mum.' Saskia wiped her eyes with a tissue. 'I can't unsee that paperwork, and I can't be part of any deceitfulness in something like that. I felt I had no choice but to tell you.'

'Thank you.' I look at the paperwork in my hand, shock still tracing its cold path down my spine. 'I know it mustn't have been easy for you to come here. Did you manage to call the helpline yesterday?'

She nods. 'They asked me to pop down to the clinic, so I went when Hugo came home. Everything is fine, they just said I'm probably doing too much.'

'You need to rest, Saskia. You're very welcome to stay here, with us tonight,' I say. 'You can have my bed.'

'No. I can't. I... I'll leave it to you to find out the truth of what happened with your dad.' She taps at her phone screen and her expression darkens. 'Hugo's texted. He knows I'm out of the house. I have to go.'

She rushes to the door, and I follow, calling her back. Nina comes out of her bedroom at the commotion.

'Saskia,' I call again. 'Please don't—' But the door closes behind her as she rushes out of the flat.

* * *

Unsurprisingly, I barely sleep a wink. Everything Saskia has said swirls around and around in my head.

At eight o'clock I ring Mum and tell her Hugo and Saskia are having problems. 'I'm sorry to ask, but could you look after Scarlet if I bring her over?'

'Of course I can! You know you don't have to ask.' She sounds delighted. 'I thought Hugo had grown up a bit, but it sounds like the classic case of the leopard who never changes his spots.'

It's the first time I've heard Mum criticise Hugo, and it feels very satisfying. But there is worse to come. I still have to break the news about Hugo's involvement with Dad.

'I'm going to pick up Scarlet, and then we're both coming up to Nottingham.'

'I'll get us something nice in for tea,' Mum says cheerily.

I blow out air, trying to calm myself down. Then I book a train to Peterborough.

By late morning, I'm in a cab travelling to Bee Cottage from Peterborough train station. I don't know if Saskia will be back home now. If she's not, Hugo will be at home looking after Scarlet, and there's a conversation we need to have.

The cab is only about five minutes from the cottage when I suddenly see Hugo's distinctive black Mercedes coming the other way. His face is like thunder as he glares ahead, both hands gripping the wheel. He's alone, so that means Saskia must be back at the house with Scarlet. I wonder if she's told him where she went in the early hours.

'Change of plan,' I tell the cab driver. 'Can you turn around and follow that black car that's just passing us?'

'No problem, love. Just like in the movies, eh?' The driver perks up, swinging the car around when the road is clear, like he's starring in a classic car-chase scene.

Hugo travels in a straight line for another five minutes and then takes a left turn onto a smaller road. A small van pulls in front of us, so we're two vehicles behind Hugo.

'Looks like he's heading for the industrial estate,' the driver says, as I spot Hugo's car take a right turn ahead.

'Is it a big estate?' I ask.

'Yeah, massive. It's mainly loads of those big storage warehouses rather than working businesses.'

Hugo had mentioned he had a business interest involving storage facilities. Maybe he's got problems with the new business. That could explain his bad mood, together with the fact Saskia left the house last night without telling him. In any case, after Saskia's visit, I know the levels he will sink to and, for the first time in my life, I truly believe I married a man capable of almost anything. A man I cannot trust to be around our daughter unsupervised.

The driver slows. 'There he is, up ahead. He's getting out and unlocking a padlock on the gate. What do you want me to do?'

'Nothing,' I say. 'Take me to Bee Cottage now, please.'

I feel relieved I won't have to face Hugo at the cottage, but he still isn't far away. I need to get Scarlet and be long gone by the time Hugo returns.

* * *

I ask the cab driver to wait while I run to knock at the door of the cottage. There's no answer.

A feeling of doom threatens to engulf me as I fear Saskia has taken my daughter somewhere, possibly to get away from Hugo. I knock again, but nobody comes.

I walk around the side of the house and sigh with relief when I see Saskia on the patio, her head bent low over a book. Then Scarlet darts out from behind the trees at the bottom of the garden. She doesn't see me and runs around looking happy and free as a bird.

I walk up to the patio. 'Saskia?'

'Oh!' She clutches her chest and breathes out a sigh of relief when she realises it's me. Her hair is done, and she has make-up on. She looks a different person to the distressed woman hammering on our flat door in the early hours. 'Eve! What are you doing here?'

'I've come to get Scarlet. How are you feeling?'

'Fine. I mean, OK. I'm bearing up, considering.'

'What happened when you got home after coming to the flat?'

'He was up, waiting for me when I got back. Scarlet was fast asleep, so she didn't witness anything. Initially, I lied and said I'd just been for a long drive, but he wouldn't accept it. It was like he knew I was hiding something. He wouldn't let it go. In the end I just went to bed.'

I glance at Scarlet, still racing around the garden. 'I just saw him in his car. He didn't look very happy.'

'Really?' She looks surprised. 'Where did you see him?'

'Near the industrial park on the outskirts of town. He turned into an industrial unit with storage facilities.'

'Oh yes.' Her face darkens. 'He goes there a lot. Business deals apparently. That's all he says if I ask him.'

I step closer to her. 'Are you sure you're OK? I'm surprised you've come back here after...'

'I'm sorry I disturbed you both; I wasn't thinking clearly. I just felt a responsibility to let you know what I'd found. I know what it's like to lose a parent. I've got some decisions to make, I know that.'

I glance down the garden just as Scarlet spots me. 'Mummyyy!' she cries out, and belts across the grass towards me.

I wave and turn back to Saskia. 'I've got a cab waiting to take us to the station. I just want to say again that I'm here, if you need anyone to talk to.'

'Thanks, Eve. I do appreciate it.'

'Mummy, you're here!' Scarlet grabs hold of me around the middle and squeezes hard.

'Hi, sweetheart, I've come to take you on a surprise visit to see Gran. The cab's waiting outside.'

'Yay!' She seems happy enough and gives Saskia a kiss on the cheek.

'I'll get her things. For what it's worth, I think you're doing the right thing taking her, Eve. Hugo is... He's not in a great place right now.' We follow Saskia inside, and she quickly packs a bag. She's pretending to be fine, but I can feel her tension. Before I can change my mind, I decide to tell her about the note I'd found from Phillipa's on Hugo's desk.

Her eyes widen in disbelief. 'What did it say?'

'Something about her paying money over to Hugo. There's no way of knowing when it was written, but it was there on his desk with the other papers he was working on. I didn't want to tell you last night with everything else that was happening.'

'Oh God, he's been acting so strangely,' she whispers almost to herself. 'Surely it's nothing to do with... I mean, I asked him if he knew anything about Phillipa, or if Simon, Fleur's ex, had said anything. I know he bumps into him occasionally.' She runs a hand through her hair. 'I think my imagination is running away with me. There's probably a perfectly good explanation for the note.'

'When you say he's been acting strangely, what do you mean?'

'Ever since he bought that big storage place for no apparent reason, and then he suddenly had money to burn... Oh, I don't know. I don't think Hugo would be involved in anything dodgy, and Phillipa definitely wouldn't.'

It sounds like Hugo all over to me. Secretive, scheming. Effortlessly pulling other people into his doomed business initiatives. If Phillipa was feeling low, that might have made her vulnerable to his outlandish business claims.

As I usher Scarlet out of the door, I turn back to Saskia, 'My advice to you is: don't put up with Hugo's rubbish for too long like I did.'

'Thanks, Eve,' she whispers, then turns away and goes back inside the house.

FORTY-FOUR

CHAD

Tweet from @ChadBsuperfan to @TheNarratorEH:

Hi Eve, can you pls follow me back so I can send you a DM?

Chad had sent the message twelve hours ago now, and there had still been no response from Eve. Could it be she didn't realise who was messaging her? He couldn't imagine she was ignoring him, being one of Phillipa Roberts's superfans as he was, not to mention running the author's biggest online fan forum. He wasn't just some random reader. The Tower series was a big part of his life.

He had her email address from Mrs Hewitt's laptop, and he also had her phone number from the older lady's address book. He sent an email and a text message saying the same thing:

Hi Eve, could you please get back to me asap. I have some information you might find interesting. Regards, Chad Belton (we met in Primark)

If she didn't respond to any of that, he'd be forced to take more direct action.

FORTY-FIVE

EVE

On the train to Nottingham, I read from one of Scarlet's favourite animal storybooks and she falls asleep. She's no doubt tired herself out with all that fresh air and running around the huge garden at Bee Cottage.

I take out my phone and call Deidre's mobile phone. I assume this is her work number and I'm expecting to leave a message, but she picks up.

'Eve! Looking forward to our session in the morning. Is everything OK?'

'I'm so sorry, Deidre, I'm not well. I've picked up some kind of sickness bug, and I feel pretty dreadful.'

'Oh no, you poor thing. No worries. Get yourself well, and I'll hopefully see you at the next session on Tuesday.'

'Thanks. I'm hoping it's just a twenty-four-hour thing.'

I feel easier knowing I have a little breathing space now. I check my emails and find there's yet another message from Chad Belton, claiming he has some 'information' for me and asking me to get back to him asap. I don't think so, somehow.

This guy is creeping me out big time. How on earth has he got all my contact details? I think about how someone must have followed me to Fleur's house to know I'd been there. Twitter is public, but my email and my phone number? He's making me feel very uncomfortable, and I want it to stop. I quickly reel off a text in reply.

I don't know how you have managed to get my contact details, but please delete my number and email from your records. I do not wish to communicate.

It's short and snotty, and I send it before I can change my mind.

* * *

When we arrive at Nottingham station, we get a cab to Mum's house. Scarlet is predictably grouchy as I've had to wake her. Fortunately, it's only a ten-minute trip from the station to Mum's small, terraced house.

'I'm tired,' Scarlet complains. 'And I'm hungry.'

'Not long now.' I kiss the top of her head. 'You've been so good, and I bet Gran has been baking so you'll probably have a fairy cake waiting!'

'Will I be back at Bee Cottage in time for my riding lesson tomorrow?' she grizzles.

'Here we go... Gran's street coming up!'

As the cab nears the road I grew up on, I feel flutters in my stomach at the thought of speaking to her about Dad. She's taken what happened very personally, as if she'd somehow been less than and driven Dad to take his own life.

It had been just an ordinary day. Dad had always been a keen fisherman. It was one of the activities he dreamed of doing more, when he retired from his forty-year stint as the manager of a large textiles factory. He'd started as a machine engineer and steadily worked his way up to being a popular manager.

That was Dad all over. Steady Eddie, Mum used to affectionally call him.

But when it came time for his retirement, he was ready.

'I can't wait until I never have to hear the drone of those machines again,' he told me. 'I even hear them in my sleep, do you know that? It gets inside your head and stays there.'

He went fishing at a variety of places around Nottinghamshire, usually with his friend, Ken. Their favourite spot though was Colwick Country Park. Set in two hundred and fifty acres of woodland and grassland. It sat by the river Trent and had three large man-made lakes, popular with local fisherman. The park was a stone's throw from Mum and Dad's house, so he never stayed out overnight there.

As with Phillipa's disappearance, when police had exhausted their efforts to find him, they'd flagged up the possibility that Dad had just taken off to start again somewhere else.

'It's more common than you'd think, Mrs Hewitt,' a well-meaning police officer had told Mum clumsily. 'Sometimes, people have just had enough and decide to leave all their problems behind for good.'

'My Derek hasn't got any problems,' Mum had snapped back. 'He has everything to live for. He's been looking forward to his retirement for years.'

She'd been so upset at even the mere suggestion Dad could have wanted his freedom more than he'd wanted us. Then the worst possible news had come. Dad's lifeless body, pulled from the river.

Mum didn't scream or shout or sob on anyone's shoulder. She simply shut down to protect herself from the devastating emotions. She stopped talking about Dad, refused to discuss his death, even with me.

'She's being selfish,' Hugo had said angrily one day when I'd got upset soon after Dad's death. 'But you can't force her to talk, and that's the truth of it. Maybe one day she'll feel able to discuss it with you.'

That day had never arrived. Mum had pushed what happened further and further away, until I started to wonder if she believed it had never happened at all.

I'd found it tough, but it was something I'd had to accept. Until today.

Now I was about to ask Mum to dredge up all her uncomfortable feelings again and talk to me about the day Dad disappeared.

The cab stops outside the house. The driver gets my small case out of the boot, and I pay him. Scarlet runs to Mum's gate – which I notice has been painted and repaired – and I stand for a moment on the pavement and look at the front door. I imagine Dad walking out of there for the last time. I've never allowed myself to say it out loud, but I miss him so much.

'Mummy, come ON!' Scarlet calls, and I wipe a solitary tear from my cheek as I walk up the narrow path.

Somehow, I must get Mum to talk, and there is only one way I can do that. I'll have to tell her the heartbreaking truth.

* * *

The door opens before I get a chance to use my key. Mum steps forward and reaches for Scarlet. 'Oh, I have missed you, pet. I have.' She ruffles her hair. 'There's a cupcake in the kitchen with your name on it.'

Scarlet yelps with pleasure and runs inside, and Mum gives me a hug. Her face looks pale and drawn.

'Nice to see you, love.' I follow Mum inside. From the back, I see her skirt and cardigan seem to be hanging looser on her than I remember.

'The front garden is looking tidy, Mum.'

'Yes, I know. It's my nice, new odd-job man. Nothing's too

much trouble for him, and he can turn his hand to anything. Now, let's get you a nice cup of tea, and you can tell me all about London. Go and sit down.'

Mum's kitchen is small with no breakfast bar or dining area. I leave my case in the hallway, slip off my coat and shoes and go into the living room.

Scarlet bounds upstairs to her bedroom, no doubt to catch up with all her favourite toys.

I look around the drab room. It feels so dark in here compared to the flat in London where the windows let in a lot of light. Mum's window is cut down by about a third due to the oppressive velvet drapes she favours.

When Dad died, it came to light he'd decimated their modest savings. He'd also defaulted on the life insurance policy, although mercifully his pension from the factory was still intact. Mum hadn't been angry at the time. She'd said, 'Shows he wasn't in his right mind. Derek has always been a saver.' They'd both lived a frugal life, putting money away for a rainy day.

Mum had always maintained Dad must have slipped and fallen into the river. She accepted he was probably depressed. 'Like all men, he kept his troubles to himself,' she'd acquiesced. But she would not entertain the idea Dad had consciously wanted to end it all. The coroner's verdict of accidental death only added weight to her argument.

She brings in a tray bearing two mugs of tea and a plate of digestive biscuits.

'Have you had any lunch, love?' She puts a mug on the coffee table in front of me. 'I could do you a sandwich.'

'I'm fine, thanks, Mum.' I feel like I'll throw up if I eat anything, even a biscuit. Not mentioning Dad's disappearance is ingrained into me. It's like a family rule – we all have them, even if they're not regarding something this serious. In some families, it means not mentioning Auntie So-and-So's drinking problem, or a brother-in-law's affair... They're like unspoken but cast-iron expectations. I haven't got the luxury of playing along with Mum's wishes anymore, but I still need time to drum up the courage. 'How are you feeling? You look like you've lost a bit of weight.'

'Do I?' She holds her arms out to the side and looks down at her body. 'Maybe a few pounds, but it was long overdue. I've felt a bit under the weather if I'm honest, but the doctor thinks I've probably had a virus or something. I'm feeling a bit better, now.' Her eyes sweep up and down. 'You look like you could do with putting a few pounds on yourself, Eve. Are you eating properly?'

'I'm fine. Just rushing about a bit more than usual, but that's a good thing.' I clear my throat. 'Mum, I wanted to come and see how you are. But there's something else I want to talk to you about, too. Something very important.'

'Oh, yes?' Mum is unfazed, sipping her tea and looking at me over the mug. 'Isn't it working out in London? I did try and tell you the risks, but you—'

'London is fine. It's not that.'

'Spit it out then.'

'You won't like what I have to say. It's about Dad and what happened on the day he disappeared... and the days before that.'

Her shoulders sag a little. For a moment or two, she looks ten years older, and I realise just how much it all still weighs heavy on her. The effort of keeping it all inside for so long has worn her out.

'You know I won't talk about it, Eve.' Stubborn to the end.

'I know you've refused to talk about it before now, Mum. But it won't go away. I'm begging you to make an exception today. For me. For yourself... We both loved Dad. I can't imagine how terrible it was for you... still is. But we need to—'

'You're not going to bully me into doing what I don't want to do.' She stood up. 'I've got things to do. I'll give you some time to get sorted, and when I come back, we can forget you ever mentioned it.'

'No, Mum. We're not going to do that. We *are* going to talk about Dad.' I swallow. 'We have to.'

She starts to move away, her eyebrows beetling. 'I don't have to do anything I don't want to do. And I absolutely do not want to talk about what happened. Not now, not ever.'

I stand up and walk in front of her, obstructing her exit.

'We haven't got that luxury anymore, Mum,' I say, placing my hand on her arm. 'Something's come up. About Dad.'

Her face drains of colour, and she covers her nose and mouth with her hands. 'What do you mean? The police haven't been in touch with me.'

'The police don't know. I've found out that Hugo knew something about Dad's disappearance,' I say. 'Maybe he was even partly to blame for it.'

'What?' Her hands drop away. 'What on earth are you talking about?'

'Saskia came to the flat in a state in the early hours of this morning,' I say. 'She was so upset. She'd felt a bit unwell, and she'd gone upstairs to Hugo's office for her maternity papers. She came across... some documentation relating to Dad.'

Mum walks back to the sofa and sits down. 'What kind of documentation?'

'Some personal information and clippings relating to his disappearance, taken from the local newspapers.'

Mum says, 'I kept some clippings too – they're in the loft with his other stuff.'

'There's more.' She stares at me, and I know the moment has come. The moment where I have no choice but to devastate her. 'Saskia found a letter. From Dad. It was hidden away in Hugo's filing cabinet.'

'A letter?' she says faintly. 'What are you trying to tell me? Hugo is an honest man, he—'

'Hugo has a side to him that isn't nice and mostly definitely isn't honest.'

'Are you talking about his affair when you were married?'

'His *affairs*. There was more than one. I'm talking about the way he tried to control me, and now he's doing the same to Saskia. I've listened to you go on for years about this lovely, lovely man I was married to, but I don't recognise your description of him.'

Mum falls silent, her lips tight. I feel lighter inside. I haven't realised how much I've wanted to say all that out loud.

'Dad and Hugo were quite close in a way, weren't they? Hugo was never interested in fishing, but they went to the Forest matches together, now and again.'

When we were first married, we'd come to Mum and Dad's for Sunday lunch most weeks, and while I helped Mum in the kitchen, Dad and Hugo would often sit in this room and watch the footie. Hugo was always telling Dad he'd get the two of them a season ticket for Nottingham Forest, Dad's favourite team, but true to form, it never materialised.

'They were no different to any father and son-in-law,' Mum says stiffly. 'I feel quite uncomfortable talking about this, Eve. You've always had an imagination that runs away with you. I admit I don't know exactly what happened to your dad; I try very hard not to think about it. I really don't want to believe he left us because he was secretly unhappy with his life.'

'Dad wrote to Hugo, Mum,' I say quietly. 'The postmark is the day he went missing. He must have posted it on his way to the river.'

Mum's face doesn't alter. It's as if her puzzled expression is frozen. 'What did the letter say?'

I take the letter out of my pocket and pass it to her, but she doesn't take it.

'Read it to me,' she whispers.

Dear Hugo,

This is a difficult letter to write.

> *I've had enough. I love Viv with all my heart, but I now know she will be better off without me. If I'd told you about this earlier, there's nothing you could have said to change my mind, so please don't feel bad and don't let anyone else feel bad, either.*

> *But there's something you can do to help when I'm gone. I want you to look after my girls.*

> *I'm attaching a breakdown of the money I lent you from our joint savings. I trust you will keep up the schedule of repayments we agreed. I never told Viv about our agreement, so there won't be any unpleasantness for you to face.*

> *I'm also leaving a sealed letter for Viv that I would be obliged if you could personally hand her and offer her support while she reads it.*

> *You've been a good son-in-law and friend to me, Hugo. I'm aware it's a big responsibility I'm leaving at your door. But I know I can trust you to look after all my girls, including little Scarlet.*

> *God bless and see you in the next life.*

Derek

Mum's face crumples. 'Where is it?' she whispers. 'Where's the letter he wrote me?'

'It's not here, Mum,' I say. 'Nor the payment schedule. Saskia didn't have time to look for them. That's why we have to talk about this.'

'There was seventeen thousand pounds missing from our savings. I know we had about twenty thousand when your dad retired. His lump sum.'

'Can you tell me roughly where Dad's stuff is in the loft?' I say urgently. 'I won't mess anything up, I'll just look through it. We need to see if there's any evidence at all up there. Maybe Dad duplicated the payment schedule and disguised it as something else.'

Like Phillipa had written things in the new book that seemed to be about the character but could be about her.

Mum follows me upstairs. Scarlet pops her head around the bedroom door.

'I'm setting up a tea party for all my toys!' she says happily.

'Sounds wonderful,' I say. 'I'll pop in and have a look in a bit.' When Scarlet has gone back inside, I turn to Mum. 'Is Dad's stuff on the left or right side when I stand at the top of the pull-down ladder?'

Her face cracks and tears run down her cheeks. 'I had a good look through everything when they found his body. I spent night after night crying, looking through that stuff, trying to find just one clue why he left me.' I can see the distress gripping her. I feel terrible upsetting her like this, but I have to go through with it now. It's the closest I've ever got to getting her to open up about Dad and we need to find anything that can help us.

* * *

Ten minutes later, we're back downstairs in the living room with two bin bags full of Dad's documentation.

'Let's look for bank statements first,' I say, and Mum helps me to sift through. I find a folder, but Mum says, 'That's HSBC, the current account. Our savings were with the Halifax Building Society.'

Eventually, Mum finds the folder. She spreads the statements out on the floor in front of us. 'See, a few months before Derek disappeared, large amounts started coming out. I knew nothing about it, never took any interest in the financials. That was Derek's forte.' She picked up another piece of paper. 'This was the statement that came through about three weeks after your dad died. Twenty thousand pounds now reduced to just three grand.' She looks at me, her eyes glistening. 'All this time I thought he might have had another woman, you know. I thought that's where the money had gone – he'd spent it on her, set her up as his mistress.'

'Oh, Mum! Dad would never have betrayed you like that.' After eighteen months of remaining silent, my heart squeezes at the effort it must have taken for Mum to voice those words.

'He lent Hugo money without telling me. That was a type of betrayal, too.'

'He should have discussed it with you, I agree. But the letter proves it was always meant to be a loan. Dad always intended replenishing your savings.' I stop and consider how accomplished Hugo has been at convincing people to part with their funds. So skilful, he's made a lifelong career out of it. Still, what on earth had he needed all that money for? He certainly hadn't splashed it out on his family. We hadn't had a proper family holiday for four years by the time he left home.

We search through the contents of the bags a second time but find no payment schedule.

'What are we going to do?' Mum says, quietly. She sounds beaten.

'I'll tell you exactly what we're going to do. I'm going back to Bee Cottage in the morning. I'm going to tell Hugo I want to see the agreed payment schedule or I'm going to the police.' Mum nods, and I reached over and squeeze her hand. 'And if it's the last thing I do, I'm going to find the letter Dad wrote you and I'm going to bring it home. I promise you that.'

FORTY-SIX

After breakfast, Mum offers to take Scarlet to the park. 'I need some fresh air and some thinking time,' she says sadly. 'What you've told me, Eve... it's made me feel hollow inside.'

I feel terrible, but I couldn't have lived with myself if I hadn't been honest with her.

My head is whirring about how I'm going to tackle Hugo. To give myself a little respite, I decide to look at the folder Fleur gave me. The first item on the pile of papers within is a colour photograph of Phillipa accepting an award as part of an online ceremony. It is one of the items we looked at together before I left.

'We'd lost track, long ago, of the number of awards she'd won,' Fleur told me wistfully. 'She was such a tremendously popular author, and she thought the world of her fans. Even though this ceremony took place online, Phillipa insisted on dressing the part for the readers.'

The photograph had been taken in what I now recognise as the lounge with the big white fireplace at her house. Phillipa's hair has been curled and pinned up and she is dressed in a sapphire-blue cocktail dress, her body and face angled towards the camera. Behind her, the television on the wall is live-streaming the presenters of the award, a man and a woman. There is also a grid of readers in the background who Fleur said had been selected by the publisher to join in by Zoom. Phillipa is smiling and looks relaxed and confident.

When I scanned the readers with Fleur, a face had popped out at me.

'This guy here.' I'd tapped his face and showed Fleur. 'Do you know him?'

Fleur squinted then nodded. 'Oh yes, he's one of her super-fans. He came to all her events, both the live ones and the streamed. He ran her fan forum.'

'I've met him. He's quite passionate about the Tower books. Creepily so.'

Fleur gave me a weak smile. 'Yeah, I know – they are a breed apart, the superfans. But Phillipa knew them all and loved them. She used to give them signed books, event tickets and stuff.'

I continued to study the photograph.

'I took that about a year before Phillipa disappeared,' Fleur said softly.

Phillipa was nearly fifty when it was taken, but she only looks in her early forties in the picture. I've seen gossip online about her having facelifts and Botox. Maybe that's how she looks so young... I don't know. She's tall and slim, and she certainly looks like a woman who looks after herself.

'She looks well,' I remarked.

'She always looked well,' Fleur said. 'Phillipa did all the right things. She exercised and ate healthily, never smoked, hardly ever drank alcohol. She was fitter than me, and I'm fifteen years younger! She looks so happy here, I think.'

Looking at it now, it's just a single picture, a snapshot in time. It can't really signify anything conclusive about Phillipa's state of mind or level of happiness. But the photograph has its place. If nothing else, it shows that, if Phillipa was going through any difficulties at that time, she was able to put on a convincing act in front of the people who knew her best.

One of the last pictures of my dad was taken by his friend, the week before he disappeared. He was out fishing. It was early in the day, the sun still rising behind him, filtering through the trees at the country park he loved so much. He looked serene, at peace. A man who'd reached the stage in life where he could spend time doing the things that made him happy. Two days later, he disappeared. No signs, no note... he'd just gone.

A week after that, they found Dad's body in the river Trent. There were no suspicious circumstances, no one else involved. According to the coroner's report, his body had been in the water for days.

I look at the photograph in my hand, consider Phillipa's wide smile, her sparkling eyes and radiant skin. This is a woman who was either incredibly happy, or one who knew how to put on a very convincing mask.

Sometimes, very sad, troubled people are exceptionally good at doing that.

* * *

I leaf through the other items in the folder. The documents cover about three months before Phillipa's disappearance.

Fleur has done a good job keeping everything catalogued, but I remind myself of something important. Fleur's choice of material is filtered through the lens of a wife. In the midst of her grief, and no doubt panic, Fleur alone decided what information was relevant and what should be ignored.

I pluck out an online biography and timeline of Phillipa's career.

The piece details her education in state schools, A levels at college until the age of eighteen, and then she attended

Newcastle University. The article goes on to cover her writing career to date, but I notice a large section of time has been skimmed over. From Phillipa leaving university to the start of her writing career and the first book in the Tower series being published, nothing has been detailed.

I had asked Fleur about the lack of information on Phillipa's pre-Tower life.

'The press tend to do that,' she said. 'They're interested in her early life and her writing career, but people rarely ask about what came in between.'

'And what did come in between?'

A few beats of silence, then, 'Phillipa didn't like talking about her life before her writing career took off. She didn't even talk much to me about it. When asked, she'd keep it general, citing a career 'travelling.' Incredibly, nobody asked too many questions because they were always so focused on her writing.'

I waited.

'Suffice to say, she went through some difficult years. People always think Phillipa is a strong person, and she is, in some ways, but... she can crumble under stress. There was a period of time she had a... bad time. A period when she found it difficult to cope.'

I almost didn't say it, and then... well, I just did. 'Did Phillipa have a breakdown?'

Fleur gave a sad smile. 'I didn't know her then and she didn't like to hark back, but yes, I think that's what happened.' She sighed. 'I had to tell the police all that of course, and I'm sure that just ticked another box for them in their theory that Phillipa took herself off somewhere when she disappeared.'

I look up from the file. 'What happened exactly, on the day Phillipa went missing?'

Fleur sighed and raised one side of her mouth.

'She was up early. As you know, it was the awards ceremony that night. I'd helped get her organised, booked in lots of appointments to save her going out: hair, nails, that sort of thing. Her dress had already been delivered. Phillipa thought it was all too much fuss, but as I'd told her, if she won, the photos would be around for a long time, so she might as well make the effort.'

I had looked at Fleur – as ever, she was flawless in her own grooming. A bad hair day wouldn't dare to even approach this woman. Her buttery blonde locks looked as if she'd casually run her fingers through, but on closer inspection, I could see it was expertly sculpted and held in place with invisible product. Her make-up, despite being at home, was perfectly applied in nude, neutral shades, for a fashionable 'no make-up' look.

Self-consciously, I had smoothed back my own brown hair. I'd hastily brushed and pulled it back into a no-frills ponytail before leaving the flat that morning. I had taken the time to rub on some tinted moisturiser and apply a bit of mascara and lip balm, but next to Fleur, I looked like I'd just fallen out of bed.

'The award was the only major award Phillipa hadn't won yet,' Fleur continued. 'It was a biggie. She knew that winning it would take her career to another level and probably seal the deal for the screen adaptation.'

'She was already top of the tree in police-procedural crime fiction,' I remarked.

'In the UK and parts of Europe, yes. But she still had some way to go to reach mega-sales status in America. Winning the award could have skyrocketed her career there. Harris-Lasson had already begun to organise a fifteen-state US book tour for the start of the following year. We'd agreed that I would fly out at strategic points to join her there.'

'Had Phillipa received any indication from the organisers that she might win?'

Fleur shook her head. 'But the press had her as the hot favourite, and her publisher seemed to be very optimistic. Her last book had shot to number one in hardback in five countries, with record sales. Phillipa was at the top of her game.' Fleur looked at her hands. 'She had no reason to run. No reason at all.'

Which meant what? That if she *had* done a runner, it was because of her personal life, not other pressures? Fleur was adamant Phillipa hadn't left of her own accord, and I completely understood that. After all, who wants to believe their loved one hated their life with you much, they decided to plan a disappearing act?

I had said nothing about my ruminations. I didn't want to interrupt Fleur's account, and most of all, I didn't want to offend her. I felt we had some getting to know each other to do before I could speak that candidly with her. Till then, I was happy to stick with the mechanics of Phillipa's disappearance.

Fleur reached for her glass of sparkling water and took a sip. 'As you can imagine, the whole morning of that day was taken up with all the stuff that had to be done. All Phillipa wanted to do was keep reading through her winner's speech, tweaking the odd word here and there.'

'She must have been confident of taking home the award,' I said.

'All nominees are encouraged to write a speech and rehearse it, so they're not caught out with nerves if they do win. But yes, all the signs were there that it could be Phillipa's year.'

'What happened in the afternoon?'

'Phillipa went upstairs for a lie down in her study after lunch. She has a daybed in there. That was nothing unusual – she's always liked a post-lunch nap.'

'And what did you do?'

'I chilled in the garden room. Watched a little TV, read a magazine. It was only an hour or two, then things moved up a couple of gears. The journalists started calling. Pre-arranged phone chats for *The Bookseller*, various magazines, radio and TV. Too many to mention. She had thirty-minute slots for two hours. When she finished, she was shattered and annoyed because we'd realised, too late, the Harris-Lasson PR department had overbooked stuff.'

'What happened when Phillipa got annoyed?' I said. 'Did she shout, throw things?'

Fleur laughed. 'The opposite. If Phillipa's annoyed with you she goes quiet. Mumbles her replies if you ask her anything. Makes excuses to disappear into her study. She's generally a lovely person, but she has a tough side. Believe me, she's not someone you'd want to get on the wrong side of.'

FORTY-SEVEN

ELEVEN MONTHS EARLIER

Phillipa cruised down the street in her convertible Mercedes and was surprised to see so many people outdoors, enjoying the weather. Sometimes she forgot there was a world out there. A real world that was set apart from the one in her head and the problems that resided there.

She was well known in the local area. She didn't have the sports car's roof down because she didn't want to be recognised. Still, the car – with her very expensive private numberplate: 1 PR – drew admiring glances as she made her slow journey across town.

Phillipa got it. She was privileged. She was living a life many other people could only dream about. They looked at her writing career, her car and her big fancy house, and they thought she had no worries, no problems to speak of. They thought she was living the dream, but in reality, she was living an ever-increasing nightmare.

In a strange way, she had felt more comfortable as a student.

In those days – too many years ago to mention – she'd scraped together money any way she could to feed herself and pay the bills on her half of a grubby flatshare.

In her working-class upbringing in Newcastle, lack of money had been an everyday fact of life. She was raised on phrases like, 'Make do and mend' and 'Pennies make pounds'. The irony was, she hadn't felt an imposter back then as a penniless student. Today, a millionaire, she did. On paper, at least.

Sometimes, the publisher asked her to do author events in schools located in deprived areas. Whenever she could, she always said yes. She recognised the signs of a difficult life in lots of the kids – hand-me-down clothing, always too large or too small, the dozens of pairs of dull eyes clouded by a longing for escape. They'd watch as she moved around talking, struggling to draw a line from their lives to hers.

There were times at home, when she saw a bill for a pair of curtains Fleur had purchased, or when the cost of just one of her wife's designer handbags landed on the credit card bill, that Phillipa felt physically sick. Not because she objected to the cost, even though that has been worrying her more and more. She didn't want to disappoint Fleur. She wanted to continue to provide for her family, but she could feel it slipping further out of her hands with every day that passed.

In some ways, she'd always felt like an imposter in her own life, and right now, she felt it more than ever.

Trouble had been a long time coming. She'd looked the other way, hoping it would disappear, only to turn back to find it had suddenly got very close. Too close. Phillipa was finding it harder and harder to keep the awful truth from Fleur, but all was not lost. Not yet. She had the beginnings of a plan and there was a slim chance she might be able to turn things around again. And today was the first step in trying to make that happen.

Phillipa drove past the local library on her left. This wasn't her destination despite what she'd told her wife. She kept driving over ten miles until she reached the low, sprawling building on the edge of a small wood. She parked the car and with a heavy heart, she gathered her things and went inside.

Nearly two hours later, she turned into the industrial park on the edge of town and parked up next to the bathroom-supplies warehouse. She waited. Her digital dashboard clock read 11.42.

She'd been here before, but it hadn't been to buy bathroom supplies then, either. She stared out across the concrete scape of the nearly empty car park. At regular intervals, a sapling tree had been planted with a wire enclosure fixed around it. The young trees looked lost in the sea of concrete. The sun was shining, but the warehouse still looked grey and grim. She pushed her fingers into the torn lining of her handbag and pulled out the burner phone which she lay on the passenger car seat, screen facing upwards.

She glanced at her clock again: 11.47. Five minutes that had felt like an hour.

Phillipa scanned the car park. The person she was waiting for was two minutes late. On the last occasion, they had been bang on time.

At 11.51, a silver BMW turned into the car park. It drove past Phillipa without slowing and continued moving steadily to the opposite end where it turned and headed back towards her. The car parked four rows away, directly in her line of sight.

Phillipa couldn't see anyone inside the car because the windows were tinted. She glanced at her phone, but there was no message.

She stared at the car and the headlights flashed once. It was the sign she'd been waiting for.

She took her handbag and the thick brown envelope and got

out of her car. She walked towards the BMW, calm and resolved.

However unpleasant it might get, she had to sort this all out, once and for all.

Right now, she felt like the loneliest woman on earth.

FORTY-EIGHT

When she hears the rattle of the keys and the bolts sliding back at last, she is ready. She is prepared. She stands up and faces the door, the padded manacle pinching into her sore flesh.

The figure stands in the doorway holding the taser.

'The book is going well,' she says, trying to keep her voice strong. 'You can let me go, and I give you my word I'll complete it.'

Her words sounded hollow even to her, and so it was no surprise when the figure threw back their head and laughed. The sound was distorted, but there was something there... the length of the laugh, the way it faded at the end.

She had heard this laugh before.

Something resonated inside her as she reached for the memory, so close now. So close...

FORTY-NINE

EVE

Mid-morning, I leave a happy Scarlet with Mum who lends me her car, so on the way back to London, I can detour to Oakham. But I'm not heading for Bee Cottage. Not yet.

I trace the route the cab took when we spotted Hugo in the car and followed him to the estate. Thanks to yesterday's call to Deidre, cancelling our recording session, I have plenty of time to look around today.

I turn into the industrial estate. As the cab driver had said, the vast metal warehouse-type buildings look to be mainly used for storage purposes. I crawl past one full of parked lorries, another with enormous cellophane-wrapped blocks of building supplies ready to be distributed to customers.

I approach the tall iron gates where Hugo had got out of his car. The large yard of this storage facility looks bare. Aside from a few large refuse bins, there's no sign of any goods or vehicles. The facility itself is a long, wide, grey metal structure with a small sign above the single side door that reads BALFOUR HOLD-INGS LTD.

I take a photograph from the gate. There's a big, locked padlock and thick chain wrapped around both gates. I'm no climber so there's no way I'm getting in. I get back into the car, turn around and go back the way I came. A few hundred yards on, a man in oil-stained overalls is emerging from the lorry park. I pull up and wind down my window.

'Excuse me?' He walks over. 'I'm wondering what business Balfour Holdings is in?' I indicate back along the road. 'There's nobody about, and I'm trying to find out who I can contact.'

He scratches his head. 'We've asked the same question ourselves once or twice, cos my boss is after expanding and that plot would be perfect for what he needs. Hardly see a soul there. It's locked up and left most of the time.'

'You said you *hardly* ever see anyone... Does that mean you have seen someone, on the odd occasion?'

He frowns, thinking. 'Couple of times. A guy comes now and again. Tried to talk to him once, but I wouldn't say he was the friendly sort. Seen a woman there, too, but that was just the once ages ago.'

'What did they look like? The man and the woman, I mean?'

'The guy looks late thirties, forties. Dark hair, fancy car as I remember but couldn't tell you about the woman, sorry, love. Didn't take that much notice and just spotted her at a distance.'

'Sorry to have bothered you,' I say, putting the car into gear before pulling away. 'Thanks for your help.'

The guy he'd described sounded like Hugo, and I already knew he'd been here. I wonder, could the woman have been Phillipa? She isn't that distinctive looking really – unless you happened to be a big Tower series fan – and he hadn't managed to get a close look. There was no date on the note I'd seen. What if Hugo had brought Phillipa here before she went missing, perhaps to invest in one of his hare-brained business schemes? That would explain her transferring money over to him.

Hugo's business background is littered with ruined small businesses. Some he'd started and others that people had built with hard work and then had the misfortune to put their faith in Hugo's next big idea and his persuasive rhetoric promising easy, fast profits.

There had been a recruitment agency for highly skilled IT professionals, a concierge service for busy businesspeople and – his last disastrous endeavour before we split up – a hire-car brokerage for luxury-end vehicles.

Somehow, Hugo always managed to just about scrape through with minimal financial damage, largely because he was so adept at getting other people to part with their own funds for his startups.

He had never involved me in his business dealings, and I could just imagine Phillipa listening to his well-practised sales pitch and deciding to invest in some super storage facility, making big bucks fast from customers that didn't actually exist.

FIFTY

The driveway of Bee Cottage is clear apart from Saskia's small car, so I park a little further down the road and fire off a text to let Saskia know I'm here.

I swing the car round and drive up to the cottage thinking again how special this place is. It must have cost an absolute fortune. Is it possible Hugo bought it with a combination of Dad's savings and the money he'd somehow extracted from Phillipa?

Saskia appears at the door. She looks nervy, looking past my car down the drive.

'It's so good to see you again, Eve.' After another quick look around, she says, 'Come inside and we'll talk.'

Inside, I decline her offer of a drink, and we sit in the kitchen.

'How's Scarlet?' she asks.

'She's fine. Happy with Mum. I've just come from there, I told Mum about Dad's letter. She's grateful to you for what you've done.'

Saskia shuffles awkwardly. 'I hope... your mum finds peace. You too.'

'That's why I'm here, Saskia. I really don't want to put you into an awkward situation, but I've promised Mum I'll get the letter Dad wrote her from Hugo. He's probably going to guess you're the one who told me about what he did.'

Suddenly, Saskia cries out in alarm. 'Oh no, he's back!'

Hugo's car pulls up on the widest part of the driveway, next to mine.

Saskia rushes to the window. 'This is it. He's going to know I've told you, but I don't care. He needs to account for what he did, taking your dad's savings. It's time for Hugo to own up and be honest for once in his life. I feel strong enough to stand up to him with you here. We can do it together.'

I reach for my handbag to get my phone. I'm prepared to call the police if he gets nasty. But then Hugo walks into the kitchen.

He looks from me to Saskia to me again. 'What's this then, a mothers' meeting?'

'I need to speak to you,' I say.

'Oh, well then, I'd better oblige! But first... where's Scarlet?'

'She's safe with my mum.'

'Well, she'd be perfectly safe with us here, too. In fact, she'd be here in a beautiful home living the life she deserves. Not stuck in virtual poverty in some nasty little back street in a rough area with a sick old woman. No family court will disagree with me and that's where I'm going to take it.'

That forces a sharp intake of breath from me. 'Don't you—'

'You can go now, Eve. I have work to do. Important work. Don't call at the cottage again unless it's been pre-arranged.'

I take Dad's letter out of my handbag and unfold it carefully. I place it on the worktop and look at him as the colour drains from his face.

'Where did you get that?' His eyes stare glassily at the wall, then his expression darkens. 'Saskia.'

She stays silent, but I speak up. 'You took my parents'

savings,' I say, making sure my voice remains calm and level. 'You stole their nest-egg that took them a lifetime to grow.'

He throws his hands in the air. 'No, that's not fair! Your dad offered it. I was always going to—'

'Pay it back? When exactly were you going to do that, Hugo? Was it when one of your pathetic schemes eventually succeeded instead of bombing in the first few months?'

'Hang on a minute. I—'

'You were there... through all of it. You saw how Mum and I suffered for that entire week after Dad went missing and before his body was found. You held my hand, told me everything would be OK. You insisted they'd find him, when all the time, you knew. You knew he was going to take his own life.'

'I... I thought he was bluffing when I got the letter. I swear, Eve. I thought it was just a cry for help. People do that all the time,' Hugo says.

'Where is it?' I ask.

'Huh?'

'Mum's letter. The letter Dad wrote to her and asked you to deliver?'

'I... I'm not sure. I don't think I kept it.' I see the signs. The darting eyes as he racks his conniving brain for a clever response, the sweat on his upper lip when he realises he's backed into a corner. I've spent enough time on the receiving end of Hugo's lies to recognise what's happening here.

'I know things about you, Hugo. I know Phillipa paid you money, too,' I say, looking around the kitchen. 'It's probably how you afforded this place. By cheating and lying, and it all started with my dad's money to get you out of a fix.'

'I don't know what you're—'

'Enough!' I bang the countertop with my fist, and he visibly jumps. 'Enough lies. Don't waste your breath because we're way beyond that, now. I know enough to go to the police right now and get you arrested. And I'm betting you didn't mention to them you were taking money from Phillipa.' His mouth drops open but I don't hesitate. 'Where is Dad's letter to Mum?'

'Look, Eve. Let's just calm down and—'

I raise my voice. 'Where's the letter Dad wrote to Mum?'

'It's... it's ages since I saw it. When you leave, I'll look and—'

'Go and get it, Hugo. Now.' I look away from him, out through the open French doors and into the beautiful cottage garden our daughter loves so much. 'I don't care how long it takes. I'll wait.'

He stares at me and shakes his head slowly. Then lets out a yell of frustration and disappears. I hear his feet on the stairs and pull in a deep breath. I'd been terrified he'd thrown it away, but the fact he's gone up there means he knows it's there.

They've just moved house, after all. He'll have sorted through all his stuff, deciding what to get rid of. Saskia had asked why I thought he'd keep something like that, and I knew the answer. Hugo was the worst kind of narcissist. He liked to remind himself of how clever he was, no matter how abhorrent his actions.

I remember he used to keep a list updated at home, full of the names of people he'd fired. It was one of the early warning signs that I'd made a big mistake in marrying him.

'I'm the hirer and firer, the man with all the power.' He'd smirk, proudly sweeping his finger up and down the list of names like they were notches on a bedpost.

Hugo would have kept Dad's letters so he could remind himself how clever he was. How he'd extracted money from a man and had the good fortune that he'd done away with himself and trusted Hugo to carry out his final wishes. Of course, if Hugo had followed my dad's final wishes and relieved us of the torture of not knowing what happened to Dad, he would have revealed his own treachery in taking the money. And burdened himself with paying it back on top of that. So it had been far easier for him to say nothing at all.

I turn to Saskia. 'Are you feeling OK? Maybe you ought to sit down.' She waves my concern away, but she looks a funny colour.

* * *

Hugo is taking a while upstairs. I wouldn't trust him not to abscond, because underneath, he's a coward who doesn't like facing his shortcomings. He's always been the sort who'd rather run from his problems and responsibilities than face them. But I can hear him upstairs, moving about, the odd bump and bang as, I presume, he searches his office.

Finally, he comes down, and in his hand is a small white envelope. Silently, he hands it to me. Mum's name, 'Viv', is printed on the front in Dad's handwriting. The letter has been clumsily torn open. Inside is a single folded sheet of paper. I peek inside, enough to see it's covered in Dad's handwriting.

'You read it,' I whisper, pain tearing at my chest. 'You read Mum's private letter.'

'I... I had to. I had to see if he'd mentioned the money, Eve. If he hadn't, I would have given it to your mum, I swear. I was just waiting until I had spare funds.'

'The same spare funds you used to buy this house?' I sweep my arm around the kitchen. 'Or the funds you used to buy your smart Mercedes outside?'

I stand up and push the letter into my handbag.

I glance at Saskia who has stayed completely silent throughout. She looks pale and nervous. 'I'm going to ask you this just once. Have you any idea what happened to Phillipa, Hugo?'

'What?' His eyes dart to Saskia. 'Of course I haven't!'

'Why did she pay you money?' I add.

'It was... just a loan. She swore me to secrecy. I can't talk about it. How did you—'

I turn and head for the door.

'Where are you going? What are you going to do?' he says, his voice rising an octave. 'Don't go to the police, Eve, don't do anything rash, I beg you. Think of Scarlet! We're just getting close again. She'll be heartbroken. She'll blame you when she's older, Eve. She'll never forget what you did.'

I look at him, sickened. This pathetic, weak man who I once thought so principled and strong. Only now am I beginning to realise just what Hugo might be capable of.

He looks so upstanding, appears so amiable. But underneath the façade lurks a monster... and that's when it hits me.

I'm describing the character from Phillipa's latest book.

FIFTY-ONE

By the time I get back to the flat it feels like it has been a very long day. I punch the code into the keypad on the front door of the house and push open the door.

'Oh, hello!' I address a crochety-looking man in his late seventies who's standing in the hallway with his arms folded, evidently waiting for me to enter the house. He has grey hair, a tidy grey moustache and wears a grey cardigan. 'You must be Joseph.' I extend a hand. 'I'm Eve. I've moved into the upstairs flat with –'

'I know who you are,' he says shortly, ignoring my hand. 'I've been watching you come and go each day.'

'I see.' I find that a bit unnerving. He must be peeking from behind the curtains whenever we take a step outside the door.

'I like to make it my business who's coming and going here,' he barks. 'That's what forty years in the army does for you. Started as a private, retired a decorated captain.'

I felt the weight of an expectation for a suitable reaction as I inch towards the stairs. 'Wow, that's... quite an achievement.' Then sheepishly, I say, 'I'm so sorry you were disturbed yesterday morning in the early hours. It was a friend in trouble.'

'I was about to call the police at the commotion outside and then I saw the young woman out of the window. She looked very upset.'

'Yes, she was. But I've seen her this afternoon and she's feeling better.'

He gave a curt nod. 'Well, no time to dally, I'm just about to put the bins out.' His brow furrows. 'I sincerely hope you two girls are recycling your rubbish, not just sticking the whole blazing lot of it into one bin bag?'

'Oh no, definitely not. We're... separating out the cardboard and glass and things. Absolutely.'

He gives a curt nod and marches past me to the front door.

'Nice to meet you,' I say faintly. Nina had mentioned he was a bit of a grump, but I wondered if something had upset him. Then I remembered Nina's party... and my bedroom being ransacked. 'Just on the off-chance, I don't suppose you saw anyone suspicious hanging around the house on Friday night at the party?'

He stops in his tracks and turns to face me. 'Party?'

'Nina's party... I hope you weren't disturbed. I was away for the night, but someone rifled through my bedroom and—'

'I know nothing about any party.' He frowns. 'No loud music nor other noise disturbance after eleven p.m. That's what the tenancy agreement states.'

'Right. As I say, I was –'

'I'll certainly speak up if I'm disturbed,' he interrupts. 'Rest assured you'll be in no doubt about that. Good day.' And he heads outside.

'How's Scarlet settled back in?' I ask Mum when I call her later.

'She's fine. She's had some tea, and now she's watching a bit of television before her bath. It's lovely to have her back again; I didn't realise just how much I've missed her.'

It feels good knowing Mum and Scarlet are back together again.

'That's great. What have you got planned for tomorrow?'

'Well, we've got my new handyman here in the morning, and Scarlet has already said she's going to help Chad with the weeding.'

'Who?'

'Chad, my new odd-job man! He mends things, he weeds, he's even good with computers and—'

My hand flies to my mouth. I feel like I'm going to vomit.

'Is his name Chad Belton?'

'Wh-what's wrong?' Mum stammers. 'I've forgotten his surname. Why?'

What does he look like?'

Mum hesitates. 'He's in his early to mid-thirties, he has sandy brown hair and I'd say he's about five foot ten or—'

'That's him! Oh my God, Mum, he's a very weird guy. I think he's trying to get to me through working for you.'

'What are you talking about, Eve?' Mum laughs. 'He's not weird at all, and he's all official. I got his details from a flyer. He's painted the gate and everything.'

'Did your neighbours get a flyer?' I'd bet my bottom dollar only Mum received one from Chad the 'odd-job man'.

'I don't know. Maureen has gone to visit her son in Edinburgh, and Edgar on the other side is staying with—'

'I don't want him anywhere near Scarlet, Mum. I want you to cancel his visit tomorrow. Just say you're ill or something.' From what Mum's just said, I now know she currently has nobody either side of her if she were to need help.

'But—'

'Promise me. I'll explain everything soon, but you have to trust me on this one.' My blood runs cold when I remember something else Mum said in passing. *He's even good with computers.* 'Has he touched the laptop?'

Mum's tone has turned sullen. 'Only to sort out my email because it was stuck on your login.'

I groan and cover my eyes with a hand. 'OK, Mum, I need to ring off now, but remember what I said. Cancel Chad's visit tomorrow. OK?'

'I heard you the first time!' Mum snaps. 'I don't know when my life stopped being my own, but I don't like it one bit – I can tell you that much.'

'I'm sorry. I promise I'll explain soon,' I say, itching to get off the phone. 'Bye for now, Mum. Love to Scarlet.'

Immediately the call has ended, I go into my email settings and change my password, selecting 'log out of all devices' before I save my changes. I can't see any meddling on my email account. Nothing in the 'draft' folder, nothing strange in my 'sent' folders.

I feel sick when I think he might have had access to Phillipa's new book through Mum's laptop. In fact, I think it's probably a given, but I'm not about to confess all to Jules and Alicia. They'll fire me on the spot.

FIFTY-TWO

I dial the number and wait. 'Good afternoon, the Sage Heathfield Literary Agency. How may I help you?'

I explain who I am and my connection to Phillipa. 'I need a quick chat with Sage if at all possible. It won't take more than ten minutes.'

'Sage is on another call right now but if you leave your details, I'll make sure she gets them,' the receptionist says, non-committal.

Twenty minutes later, my phone rang.

'Sage Heathfield here.'

'Thanks so much for returning my call, Sage. As you know, I'm recording Phillipa's latest book for Harris-Lasson, and I just wanted to ask you a couple of questions about the time she went missing.'

'I don't see the connection,' she says shortly. 'Between working on the audiobook and wanting to speak to me about her disappearance.'

Sage is evidently not someone who sees the need to indulge in small talk.

'It's for my own benefit,' I admit. 'I had some personal problems at the time Phillipa disappeared, and I just want the full picture so I can settle some little niggles I have and give my all to the job, if that makes sense.'

'It doesn't make much sense, actually.' Sage sniffs. 'But I can tell you what I know, which I have to say, isn't that much. Like you, Phillipa going missing impacted us in a big way here at the agency. I'd made a big mistake, too. Plus I lost my assistant of ten years at about the same time.'

'Was that Jasmine?'

'Yes. The two of them used to be good friends. I don't know what went wrong, but Phillipa detested her in the end and Jasmine wasn't keen, either. But then Jasmine overheard Phillipa talking to me.'

'Talking to you?'

'Yes, Phillipa had heard some gossip that Jasmine had been leaking confidential information from the agency.'

'Was this information about Phillipa herself?'

'I'm afraid so. At least Phil thought so. She said Jasmine had been spreading rumours that Phillipa wanted to stop writing the Tower series.'

'And that wasn't true?'

'That's hardly the point,' Sage says. 'Whether it was true or not, we have to be watertight about our authors' personal information.'

'Yes, of course.' She still hadn't answered my question.

'Anyway, I felt I had no choice but to suspend Jasmine pending an investigation, but she left anyway. I soon realised my mistake when it became apparent just how much Jasmine did in the office. I tried to rectify it, offer her the job back, but by this time she had decided to pursue a lifelong dream to go and help run a wildlife retreat in Zimbabwe.'

'That seems like a radical change. Did she keep in touch?'

'She emailed a couple of times, said she'd set up an Insta-gram account with pictures if I wanted to follow her progress.

My new assistant showed me the account, but I'm not really interested in what Jasmine is up to.'

'So within a short time you lost your assistant and then your biggest author?'

'That's right. But of course, no one's heard a word from Phillipa.'

'Was there anything that jumped out at you at the time, anything you noticed strange about Phillipa's behaviour or mood?'

'She did seem rather low and distracted. And then there was the new software she was having problems with. I never quite understood that.'

My ears prick up. 'Software?'

'Yes. I told the police about it. She told me she'd spent a fortune on some new-fangled technology for book ten and then hardly wrote a word. It was very odd. There was definitely something different about her, but I can't put my finger on what. Maybe she was just sick of the whole publicity juggernaut around her.'

When I come off the call, I open Instagram on my phone. I have a personal account, but I don't maintain it. I'd never really taken to Instagram, didn't see the point in just posting photographs and stories rather than writing a post on Facebook.

I type 'Jasmine Sanderson' into the search bar. Several accounts load and I instantly spot the correct one based on the photographs I'd seen of Jasmine in Fleur's folder.

There are only about a dozen photos and the last one was posted a month ago. Jasmine herself doesn't appear on any of the photographs. Apart from a couple of sunsets, they are mainly of animals and the construction of an animal sanctuary. Each one has a short tagline from Jasmine. *Helped with the new roof today!* Or, *Feeding the hippos!*

A hand-painted wooden sign in one picture reads: *Wild and Free in Harare.*

I google the phrase and a website for an animal sanctuary in Harare comes up as the first result. I click on the link and the site loads. On the home page, a gallery forms part of the home-page. The pictures are all in thumbnail, but when I peer closer, I see why my eye had been instantly drawn to them.

These are the exact photographs Jasmine Sanderson had posted on her Instagram account. She'd wanted it to appear like she'd taken the photographs herself on any given day, but in actual fact, every single image she'd posted had been taken from this website. Why would someone do that? Why not post original photographs that reflected the true situation? I can only think of one valid answer: she wasn't at the Wild and Free sanctuary in Harare.

Had Jasmine ever gone to Zimbabwe in the first place... or did she just want everyone to think she had?

FIFTY-THREE

When Nina gets in from work, late afternoon, she looks exhausted. 'I'm still recovering from the party.' She's still clearly feeling guilty about what happened in my bedroom because she can't meet my eyes. 'I'm going to take a shower and then lie on my bed and read a bit.'

I don't want to explain everything about Chad to her – it will take too long. I'm sure she's getting sick to death of my problems coming to the flat door.

'Joseph was downstairs when I got back. I apologised about Saskia disturbing him, but he didn't seem too bothered about your party.'

She pours herself a glass of water. 'You talked about the party?'

'I asked him if he'd seen anyone suspicious as he seems to notice everyone's every move. I thought he'd moan about the noise, but he didn't seem fazed.'

'Typical. He snoops twenty-four-seven but can't tell us anything useful when something actually happens.'

When Nina has gone to her room, I realise I need to decide what to do about Chad. I feel like he's trying to infiltrate my life and yet, if I go to the police, he's not actually done anything wrong. In fact Mum seemed completely charmed by him.

I check I've double-locked the front door and go to my room. The sun has been blaring in all day and it smells fusty and hot.

I crack open my window and take in a gulp of fresh air, and that's when I see something move over in the graveyard. The late sun is low in the sky, and I have to squint my eyes, but I can just about make out a figure. It ducks down and disappears from view so quickly, I wonder if I imagined it.

My phone starts to buzz, signifying an incoming call. I look down and see a mobile number I don't recognise, but something makes me answer it.

'Hello, Eve? It's Chad Belton here. I really need to—' For a second I'm speechless. Then I let rip.

'What the hell are you playing at?' I snap, keeping my voice down. 'I know you've wormed your way into my mum's house and been snooping around my emails.'

He's quiet for a second or two, and then he says, 'Please, Eve, just listen to me. I've something I need to discuss with you. Can I come up to the flat? I'm outside.'

'You're *what*?' Dread fills my chest. 'Was that you sneaking around in the graveyard just now? How do you know where I live?' My breathing is erratic with rising panic. But I know the answer to my questions... He's got all his information through wheedling his way into Mum's life.

'It won't take long; I can meet you outside if you like.'

'No, I definitely do not like! If you don't leave the vicinity of the flat, I'm going to call the police.' Then I think of a more powerful threat. 'I'll ring Harris-Lasson and tell them what you've done. They won't let you anywhere near their authors or their events again.'

'No, don't do that. Look, this is about Phillipa. I—'

'Go away!' I yell down the phone. 'Leave me alone!' I'm

about to end the call when something else occurs to me. 'Go near my mother's house again and I'll have the police arrest you for impersonating a tradesman to take advantage of a vulnerable person!'

I end the call and try to collect myself.

FIFTY-FOUR

She's working as fast as she can. Writing, getting the words down.

The sense of danger is increasing as her flashbacks become more frequent. Discussions about money, threats... Everything collapsing around her... Infuriatingly, the people around her stand in the shadows, faces and identities still blurred and hidden.

She's desperate to finish the book and also terrified. Will she be freed as promised?

How can she trust a faceless stranger?

She's been stretching and doing a few squats and lunges in the bathroom for a while now. Is she strong enough to try a bid for freedom again?

The thought of returning to the basement room fills her mind. The damp, the stench, and she covers her face with her hands and cries.

FIFTY-FIVE

CHAD

Chad stood in the shade of a tree set back from the road outside the flat where Eve Hewitt lived.

She was an infuriating woman – she would not listen and seemed to despise him for no reason at all. Yes, he had done doing a few hours' work for her mother, but he was a skilled odd-job man. He wasn't frightening the old woman, and anything she'd told him had been completely voluntary.

Chad had heard on the fan-forum grapevine that the narrator of Phillipa's new book had been asking around about her disappearance.

He'd had a caution for 'stalking' before, and he didn't want to admit he'd been up to his surveillance tricks, yet again.

Sadly, Eve had made it painfully clear she wanted nothing to do with Chad at all, so he had no choice but to move to Plan B.

He'd tried everything to get closer to Eve, close enough she would be forced to spend time with him.

She had rejected all his efforts, and since discovering he'd been employed by her mother, she had also threatened to call the police. But the last time he looked, working part-time offering repairs and maintenance wasn't a crime.

The police couldn't do anything about him working for Mrs Hewitt. Nobody could touch him for anything he had or hadn't done because they'd all under-estimated him and what he was capable of. Including Phillipa Roberts who had dismissed him at her peril.

Still, Chad couldn't risk Eve contacting the police because he didn't want them sniffing around his life and, more importantly, his basement.

A few years ago, he'd been accused by a neighbour, who lived alone, of stalking. It had been a ridiculous notion. There had been a spate of burglaries in the area, and Chad, a member of the local Neighbourhood Watch scheme, had simply sat outside the young woman's house after dark each night for a couple of hours watching the street. How was he to know she was in the habit of getting changed with her bedroom curtains open?

He'd been cautioned, not charged, but it had still been mortifying. Thank goodness his dear mother hadn't still been alive. The incident would surely have finished her off before her time.

Chad had tried, on several occasions, to reach out to the police with his theories about Phillipa Roberts's disappearance. On his third attempt they had taken him through to an interview room, a couple of male officers asking him questions and winking at one another like he'd given them a bit of sport.

'Have you actually met her then, this famous author? Oh, I'm impressed. I bet she loved *you* attending all her events. Her heart soared when you were first to arrive, I'm sure.' Cue laughter and the rolling of eyes.

It had been a complete waste of time when Chad had tried to explain he understood Phillipa in a way her other fans did not. Their mirth and attention span were short-lived. After ten minutes, the officers stood up and told him in no uncertain terms they did not want to see him at the station again.

'You are what we generally refer to as a timewaster, Mr Belton,' one said.

'Or, unofficially known as a *crackpot*,' the other one sniggered.

'Either way, you're someone who adds nothing to an investigation, just sucks out valuable resources in an effort to bring some meaning to your sad little life. We're focusing on just the worthwhile leads. So, if you know what's good for you, you'll stay away from the station. Stay well away.'

One of the officers escorted him off the premises and as they walked down the stark, brightly lit corridor back to reception, the man dropped his voice menacingly.

'We're aware of your peeping Tom activities a few years ago, by the way. And, if we see you again, we might be tempted to take a closer look at your activities and turn your caution into a full-blown conviction. So think on.'

So Chad took Eve Hewitt's threats to report him seriously. The time had come to risk everything.

And if Eve knew what was good for her, she'd come quietly.

FIFTY-SIX

EVE

I leave the flat and walk across the road to the car.

'What are you doing here?' I snap when Chad Belton appears from behind the oak tree across the road on the dimly lit street. 'I told you to stay away from me and my family.'

He holds his hands up in the air. 'Please, Eve, I beg you to just listen. I want to –'

'I don't care what you want! I'm telling you to leave us alone.'

Chad moves closer, and I fish in my bag for my phone. 'I warned you. I've had enough of this. I'm ringing the –'

Suddenly, Chad's arms are around me, restricting my arms. My handbag drops to the ground, and I let out a strangled yelp. 'What the hell –'

He pushes me towards a white van without too much difficulty. He is bigger and stronger than me, and I'm losing the battle. I open my mouth to scream, and he clamps a hand over my face and pushes. The tops of my thighs hit the metal floor of the van, and I stumble, the top half of my body falling forward.

His hand falls away from my mouth and I take a breath, ready to scream again, but the air is forced out of my lungs as

I'm picked up bodily and launched into the back of the van. Before I can collect myself, the metal doors are slammed shut. The harsh clunk of a shifting hook lock and then... darkness.

I bang on the wall of the van, yelling at the top of my voice.

'Let me out! Please... someone help me!'

The engine starts up and then the vehicle is moving. Within seconds we are travelling very fast, away from my street. I feel around the dusty metal floor. There's a crumpled sheet spread out underneath me, and I find a couple of empty plastic bottles that probably contain oil remnants or similar. But my handbag isn't in here.

Then I remember. I dropped my bag in the scuffle. I have no handbag and no phone and therefore, no means of calling for help.

FIFTY-SEVEN

I sit awkwardly, trying to find my balance and grip on the wheel arch so I can try and avoid being thrown around and feeling every single bump and blip in the road.

So far, we've been moving fast on well-maintained surfaces. But the van has just taken a sharp left turn and is now lurching down what feels like a rough track. We have been travelling for what seems like hours although I know it can't be that long. I curse myself for rushing out of the flat and leaving my watch on my bedside table. I feel disorientated and sick. My head is pounding where I hit it on the van door as he pushed me in.

The truth of what I've done dawns on me. I've made a cardinal error in my powers of judgement. My dad had a favourite saying: *Don't under-estimate your enemy.* And that is precisely what I have done. I've been so desperate to try and discover the mystery of what happened to Phillipa that I've completely missed the 'harmless' psychopath under my nose.

Chadwick Belton. Phillipa's superfan. Weird, creepy but, according to everyone I've spoken to, completely harmless. Well, this "harmless" fan now has me imprisoned in his van and is currently transporting me somewhere against my will.

I feel like I'm going to be sick. Not with the bumpy ride but because of the sharp tang of raw fear that's squeezing my stomach. Two questions are playing on loop in my head.

Am I about to find out what happened to Phillipa Roberts?

Am I the next person who's about to disappear?

The van stops, and everything remains quiet for a while. I can't hear any voices, or any other traffic. It feels like we're in the middle of nowhere. I bang on the metal side of the vehicle. 'Chad... can we talk? Let me out!'

Silence.

Then a petulant reply. 'I tried to talk to you, but you made it impossible.' He's talking loudly from the driving seat, and I can hear him perfectly well in the back through the thin metal partition. His voice sounds strange, forced.

This man is dangerous. He's managed to fool everyone around him to think he is harmless but what he's done to me proves I shouldn't under-estimate him any longer. It's time to try another tack.

'I'm sorry if you think I've been unreasonable. Maybe I have brushed you off, but I hardly know you, Chad. I do know you're respected by Phillipa and her publisher, so I should have listened. I'm sorry, OK? If you let me out of here, we can talk.'

He stays quiet while he considers my words. Evaluates them.

'I'm not going to open the doors so you can save your breath.' He says eventually and my heart drops in my chest. 'But I need you to listen to what I have to say.'

I want to scream. I'm hot and uncomfortable, and I'm scared. Scarlet's face flashes into my mind and Mum's, too... He's got full access to the people I love most in the world. I can't afford not to play the game his way, at least for now.

'OK, I'm listening.' I sit back against the wheel arch and try to breathe in the airless, dark space. I use the back of my hand to wipe beads of perspiration from my upper lip.

'I've read Phillipa's new book, the original one they found,' he says. 'I got it from your emails on your mother's laptop.'

I knew it. I knew he wouldn't have missed the chance. After I'd changed the password, I'd checked my email account and everything looked in order. I thought I'd acted in time. It appeared he hadn't forwarded Jules's emails to himself because I'd been sure to check the sent folder, but he must have covered his tracks by deleting them from there, too.

Play the game. It's the only chance I have to get out of here. So, instead of yelling at him, I keep my voice calm.

'What did you think of the book?'

A soft laugh, as if he knows I'm trying to humour him. 'I'd like to know what *you* think to it first, Eve.'

This guy is no idiot when it comes to the Tower series. He's obsessed with Phillipa Roberts and her books. If I don't tell the truth, I'll never win his trust.

'Right from the very beginning, I thought the book was strange. I spotted inconsistencies, big ones. I was so concerned, I spoke to Phillipa's editor about it. They've edited out the anomalies and they're going ahead to publish it. They don't seem worried at all.'

'Phillipa hid it for a reason!' he said, frustrated. 'She knew it wasn't right. They should have viewed it as a cry for help, not tried to patch it up like that.'

A shudder runs through me as something ignites in my head. Dad didn't reach out to us, his family, for help because he thought he was a burden on others. All this time I couldn't work out why Phillipa would write a book and then hide it away, but maybe Chad is right. Maybe she had lost all her confidence for some reason, and she was ashamed of facing it.

'It's time for us to be honest with each other,' I call into the musty darkness. 'Do you know what's happened to Phillipa?'

His voice drops, and I can't catch what he says.

'I can't hear you.'

He clears his throat. 'I said, I think I might know where she is. That's what I've been trying to tell you all this time.' He hesitates before adding, 'But you're not going to like it, Eve. You're not going to like it at all.'

FIFTY-EIGHT

I hear the door of the van open and then slam shut again. I wait, holding my breath.

Silence. No footsteps, no sounds at all.

'Chad?' I call out, keeping the concern I feel out of my voice.

He's basically just admitted he knows where Phillipa Roberts is and that I'm not going to like what he's about to tell me. Is she alive or dead?

A couple more minutes pass and the silence continues. The fear is growing inside me. I've pushed him to tell me the truth about Phillipa, and now he might feel he has to silence me in some way.

Perhaps Chad is quietly debating what to do... What if he's standing outside the doors right now with a weapon, deciding whether to attack me or not? I start to search the metal floor of the van again with flat hands. Sweeping and patting softly, trying to find something loose and hard I can try to defend myself with.

Then I hear his footsteps... He's walking down the side of the van and around to the back doors. I swallow down bile as my hands pat every inch of the floor frantically and then... my fingers close around a small spanner. It's hardly bigger than my hand and has obviously gone unnoticed being so small and lying in a metal groove. But it's something. Something I can use to defend myself if things get nasty.

He unlatches the bolt on the doors. The raw metal scrape reverberates around the space as I crouch, still in darkness, grasping the little spanner with my daughter's face in my mind and trying to prepare myself for what Chad might do next. My heartbeat is up in my throat, I feel so sick and then... then the doors open and, before I can overthink it, I spring forward and roll out onto rough earth with plants and trees. I scrabble to my feet and begin to run.

'Eve, wait!' Chad spins around, his face an angry mask.

'You're crazy!' I yell. 'Stay away from me.'

I haven't a clue where we are. My handbag is probably in the front of the van and in it, my phone. But I can't risk going back there. This is a man whose admitted knowing where Phillipa is. Someone who has infiltrated my mother's house, putting both her and my daughter at risk.

I have to get out of this wood and find a road to flag a passing vehicle down.

'Eve, stop!' Twigs snap behind me, I can hear his heavy breathing... He's coming after me. I turn to glance behind me and trip. Next thing, I'm flat on my stomach, the side of my face buried in dirt, my head pounds where it hit the parched, packed earth.

I push myself up with an arm, managing to roll over on to my back and suddenly, he's there. Towering over me, eyes wild and fists balled. But I note there is nothing in his hands, No weapon.

In one sudden movement, he steps and bends forward, and I cower, holding the crook of my arm in front of my face, ready to strike him with the metal tool in my other hand.

'Eve?' When I open my eyes, he's holding out a hand to help me up.

I ignore it and get to my feet. I've got a cracking headache coming from the bump.

'I'm sorry. I didn't mean to force you to come here, I –'

'You didn't mean it? We've been driving for ages, you had plenty of time to change your mind.'

He shook his head and looked down at his feet. 'I had to get you here. I had to. You wouldn't have believed me.'

'I wouldn't have believed what?' I can taste metal where I must have bit my lip when I fell. 'Do you have my handbag? I need a tissue.'

'Come back to the van,' he says. 'I'll give you your handbag and explain everything.'

When we get back to the vehicle, he reaches into the passenger side and pulls out my handbag. When he goes around the back to close the doors, I pull out my phone and press 999.

'What are you doing?'

I press the call button and turn to run back to the trees.

'Do you want to know the truth about your husband, the man who's trying to get custody of your daughter? Or are you going to carry on sticking your head in the sand like you've always done?'

I stop dead in my tracks. I look down at the phone and see my emergency call failed.

'No masts around here,' Chad says with a sly smile.

The fact he knows about Hugo's threat to go back to court to try and get custody – information that's obviously been gleaned from my mother – fills me with rage. 'You've no right to keep violating my privacy like this,' I yell at him.

'Eve, listen to me. I have every reason to believe Phillipa is in Hugo's storage facility.'

I laugh. 'What?'

He taps his phone and slides through several photographs. It's Hugo unbolting the padlock on the storage facility's gates. Hugo carrying supermarket food bags over and unlocking the door. Hugo putting the bags inside the door and relocking it, before closing the gates securely and leaving the premises.

'I was watching him yesterday through the zoom lens of my camera. Those bags were full of groceries and – you can't see it from the angle of the photographs – but he had a large flask tucked under his arm. Put it this way, I don't think he was planning a picnic.'

'But how did you get this lead? How did you know Phillipa and Hugo even knew each other?'

He sniffed. 'Sometimes I like to follow people. I know people like you would find that weird, but... well, people are interesting and it's better than sitting in the house on my own all day. I'm not doing any harm. I followed Phillipa to Hugo's storage place before she went missing. She had a look around it, sort of viewing it like a business visit. It was only when I bumped into you in Primark that I realised Hugo was your husband and saw a possible link.'

'I'm not sure you bumped into me at the shop or at the bar, Chad. I think you were doing one of your following exercises.'

He flicks through the photos again and doesn't answer. 'Hugo didn't stay. Just unloaded the goods and off he went.'

'You didn't see anyone else?'

'No, but that might change today.' He looks around us. 'Do you know where we are?'

I shake my head.

He points to the trees where I tripped. 'If we walk that way for about three minutes, we'll get to the perimeter fence at the rear of Balfour Holdings.'

'We're here? I had no idea. So, you think Phillipa is inside the storage unit?'

'Yep, I reckon Phillipa is in there and she could be in trouble. There's a small window at the back of the unit that I spotted when I did a reccie here. It's too small for me to clamber through, but I think you could get inside. If Phillipa is in there, all you have to do is shout to me and I'll call the police.' I think about Phillipa and what she might be going through in there, if Chad is right.

Would I ever forgive myself if I walk away now and she's in terrible danger?

'Show me the window,' I say.

FIFTY-NINE

She's curled up in a ball on the bed when she hears glass breaking. She sits bolt upright, listening.

This is not just a drinking glass being dropped or something small, it's a lot of glass. Like a window, and now there's banging and tapping noises. Then more glass falling.

She rushes over to the door and presses her ear to the wood. 'Hello?' she calls. 'Is someone there?'

The sound of breaking glass has stopped but there's another noise... a sort of shuffling and then a muffled bump. She bangs on the door. 'Hello? Who's there?'

Could it be an intruder? She thinks she's alone here when her captor locks her in. A stripe of fear drives through her and she wonders if she ought to hide. And then... footsteps running, getting closer, then the door is unlocked, the bolts slid across and the footsteps carry on down the long corridor outside the room.

She feels nauseous with fear, with hope... Dare she begin to believe the ordeal is almost over? She reaches with a shaking hand and pushes. The door opens easily, and she steps out into the corridor. She walks cautiously, follows the route she came from the basement room.

It feels like she's in a dream, like nothing around her is real. Until she sees it at the end of the corridor. A small broken window. Small, but big enough for someone to climb through. Shards of glass and half a brick scatter the floor. A grubby sheet, draped over the sill of the window to prevent skin being sliced and scraped.

She stops dead in her tracks and listens. Human voices. Ordinary human voices, with no distortion. These people are very close but around the corner so she can't see them and they can't see her. A laugh, a yelp of delight.

'Oh, thank God!' she hears a woman cry.

'Hello?' she calls out herself. 'Someone help me, please...'

SIXTY

EVE

I'd jumped down from the window and landed on the floor with a thump.

'Don't forget,' Chad had hissed before I jumped. 'Just give me the sign and I'll call the police.'

When I looked up, I saw a figure at the end of the corridor, half-hiding behind the corner. Still, I could see immediately it was a figure that looked familiar to me.

'Is that... is that you, Phillipa?' I'd called faintly. 'It's Eve. Eve Hewitt.'

The figure took a step towards me. Then another... and another until now she's running and we're in each other's arms and Phillipa is sobbing on to my shoulder.

I can barely speak. She looks thin and tired. 'Oh God, are you OK?' I hold her shoulders and look into her face. 'Are you hurt?'

She shakes her head. 'I'm OK. I'm fine.'

'Phillipa, what happened? Has somebody kept you here against your will... all this time?'

Her eyes well up with tears and she looked over her shoulder fearfully. 'Is anyone else here?' I whisper, adrenalin running through my body. Chad had said Hugo had been and gone, but there was always a chance he'd missed him returning when we'd been in the wood.

'Just her,' she whispers. 'She's here, and she's got a taser.'

'Who are you... Oh!' Another figure appears. A woman dressed in black. She doesn't move, just stands there.

Phillipa grasps my arm and sobs. 'It's her. It's Jasmine. She's kept me here... she's hurt me.' She's acting strange, she sounds paranoid, but maybe there's no wonder after what she's been through.

Clearly my hunch about Jasmine's Instagram account had been correct. She had never left the country but had used generic photographs of a location to fool anyone who looked to think she was long gone. Yet she'd been here all this time, keeping Phillipa a prisoner.

'Wait here.' I dash back to the broken window and scream, 'Chad, call the police!'

I hear him shout something urgently, although I can't discern exactly what.

I rush back to Phillipa and stand slightly in front of her in a protective manner, although I don't know what I'll do if Jasmine rushes at me with a taser.

A silence descends on the corridor. The figure looks threatening. She's dressed in black and just standing there, not moving an inch.

The police are on their way,' I shout. 'Stay where you are.'

A bang and crash sounds from somewhere close in the building. Then I hear a door fly open and voices. Surely it can't be the police already?

Hugo. That's what Chad must have been saying, trying to warn me.

'Hugo and Jasmine have kept you here?'

Phillipa nods.

'Hugo!' I yell as loud as I can.

Then suddenly, he's there. In front of me. 'Eve,' he says faintly.

His face is the colour of chalk. He looks at Phillipa, and then... then he sees the other figure. Jasmine.

'Who the hell—'

Chad runs in looking from one of us to the other. His eyes rest on Jasmine. 'You!' he exclaims.

Hugo stares out of the open door as three police cars, with lights flashing zoom on to the forecourt blocking in Hugo's car.

'What the hell is happening here?' Hugo mutters. 'Phillipa?'

Moments later, the place is swarming with uniformed officers.

Phillipa limps towards the senior officer.

Her voice sounds weak. 'My name is Phillipa Roberts,' she says, looking and sounding exhausted. 'I'm an author, and ten months ago I officially disappeared. I was abducted by Hugo Jones and Jasmine Sanderson.'

'That's rubbish!' Hugo shouts, looking at me. 'Eve, you have to believe me. I had nothing to do with – get your hands off me!' he yells at the officers.

'Hugo Jones, I am arresting you on suspicion of the abduction and imprisonment of Phillipa Roberts...' The senior officer's voice fades as I try to take in what's happening.

'Can someone tell my wife I'm OK and to please come and get me?' Phillipa begins to cry.

'You're making a big mistake,' Hugo cries out. He can't tear his eyes away from Jasmine as two officers approach her. Finally, she speaks, her voice sounds scratchy, like she has a sore throat.

'You... you've got this all wrong. Phillipa Roberts imprisoned me. She drugged me and brought me here. I've never met this man.'

'Phillipa paid me to rent these premises and to bring regular provisions and—' Hugo yells out as his arms are yanked further around his back. His wild eyes alight on mine. 'Eve, for God's sake, tell them! This is madness.'

I stand there, mute. I know Hugo well enough to see he is genuinely distressed and trying to get his point over.

'Phillipa...' He mutters her name from between bared teeth, like he is warning her. 'What are you up to? Why are you doing this?'

'Right, come on. Let's get you outside,' the senior officer says to Hugo.

'No, wait, please. I need to speak to Eve, my ex-wife. I need to...'

I lose Hugo's words as they drag him out, kicking and yelling, to the cars.

Phillipa turns to me, her face shining with relief. But something doesn't sit right. Someone isn't telling the truth here, and I think it's Phillipa.

I hear a shuffling sound behind me. I turn and see Chad. I'd forgotten he was here. He's stood quietly without saying a word until now.

'Phillipa, I think you know I am your biggest fan,' he says, and she smiles graciously at him.

'Thank you, Chad.'

'But something isn't right. I read the book you wrote and then tried to hide away. Why did you do that? Because you knew it betrayed you?'

'What?' Her expression changes to one of pure alarm. 'How do you...'

'Didn't Hugo tell you they found your book?' I said.

She shook her head slowly. 'They found the tenth book?'

'It wasn't like your other books, Phillipa,' Chad said quietly. 'Why was that?'

'Because I wrote the Tower series, all of them,' Jasmine screams, her words echoing around the walls. Her face is swollen and wet as the tears run freely down her cheeks. 'And when I refused to write any more, she brought me here to force me.' She's sobbing so hard, I have to really focus to understand what she's saying.

I look at Phillipa and something in her face looks beaten. She wobbles, unsteady on her feet.

'I'm so tired of running,' she says suddenly. 'It's all lies. They didn't abduct me. I've made a terrible, terrible mistake.'

SIXTY-ONE

BBC RADIO NEWS REPORT

ONE DAY LATER

Bestselling crime fiction author Phillipa Roberts, who became one of the UK's most high-profile missing persons some ten months ago, has been found safe and well in a remote location that currently remains unknown.

Roberts's location was discovered by Tower series superfan and online forum administrator, Chad Belton. 'I carried out a surveillance operation of my own and established the whereabouts of Phillipa. I wanted to be sure my hunch was correct before informing the police.'

But as with all the best crime fiction, all was not as it first seemed as it was revealed Roberts herself was holding an as yet unnamed person hostage.

Belton contacted his associate, Eve Hewitt, the audio narrator of Roberts's globally successful DI Jane Tower series, and together, they discovered what a source described as 'a grim scene.' It is thought Roberts pulled off her staged disappearance with the help of a local businessman – as yet unnamed – who is said to have been unaware of another person being imprisoned by Roberts in his facility.

Police have confirmed there are no casualties, but two arrests have been made with both suspects now released pending investigation.

A spokesperson for Roberts's wife, Fleur de Bois, said, 'Miss de Bois is devastated her wife was involved in a serious crime. She is seeking legal advice and asks for privacy and understanding at this very challenging time.'

A hidden manuscript was recently discovered in the house they shared together with Miss de Bois's son. Harris-Lasson, Phillipa's publishing house, are currently working to release a hardback and audiobook of Roberts's yet-to-be-titled new novel next year. It is unknown whether the publication will now go ahead. Harris-Lasson remain unavailable for comment.

A spokesman for the Metropolitan Police said, 'The investigation into Phillipa Roberts's disappearance has been lengthy and ongoing, and we are relieved it has been concluded. Our team will now seek to establish details and establish a thorough timeline of events.'

More details on this story are expected soon.

SIXTY-TWO

TWO DAYS LATER

Phillipa sits in the airless interview room with the two detectives, a woman and a man.

'So you're saying that Jasmine Sanderson, who worked for your literary agent, was the author of the DI Jane Tower series, not yourself?' the woman says.

'Yes, but up until book seven we'd worked together on the books. She was a very talented writer, but I came up with lots of ideas, plot twists.'

'But the last two published novels, books eight and nine, she wrote completely without your input?' Phillipa nods. 'Why did you stop contributing ideas?'

'A year ago, I noticed certain things became much harder. I had difficulty concentrating and memory lapses. Sometimes my hands would jerk when I tried to write by hand, or type. I felt so anxious and depressed.' Phillipa looks down at her hands. 'I consulted a private neurologist who carried out some tests and diagnosed Huntington's disease.'

'This is a condition that stops parts of the brain working,' the male detective says matter-of-factly.

'Correct. It's caused by a faulty inherited gene. On reflection I think my father probably had it, but he was undiagnosed and died in an industrial accident.' She sighs. 'Anyway, I was able to hide most of my symptoms.'

'You didn't tell your wife?'

'No. I mean, I knew I'd have to at some point because it's a progressive brain disorder. There's no cure, and symptoms just get worse. But I didn't want her to worry, and I was still coming to terms with the diagnosis myself.'

'She didn't notice the changes in your behaviour, the ones you've described?'

'No. But at a low moment I took an overdose of sleeping tablets. I said it was a one-off low moment, but of course she knew something was wrong. I brushed her concerns away. I purposely spent a lot more time out of the house. I'd cover my medical appointments by saying I had to pop to the library, or somewhere else. If I was having a bad day where I was particularly clumsy or had difficulty moving as freely, I'd hole myself up in the office.' The detectives fall quiet, allowing her a moment to reflect before she continues.

'I simply couldn't focus on the storylines anymore.' Her voice quieter now. 'But I didn't tell a soul, until Jasmine refused to write the final book and I decided to confide in her, to try to appeal to her better nature.'

The woman refers to her paperwork. 'You're referring to book ten in the series?'

'Yes. The final book in my contract before I signed a new one. Except I knew, when Jasmine refused to continue with our arrangement, it would have to be the final book in the series. But I remained hopeful I could change her mind, so I hadn't told my publisher yet. I'd tentatively discussed it with my agent.'

'Your agent was unaware of the arrangement you had with

Jasmine even though Miss Pateman also worked at the literary agency?'

'That's right. Sage knew nothing about our arrangement. I focused on trying to convince Jasmine to write the final instalment, but she put paid to that when she demanded my entire advance.'

'This is the payment you receive from the publisher before the book is even published?'

'Yes. They pay it in stages, and a big chunk comes when they receive the first draft of the book. If I'd given it all to Jasmine, I would've found myself in severe financial difficulties because I'd had some pretty big expenses recently.'

'But Jasmine still refused to write the last book after you'd told her about your diagnosis.'

Phillipa nods, worry etching her face. 'I realised I'd made a big mistake confiding in her. When I refused to pay her the entire advance, she said I had until the night of the award ceremony to change my mind. There were still a few months to go to the event at that point. If I didn't agree, she said she'd announce my diagnosis live on stage. She'd also confess that she'd been the author of the books and that I was a fraud.'

'Although she'd also have been revealing herself as taking part in the scam,' the male detective remarked.

'She didn't care about that. She had no family, was raised in foster care. She said she would go and work abroad, something she'd wanted to do for years. She'd have done it for pure spite.'

'So what did you do?'

'I knew if I got that one book out, I'd be able to retire from my career. There was a screen-adaptation deal coming for all ten books which would make me financially secure. I knew I'd have to pay Jasmine for her silence, but with the TV pay-off and my ongoing royalties, my family would have been comfortable for life.

'So I decided to write the book myself but... it was hopeless.

I panicked. I no longer had the skills needed to write a novel and to knit together the intricacies of a plot. I spent hours, days, weeks thinking about what to do. The brain fog was like nothing I'd experienced before, it felt like a brick partition had been erected in my brain almost overnight. I couldn't recall character traits, plot threads... it was so frustrating. I even bought some expensive software to help me try to put my thoughts in order, but nothing worked. In the end I just hid the book away under mountains of paperwork, just in case I improved and could revisit it at a later date.'

'So that's when you moved to Plan B?'

'Well, I had three choices, as far as I could see it. One: I could come clean to my publisher and readers and confess that I was a fraud. Two: I could just stop writing, but Jasmine was blackmailing me for more money to stay quiet. Three: I could force her to write one last book. After much deliberation, I chose the last option.'

'An option fraught with problems.'

'Yes. I knew I'd have to imprison her to force her to write the book. I hadn't given too much thought to how I might get out of the fix.'

'So all this time, you've been staying in the storage facility with Jasmine? How did you get the idea to use that place?'

'I'd kept in touch with Saskia, and we had a catch-up. She told me Hugo was getting into the storage-facility business. Big vast warehouses with tonnes of space in the middle of nowhere. I'd met Hugo several times through Eve. I knew he was a bit of a shark, would do anything for money. Initially, Hugo tried to get me to invest in his storage-facility business. I declined but told him about my other proposal. Which he jumped at. Hugo fitted me out a couple of rooms so it was like being in an apartment. I'd had all my tests and had been given my medication by that point and frankly, it was a relief to have time to think, to try and get myself on a level mentally. With the amount I offered to pay Hugo, he couldn't do enough for me.'

'But Hugo knew nothing about your real plan? He didn't know you were keeping Jasmine prisoner there?'

'No. The least he knew the better. I confided in him about my recent diagnosis and said I needed complete respite from the world while I tried to write my book. I hired a limo under a false name to drive Jasmine to the awards ceremony. When I turned up as her driver on the big night, she thought I'd finally caved into her demands, but I diverted our route. I spiked her drink and managed to get her inside the storage facility using a wheelchair. The next day, Hugo returned the car for me none the wiser.'

'What did you plan to do with Jasmine when she finished the novel?'

'I was hoping to pay her off, to buy her silence. I knew with the drama of my disappearance, the royalties for book ten would be through the roof. I knew it would also give time for the streaming deal to drop into place. If Fleur and I downsized our lifestyle and sold the two houses, we'd be reasonably well-off. I'd solve my financial problems and set my family up with this final instalment that would keep them secure when... when I deteriorated. I was between a rock and a hard place Then I'd come clean and tell my readers about my diagnosis. That was the plan. It all fit together nicely on paper.'

The female detective cleared her throat. 'I understand your wife, Fleur, hasn't made contact with you since officers informed her you'd been located and gave her brief details of the situation?'

Phillipa looks down, her head thumping, her heart squeezed dry.

'No. She's apparently sent a message that she wants a divorce.'

SIXTY-THREE

EVE

ONE WEEK LATER

When Saskia shows me into the living room, Hugo sits on the sofa with his head in his hands. I stand there and wait until he looks up.

'Eve,' he says, his voice breaking. 'I'm so sorry.'

'Sorry you did it, or sorry you got caught?'

'I'm sorry I let you and Saskia down,' he says forlornly.

'You let Scarlet down, too. And Mum. In fact you've let us all down, including yourself, Hugo. To keep Dad's last words to Mum to yourself, to let her think he'd squandered their savings...'

He hangs his head again. 'This house is being sold and then the money I loaned from your dad will be repaid to Viv. I'm ashamed about the letter, truly I am.'

'How could you? How could you involve yourself in Phillipa's plan? All the time knowing how distressed her family were. Knowing I was trying my level best to find out what had happened to her.'

He lifted his palms up. 'Phillipa's money got me out of a

very sticky situation, Eve. It was an offer I couldn't refuse. I tried my best to put you off, get you away from Harris-Lasson, but as usual, you were too stubborn to take the hints.'

I frown. 'What do you mean?'

He shrugs. 'Your ransacked bedroom, the anonymous letter... stuff that was supposed to make you nervous enough to back off. For your own good.'

'How unselfish of you, doing all that for my own good,' I snapped. 'And how did you...' A lightbulb flashes on and off in my head. 'Nina.'

Hugo nods sheepishly.

I haven't seen Nina since Phillipa's arrest. Jules told me she had big personal problems at home and was on extended leave until further notice. Very convenient.

Joseph was confused when I mentioned the party that day in the hallway because there hadn't been one. She'd ransacked my room so I'd think people were watching me. There was no sinister person pushing letters through the door. Nina had been responsible for that, too.

'I offered to pay her a decent fee if she'd creep you out a bit. She's desperate to get her own place so it wasn't too difficult to convince her, but she took a while to accept. She said she really liked you and felt bad.'

'But not quite bad enough to refuse to do it,' I say. 'You people all deserve each other.'

SIXTY-FOUR

CHAD

ONE MONTH LATER

Chad set out the biscuits and teacups on the table and checked his watch. The first visitors would be here in just over half an hour. Just time to get spruced up for the obligatory photograph and then he'd be ready.

Since the discovery of Phillipa's hideout, he'd barely had a moment spare. The Phillipa Roberts–forum membership had exploded, and his diary had been full of press interviews for newspapers and websites all over the world. Everyone was obsessed with the story of the author who'd turned bad and he, Chad, was the man with the inside story.

No longer was he ashamed of his Phillipa-themed basement – although he had, of course, removed the photographs that might have got him arrested – the press were mad for pictures of it. Chad gave them a tour while telling them the story of how his admiration for the bestselling author had been turned to shock and disbelief when he'd discovered she was captor, not captive.

Several members of the Phillipa Roberts's forum had

become good friends and been a tremendous support to Chad. There were no more long nights spent alone in front of the television, no more surveillance trips out with his zoom lens... there were too many real people who wanted to spend time with him.

He'd even met up with Eve Hewitt in the bar brasserie she used to work in. Chad had been able to apologise again for forcing her into the van against her will.

'I know it's inexcusable, and I'm ashamed I resorted to that,' he told her over coffee. 'I've always known people have thought me a bit odd, a bit strange compared to others, but I'm not a psychopath. I'm not dangerous. I'm just different.'

Eve had gracefully accepted his apology. Harris-Lasson had offered her a big contract to narrate their authors' books after she had refused to speak to the press and maintained a dignified silence. And ironically, Chad was all the more in demand with the press because of that.

He stood up and gave his hair one last comb in the old gilt-framed mirror above the fireplace. Chad looked out of the window and smiled to himself as press vehicles started to arrive for his first appointment of the day.

Life was good... for him at least. Phillipa Roberts, on the other hand, was now facing the very serious charges of abduction and imprisonment.

But he would never turn his back on her. Not now. Not ever.

SIXTY-FIVE

EVE

ONE MONTH LATER

When I arrive at Mum's, she meets me at the door and takes my overnight bag.

'Come on in, love. Let's get you settled.'

Scarlet, my little whirlwind, flies down the hall and throws her arms around me. 'Mummyyy, you're home!'

'I've missed you so much, my darling.' I kiss her head and inhale her clean, outdoors smell.

Scarlet races off to get a picture she's painted, and when I look up, Mum has tears in her eyes. 'I don't know what I'm going to tell her,' I whisper.

* * *

When Scarlet has shown me her artwork and the cress seeds she's planted that are starting to sprout, Mum announces it's time for Scarlet's holiday activity club.

I walk her to the school, and we talk about all sorts of things.

I just found out yesterday Hugo has been charged with being an accessory to a crime. There's a real chance he could go to prison.

Scarlet refers to Hugo a couple of times during our walk. I've taken her to see him on a couple of occasions this past month, but now I must gently introduce the fact that her daddy might have to go away to work.

'You might not see him for a while,' I say softly. She nods and skips along undaunted.

'I hope he's back for when my baby brother is born,' she sings happily.

My stomach fills with dread. Saskia has already moved back home to her parents' house down south. She has ended her relationship with Hugo, but we are in touch and I've promised to take Scarlet to visit when the baby comes.

I've signed a new two-year contract with Harris-Lasson as a freelance narrator for their audiobook imprint. Ironically, Phillipa's books are more popular than ever after all the drama so they're going ahead with publication of her original book ten. They're re-editing it and I'll have to start the recording process again, but that's fine. It gives me some time with Scarlet and Mum.

When the contract starts, I'll work two to three days in London and commute from my now permanent home with Mum and Scarlet. Nina has left Harris-Lasson, and I'm renting my old room with a new publishing colleague.

Phillipa has asked if I can visit her, but I'm still thinking about it. I'm not sure how I feel, but she has no one now. Ironically, neither has Jasmine Sanderson. I heard she's in a bad way in hospital, recovering from a breakdown. Fleur is currently holidaying abroad with Simon and Milo, and apparently they are talking about getting back together.

When I get back from school, Mum is cleaning the oven. She cleans morning, noon and night. The house is spotless, but

Mum is thin and pale. But I can't leave what I have to tell her for a moment longer.

'Mum, please,' I say gently. 'Leave that just a minute.'

'Let me finish, Eve, I'll—'

'Mum.' She grimaces and straightens her back and I force her to look into my eyes. 'Please. Just this once, leave it.'

I lead her into the living room, and we sit down.

'What's all this about, love?' Her foot is tap, tap, tapping on the floor. Her nail chafes on the side of her thumb, reddening the skin.

'A little while ago, I made you a promise, Mum. I told you I'd bring Dad's letter home, the one he wrote to you before he died... and that's what I've done.'

I pass her the envelope. 'Hugo opened it. But the words in there are meant for you.'

She stares at the letter a few moments and I see a whole range of emotions pass over her face. Denial, hope, dread...

But with shaking hands she takes out the letter and unfolds it. Her voice is little more than a whisper, but finally, she reads aloud the words that Dad so wanted her to hear.

My darling Viv,

I want to start by telling you how much I love you. That love will be with you always, until the day we can be together again.

I know I can't make you understand why I felt I had to leave you, my love. I have tried and failed a thousand times to tell you, but the simple truth is that there are no words that can describe the sadness and weariness in my heart.

It's because I love you so much I had to go. Do you see? So you and the girls could be free of the shadows I cast over your lives. I know it's so terribly hard for you to hear.

I just need you to know that the decision I took was all

mine, my darling. None of my woes were ever caused by you – you only brought love and light into my life.

Hugo will take care of you all when I am gone. He is a good man, an honest man. There are things I have asked him to do, and I believe with all my heart he will make a good job of my requests.

I love you with every fibre of my body. My aching heart is yours alone, and one day, when we meet again, I will wrap my arms around you, and nothing will ever part us again.

Until then, you will feel me with you in the whisper of the wind, in the warmth of a winter fire. You will see me every day in our beautiful daughter and our wonderful granddaughter.

Until the day I hold you in my arms again, my love…

Forever yours,

Derek

Mum's face crumples and the tears come as finally, she allows her grief to envelop her. I move closer, wrapping my arms around her.

'Dad loved us so much, Mum, and he'll always be with you. Looking down, keeping you from harm.' She nods, takes a tissue from her sleeve to dab her eyes. 'But Dad would want more than anything for you to live, for us to enjoy our lives together and that's what we're going to do. We have the chance to make a new start now. Me, you and Scarlet. Do you think we can at least try?'

Mum nods and looks at me, her faded blue-grey eyes tired but with the tiniest spark of hope.

'We'll do it for your dad.' She smiles. 'I know he'll be with his girls every step of the way.

And that's good enough for me.

A LETTER FROM K.L. SLATER

Thank you so much for reading *The Narrator*, I hope you enjoyed reading it as much as I enjoyed writing it.

If you did enjoy it, and want to keep up to date with all my latest releases, just sign up at the following link. Your email address will never be shared and you can unsubscribe at any time.

www.bookouture.com/kl-slater

I've been lucky enough to visit the Audible Studios in London on a few occasions. Seeing your book being brought to life by a skilled narrator is a milestone moment for any author! It occurred to me that narrators are sometimes in the unique position of being one of the first people to read a manuscript, often before a book is even published.

When it was time to write another Audible Original, I found myself thinking...What if a narrator happened to spot some anomalies in such a manuscript? Is it possible she could see clues that other people had failed to recognise? And what if the author had since disappeared? A rather pleasing mystery began to develop and when I gave the narrator a troubled personal life, then *The Narrator* really began to take shape!

I love the steps of reaching my next writing idea, initially built from the smallest building blocks. Often, characters and plotlines occur to me during the writing process, but it all has to start somewhere.

One of the best parts of writing comes from seeing the reaction from readers. If you enjoyed *The Narrator*, I would absolutely love it if you could leave a short review. Getting feedback from readers is amazing and it also helps to persuade other readers to pick up one of my books for the first time.

Thank you for reading.

Love,

Kim

https://klslaterauthor.com

 facebook.com/KimLSlaterAuthor

twitter.com/KimLSlater

 instagram.com/klslaterauthor

ACKNOWLEDGEMENTS

Thank you to my fabulous editor, Lydia Vassar-Smith, for publishing *The Narrator* in ebook and paperback formats. Thanks as always to Head of Editorial Management Alexandra Holmes and the rest of the Bookouture team for their excellent work in readying the book for publication, including proofreader Maddy Newquist.

Thanks also to Camilla Bolton, my amazing literary agent, and to Jade Kavanagh, her assistant. Their ongoing support and championing of my work means the world.

Thank you to the talented Henry Steadman who created the striking and memorable cover for *The Narrator*.

The Narrator started life as an Audible Plus title and I'd like to record here my thanks to Harry Scoble, Senior Manager at Audible, who championed *The Narrator* and had such faith and enthusiasm for the book. Huge thanks to freelance editor Sophie Wilson, whose keen eye for detail helped to make the book the best it could be. I'm in awe of the excellent voice actors, Clare Corbett and Kristin Atherton, who brought their unique talents to the story. Not forgetting the talented production team at Audible who brought the book to life and the many other Audible staff for their valued input along the way... thank you all!

Thank you to the bloggers and reviewers who do so much to support authors and thank you to everyone who has taken the time to post a positive review online or has taken part in my blog tour. It is always noticed and much appreciated.

Last but not least, thank you SO much to my wonderful readers and listeners. I love receiving all your wonderful comments and messages and I am truly grateful for each and every one of your support.